Communicating Artificial Intelligence (AI)

Despite increasing scholarly attention to artificial intelligence (AI), studies at the intersection of AI and communication remain ripe for exploration, including investigations of the social, political, cultural, and ethical aspects of machine intelligence, interactions among agents, and social artifacts. This book tackles these unexplored research areas with special emphasis on conditions, components, and consequences of cognitive, attitudinal, affective, and behavioural dimensions toward communication and AI. In doing so, this book epitomizes communication, journalism and media scholarship on AI and its social, political, cultural, and ethical perspectives.

Topics vary widely from interactions between humans and robots through news representation of AI and AI-based news credibility to privacy and value toward AI in the public sphere. Contributors from such countries as Brazil, Netherland, South Korea, Spain, and United States discuss important issues and challenges in AI and communication studies. The collection of chapters in the book considers implications for not only theoretical and methodological approaches, but policymakers and practitioners alike.

The chapters in this book were originally published as a special issue of *Communication Studies*.

Seungahn Nah is Professor at the University of Oregon, USA. Dr Nah specializes in digital media, community, and democracy. His works have appeared in prestigious journals. He currently serves as an associate editor of the *Journal of Communication* and *Mass Communication & Society*.

Jasmine E. McNealy is Associate Professor at the University of Florida, USA. Dr McNealy specializes in media, information, and emerging technology, with a view toward influencing law and policy. Her current research focuses on privacy, surveillance, and data governance with an emphasis on marginalized communities.

Jang Hyun Kim is School Head (Chair) for School of Convergence, Sungkyunkwan University, South Korea. Dr Kim is also an Associate Professor in the Department of Interaction Science. His research interests include social/semantic network analysis, reputation/crisis communication, and future media.

Jungseock Joo is Assistant Professor in Communication at University of California, USA. His research primarily focuses on understanding multimodal human communication with computer vision and deep learning. His research has been supported by the National Science Foundation, Hellman Foundation, and other industrial sponsors. He was a research scientist at Facebook prior to joining UCLA.

Communicating Artificial Intelligence (AI)

Theory, Research, and Practice

Edited by
Seungahn Nah, Jasmine E. McNealy, Jang Hyun Kim, and Jungseock Joo

NEW YORK AND LONDON

First published 2021
and by Routledge
52 Vanderbilt Avenue, New York, NY 10017

by Routledge
2 Park Square, Milton Park, Abingdon, Oxon, OX14 4RN

Routledge is an imprint of the Taylor & Francis Group, an informa business

Introduction, Chapters 2–6 © 2021 Central States Communication Association
Chapter 1 © 2020 Maurice Vergeer. Originally published as Open Access.

With the exception of Chapter 1, no part of this book may be reprinted or reproduced or utilised in any form or by any electronic, mechanical, or other means, now known or hereafter invented, including photocopying and recording, or in any information storage or retrieval system, without permission in writing from the publishers. For details on the rights for Chapter 1, please see the chapter's Open Access footnote.

Trademark notice: Product or corporate names may be trademarks or registered trademarks, and are used only for identification and explanation without intent to infringe.

Library of Congress Cataloging-in-Publication Data
A catalog record for this title has been requested

ISBN 13: 978-0-367-67995-8

Typeset in MinionPro
by Newgen Publishing UK

Publisher's Note
The publisher accepts responsibility for any inconsistencies that may have arisen during the conversion of this book from journal articles to book chapters, namely the inclusion of journal terminology.

Disclaimer
Every effort has been made to contact copyright holders for their permission to reprint material in this book. The publishers would be grateful to hear from any copyright holder who is not here acknowledged and will undertake to rectify any errors or omissions in future editions of this book.

Contents

Citation Information		vi
Notes on Contributors		viii
	Introduction: Communicating Artificial Intelligence (AI): Theory, Research, and Practice *Seungahn Nah, Jasmine McNealy, Jang Hyun Kim and Jungseock Joo*	1
1	Artificial Intelligence in the Dutch Press: An Analysis of Topics and Trends *Maurice Vergeer*	5
2	I-It, I-Thou, I-Robot: The Perceived Humanness of AI in Human-Machine Communication *David Westerman, Autumn P. Edwards, Chad Edwards, Zhenyang Luo and Patric R. Spence*	25
3	A Bot and a Smile: Interpersonal Impressions of Chatbots and Humans Using Emoji in Computer-mediated Communication *Austin Beattie, Autumn P. Edwards and Chad Edwards*	41
4	Predicting AI News Credibility: Communicative or Social Capital or Both? *Sangwon Lee, Seungahn Nah, Deborah S. Chung and Junghwan Kim*	60
5	Privacy, Values and Machines: Predicting Opposition to Artificial Intelligence *Josep Lobera, Carlos J. Fernández Rodríguez and Cristóbal Torres-Albero*	80
6	Making up Audience: Media Bots and the Falsification of the Public Sphere *Rose Marie Santini, Debora Salles, Giulia Tucci, Fernando Ferreira and Felipe Grael*	98
	Index	120

Citation Information

The chapters in this book were originally published in the *Communication Studies*, volume 71, issue 3 (August 2020). When citing this material, please use the original page numbering for each article, as follows:

Introduction

Communicating Artificial Intelligence (AI): Theory, Research, and Practice
Seungahn Nah, Jasmine McNealy, Jang Hyun Kim and Jungseock Joo
Communication Studies, volume 71, issue 3 (August 2020), pp. 369–372

Chapter 1

Artificial Intelligence in the Dutch Press: An Analysis of Topics and Trends
Maurice Vergeer
Communication Studies, volume 71, issue 3 (August 2020), pp. 373–392

Chapter 2

I-It, I-Thou, I-Robot: The Perceived Humanness of AI in Human-Machine Communication
David Westerman, Autumn P. Edwards, Chad Edwards, Zhenyang Luo and Patric R. Spence
Communication Studies, volume 71, issue 3 (August 2020), pp. 393–408

Chapter 3

A Bot and a Smile: Interpersonal Impressions of Chatbots and Humans Using Emoji in Computer-mediated Communication
Austin Beattie, Autumn P. Edwards and Chad Edwards
Communication Studies, volume 71, issue 3 (August 2020), pp. 409–427

Chapter 4

Predicting AI News Credibility: Communicative or Social Capital or Both?
Sangwon Lee, Seungahn Nah, Deborah S. Chung and Junghwan Kim
Communication Studies, volume 71, issue 3 (August 2020), pp. 428–447

Chapter 5

Privacy, Values and Machines: Predicting Opposition to Artificial Intelligence
Josep Lobera, Carlos J. Fernández Rodríguez and Cristóbal Torres-Albero
Communication Studies, volume 71, issue 3 (August 2020), pp. 448–465

Chapter 6

Making up Audience: Media Bots and the Falsification of the Public Sphere
Rose Marie Santini, Debora Salles, Giulia Tucci, Fernando Ferreira and Felipe Grael
Communication Studies, volume 71, issue 3 (August 2020), pp. 466–487

For any permission-related enquiries please visit:
www.tandfonline.com/page/help/permissions

Notes on Contributors

Austin Beattie is Post-Graduate Fellow in the Communication and Social Robotics Labs and Communication PhD candidate at the University of Iowa, USA.

Deborah S. Chung is Associate Professor in the School of Journalism and Media at the University of Kentucky, USA.

Autumn P. Edwards is Professor in the School of Communication at Western Michigan University, USA and Co-director of the Communication and Social Robotics Labs (combotlabs.org).

Chad Edwards is Professor of Communication in the School of Communication at Western Michigan University, USA.

Fernando Ferreira is Co-founder and Partner of the data science company Twist (https://twist.systems/), located at the Science Park of Federal University of Rio de Janeiro (UFRJ), Brazil. He is also a postdoctoral research associate at the Signal Processing Laboratory (COPPE-UFRJ-Brazil) and is a collaborator researcher of NetLab/UFRJ.

Felipe Grael is Co-founder and Partner of the data science company Twist (https://twist.systems/), located at the Science Park of Federal University of Rio de Janeiro (UFRJ), Brazil. He is also a collaborator researcher of NetLab/UFRJ.

Jungseock Joo is Assistant Professor in Communication at University of California, USA.

Jang Hyun Kim is School Head (Chair) for School of Convergence, Sungkyunkwan University, South Korea and Associate Professor in the Department of Interaction Science.

Junghwan Kim is Assistant Professor in the Department of Mass Communication at the Pukyong National University, South Korea.

Sangwon Lee is Assistant Professor in the Department of Communication Studies at the New Mexico State University, USA.

Josep Lobera is Lecturer in Sociology at the Autonomous University of Madrid, Spain and the Tufts University & Skidmore College international program.

Zhenyang Luo is a doctoral candidate in the Department of Communication at North Dakota State University, USA.

Jasmine McNealy is Associate Professor at the University of Florida, USA.

Seungahn Nah is Professor at the University of Oregon, USA. He currently serves as an associate editor of the *Journal of Communication* and *Mass Communication & Society*.

Carlos J. Fernández Rodríguez is Senior Lecturer in Sociology at the Autonomous University of Madrid, Spain.

Debora Salles is a PhD candidate in the Information Sciences Graduate Program at the Federal University of Rio de Janeiro (UFRJ), Brazil, acting as a fellow researcher in the NetLab research group.

Rose Marie Santini is Professor in the School of Communication, Federal University of Rio de Janeiro (UFRJ), Brazil.

Patric R. Spence is Associate Professor of Communication at the University of Central Florida, USA.

Cristóbal Torres-Albero is Full Professor of Sociology at the Autonomous University of Madrid, Spain and founder of the *Spanish Journal of Sociology*.

Giulia Tucci is a PhD candidate in the Information Sciences Graduate Program at the Federal University of Rio de Janeiro (UFRJ), Brazil. Giulia is currently a fellow researcher of NetLab.

Maurice Vergeer is Assistant Professor in the Department of Communication Science, Behavioral Science Institute of the Radboud University, the Netherlands.

David Westerman is Associate Professor in the Department of Communication at North Dakota State University, USA.

Introduction

Communicating Artificial Intelligence (AI): Theory, Research, and Practice

Communicating Artificial Intelligence (AI): Theory, Research, and Practice

In more than 60 years since the founding of artificial intelligence (AI) as a formal academic discipline, rapid advances in technology have driven an enormous increase in interest in the field of study. AI subfields, including machine learning, neural networks, and the social implications of AI, have initiated new approaches to research and emergent questions. Of particular interest is the study of AI at its intersection with the study of communication.

Like AI, communication, too, overlaps with other fields like sociology, anthropology, economics, and computer science, among others, while focusing on human information exchange in its various forms. Despite an increasing scholarly attention of artificial intelligence, AI/communication studies concerning social, political, cultural, and ethical aspects of machine intelligence, interactions among agents, and social artifacts remain ripe for exploration. This special issue tackles these unexplored research areas with special emphasis on conditions, components, and consequences of cognitive, attitudinal, affective, and behavioral dimensions toward communication and AI.

This special issue epitomizes communication scholarship on Artificial Intelligence (AI) with a total of six articles. Topics vary from interactions between humans and robots through news representation of artificial intelligence to AI-based news credibility. The collection of the special issue offers implications for not only theoretical and methodological perspectives, but policy-makers and practitioners alike.

Artificial Intelligence in the Dutch Press: An Analysis of Topics and Trends

The first article by Maurice Vergeer gets to the heart of questions about communication and artificial intelligence by examining the crucial role of the press in shaping our ideas about emerging technology. Using a mixed methods approach, including content analysis, topic modeling, and sentiment analysis, Vergeer explores both the salience of AI and topics about it, as well as key themes and attitudes to the technology over time. He finds that different categories of newspapers – popular press, national newspapers, religiously oriented, economics-related – had both reported on different topics and also conveyed very different sentiments on AI. Importantly, some newspaper types failed to report on AI-related topics that would seemingly be of interest to their audiences. That said, Vergeer's investigation reports that sentiments found in the reporting about AI remained relatively stable over time.

I-It, I-Thou, I-Robot: The Perceived Humanness of AI in Human-machine Communication

Westerman et al. investigate the applicability of existing interpersonal and computer-mediated communication theories in the context of Human and AI communication. The authors argue that humans may perceive artificial intelligence and its products as communication partners when using them. This is evident from various real-world applications of AI, such as Amazon's Alexa, which has a capability of natural language processing and speech recognition and can interact and communicate with human users. As AI technology offers significantly more advanced functionalities to support human-like communication than traditional methods in computer software, human users may indeed respond to AI agents as if they are communicating with other human beings. Indeed, AI researchers from its early stage well understood the importance of human-machine communication capabilities of AI systems. In this sense, the ultimate goal of AI research will be to develop an automated system which humans perceive as human beings. The authors also point out that studies and lessons from human-machine communication can help better understand human-human communication because humans frequently utilize scripted and robotic ways of interactions and communications with other people, which may relate to how robots will interact with real humans and also explain why humans can accept the robotic way of communication when interacting with AI.

A Bot and A Smile: Interpersonal Impressions of Chatbots and Humans Using Emoji in Computer-Mediated Communication

Although chatbots are emerging as important conversational partners, past studies have rarely explored how bots' use of emoji impact perceptions of communicator quality. Beattie, Edwards, and Edwards examined the impact of emoji use on impressions of interpersonal attractiveness, CMC competence, and credibility in a computer-mediated context. Furthermore, their study tests whether impressions formed of human versus chatbot message sources were differed significantly in view of the CASA paradigm and the human-to-human interaction script framework. Results indicated that participants rated emoji-featuring messages greater than verbal-only messages on all three dependent variables of social attraction (H1), CMC competence (H2), and credibility (H3). It further demonstrated that scores for the interpersonal impression variables did not differ significantly between human or chatbot message sources, implying the participants perceived chatbots similar to humans, which is congruent with the findings of earlier studies of perceptions of Twitterbots. This study supports CASA paradigm and the utility of emoji use in CMC.

Predicting AI News Credibility: Communicative or Social Capital or Both?

Lee, Nah, Chung, and Kim challenge the tradition of news credibility scholarship by posing an important research question concerning the credibility on artificial intelligence (AI) based news as an essential democratic value. While prior scholarship on news credibility is media-centric, the authors expand not only media use but also interpersonal discussion, leading to AI-based news credibility. More importantly, the authors shed light on the roles that social capital, such as social trust, can play in predicting credibility on algorithm and automated news. In doing so, the authors extend the theory testing how communicative and social capital interplay using data collected through a national online survey in South Korea. Major results indicate that media use through television, social network sites, and online news sites, as well as public discussion, was the main predictors of AI news credibility. In particular, social trust plays a vital role in moderating the effect of interpersonal discussion on credibility where the relationship between discussion and credibility was even stronger for those who have a higher level of trust in others.

Privacy, Values and Machines: Predicting Opposition to Artificial Intelligence

While Vergeer considers how the press helps to shape our AI imaginations and sentiments, the research team of Lobera, Rodríguez, and Torres-Albero investigates social determinants of opposition to AI. Using a national survey deployed in Spain, the team explores the predictive value of sociodemographic indicators, including age, gender, income, and work status, as well as traditional theories of opposition to technology, cultural values, and attitudes to science. The traditional theories of opposition to technology show only moderate explanatory power. On the other hand, cultural values, including egalitarianism, resistance to innovation, privacy concerns, and distrust toward science and technology, demonstrate stronger effects on opposition to AI. At the same time, the team finds that a significant portion of the survey respondents held similar attitudes toward AI and technology.

Making up Audience: Media Bots and the Falsification of the Public Sphere

The article by Santini, Salles, Tucci, Ferreira, and Grael examines the extent to which media outlets in Brazil utilizes AI-based communication strategies to create social media metrics so that they can increase their relevance on Twitter. Specifically, the authors examine the roles that media bots can play in this process. Based on data collected through Twitter API, URL metadata, and Twitter trending topics, the authors found that media bots do help legacy media outlets in Brazil, including TV broadcast programs, to amplify their links as do automated accounts. That is, the authors uncover the manipulation strategies that adopted mainstream media adopted, resulting in audience misperceptions, distrust in media outlets, and manipulated public opinion.

The six articles offer valuable insights and implications concerning communicating artificial intelligence in terms of theory, research, and practice. We hope future scholarship extends its scope covering multifaceted, multidimensional, and multilevel aspects of artificial intelligence in the following areas.

- communicative practices between humans and digital interlocutors
- interpreting the social adoption of AI as technology acceptance and/or diffusion of innovation
- integration of artificial entities into political, health, science, environmental, and risk communication
- incorporation of AI into journalism, news, and civic and community life
- impact of machine learning-based algorithmic content recommendation in social media (e.g., filter bubbles)
- social bots or fake accounts in social media empowered by AI and their influences on public opinion
- cultural discourse surrounding digital and robotic interlocutors

- critical perspectives of communicating AI in society and societization of AI
- reinterpretations and representations of humans as digital entities
- legal, ethical, and policy implications concerning AI, algorithmic content and/or systems communication about AI and the explanation of advances in the field

Seungahn Nah ⓘ

Jasmine McNealy

Jang Hyun Kim ⓘ

Jungseock Joo

Artificial Intelligence in the Dutch Press: An Analysis of Topics and Trends

Maurice Vergeer

ABSTRACT
The present study focuses on newspaper articles published in all newspapers in the Netherlands from 2000 up to 2018 on how they report on artificial intelligence. The study showed how reporting changes over time and how different types of newspapers report differently about various topics in the field of artificial intelligence. The findings show that newspapers increasingly report about AI from 2014 onward. Newspapers do so on a wide range of topics related to AI. Several types of newspapers showed distinct coverage of many artificial intelligence-related topics. Although robots and their football capabilities appear to be ever-present in newspapers, recent articles about tech giants and fake news are more prominent in newspapers. One of the most notable findings was that religious newspapers published less about AI topics, even though some topics on artificial intelligence have religious connotations (cf. singularity, consciousness). Sentiments about AI in newspaper articles remained balanced between positive and negative sentiments over the years.

Artificial intelligence (AI) has been a promise to society for a long time. Turing (1950) is the first to mention intelligence in a computing machine, which became known later as AI. The technological advance of AI has been slow but steady. It encountered beautiful summers when the sky was the limit: quick progress in algorithms in times with unlimited funding. However, it was also met by severe winters when the development ground to a halt for extended periods, and funding was cut back (Crevier, 1993). Since the early 2010s, AI has seen a strong revival, due to new perspectives, particularly the use of neural networks algorithms for deep learning, particularly Hidden Markov Models, combined with the availability of Big Data to train these algorithms. At the same time, trained AI models are accessible for software developers, using Application Programming Interfaces (APIs), as provided by companies such as Google, Amazon, and Microsoft. In the late 2010 s, many people use AI in consumer products, knowingly or unknowingly. Devices such as iPhones, Android phones, Google Home, Amazon's Alexa, computer games, chatbots on websites that often have AI-driven apps. So, does this mean AI is an accepted technology? To make that decision, people can rely on direct experiences by using the technology first-hand, using these applications. Mostly, these applications are for fun and play and have become quite popular. People can also use external information sources to learn what lies ahead in the near and distant future.

This is an Open Access article distributed under the terms of the Creative Commons Attribution-NonCommercial-NoDerivatives License (http://creativecommons.org/licenses/by-nc-nd/4.0/), which permits non-commercial re-use, distribution, and reproduction in any medium, provided the original work is properly cited, and is not altered, transformed, or built upon in any way.

In 2019, the Dutch government presents its view on furthering the development of artificial intelligence in the Netherlands (Ministry of Economic Affairs and Climate, 2019). To push forward this development, the Dutch government intends to increase public funding in the coming years to intensify public-private partnerships to increase research on AI. One part of the action plan focuses on facilitating the societal acceptance of artificial intelligence.

As with other technological developments, the increased application of AI in society is highly relevant for citizens. Unfortunately, these techniques are highly abstract and complex. People's experiences with AI are mostly hidden behind a fancy user-interface or mediated by news reports on TV and in newspaper articles about AI. Also, artificial intelligence has been a popular angle for science fiction movies. Notable is the acting performance of H.A.L. 9000 in Kubrick's "2001: A Space Odyssey" (1968), a movie about astronauts on a quest accompanied by their super-intelligent but "malfunctioning" computer, while Scott's Blade Runner (1982) shows a future with intelligent replicants, who have a set limited lifespan of four years to prevent them from developing unstable emotions. These movies mostly set AI in a bleak and doom scenario, where humans are victims of AI technology gone awry. Other than watching and reading news reports and seeing these movies, people hardly have any experience with AI technology. If people do use AI technology, they are hardly aware of it (cf., Netflix' view suggestions, or image improvements on smartphones).

In order to inform citizens about science, here AI, journalists build a bridge between scientists making discoveries and citizens who want to learn about it and value these discoveries. A Dutch survey among journalists (Pleijter, Hermans, & Vergeer, 2012) shows their primary role is "making complex information accessible for the public" ($M = 3.40$, $SD = .67$ on a scale of "not important at all" (1) to "very important " (4)), directly followed by "provide interpretation and analysis" ($M = 3.23$, $SD = .71$), and "signaling new trends" ($M = 3.20$, $SD = .63$). These primary role perceptions are particularly applicable to science journalists. Journalists, therefore, can be considered vital for determining the acceptance or rejection of AI in daily life. To increase our understanding of how newspapers report on AI, the present study will answer the following research questions:

(1) How do newspapers in the Netherlands report about artificial intelligence?
   (a) What specific topics are associated with artificial intelligence in newspaper articles?
   (b) What kind of sentiments (positive versus negative) are associated with artificial intelligence in newspaper articles?
   (c) How does reporting about artificial intelligence change over time?

Artificial Intelligence in Society

AI is a complex topic, from a scientific perspective, as well as in terms of its societal implications. Most classifications of AI at least distinguish between narrow AI (weak) and general (strong) AI. Narrow AI can perform delineated specialized tasks very well and acts like it thinks, while strong AI can think (Searle, 1980). Although some people raise concerns about general AI (Baidu Forum, 2015), it is still not well developed. The development of narrow AI, however, has made substantial leaps from 2010 onward. These developments found their way in different applications: consumer products for general use. For instance, many countries with higher levels of welfare experience an aging population due to an increased life span and decreasing newborns. As a result, the health care system for the elderly becomes very expensive. Using robots and AI is considered a viable option to resolve the stress on the health care system. Particularly Japan, a country with the highest population age, socially assistive robots are studied to support the elderly (Bemelmans, Gelderblom, Jonker, & de Witte, 2012). Another area is economic productivity, where AI can assist human labor when it comes to tedious or dangerous work. The automobile industry introduced robots in the 1970 s. In those days, robots were merely mimicking exact movements programmed by a human. In the 2010 s, companies such as Boston Dynamics manufacture autonomous robots performing complex tasks in an uncontrolled environment.

Autonomous driving is another field of applications of AI: cars that can drive autonomously among other vehicles in open public spaces. Companies like Tesla, Google, and Uber are front runners in this field. More human-like AI applications are so-called smart assistants that are implemented either in smartphones or home speakers. Smart assistants, like Google Home, Apple's Siri, Amazon's Alexa, and Samsung's Bixby. These smart assistants allow users to communicate with them using plain voice commands instead of keyboard or finger gestures. Also, traditional recommender systems have become much more advanced: YouTube and Netflix have automated viewing suggestions, "helping" people to choose the next video or movie. Helping is put between quotation marks, because these technologies are not solely for the benefit of the end-users, but mostly to increase viewing time and thus to increase advertising revenues (Gomez-Uribe & Hunt, 2015). These systems have evolved over time at such a pace that it seems the system "knows" the end-users' preferences very well. Finally, AI was introduced in computer games. Algorithms, able to emulate a human player in the games for a single player to make "social" interactions in computer games.

Putting AI on the Agenda: Understanding News Reporting about AI

Due to people's lack of direct and explicit AI experience, the general public is mostly dependent on journalists reporting about AI. Journalists build agendas (McCombs & Shaw, 1972) in newspapers and on TV, either in current affairs programs or TV documentaries. These programs and articles are to inform viewers and readers about essential issues that – in the short or long run – may affect them. Choosing a perspective and a topic in AI is framing the issue of AI in general. Framing refers to journalists who "select some aspects of a perceived reality and make them more salient in a communicating text, in such a way as to promote a particular problem definition, causal interpretation, moral evaluation, and/or treatment recommendation" (Entman, 1993, p. 52). As the field of AI is quite diverse, it allows journalists to pick from a wide array of perspectives, ranging from science-centered, technology-centered, and society-centered perspectives and topics, from factual, ethical, and philosophical perspectives.

The composition of these agenda's and the frames in news media are the result of selection processes in the newsroom: choices made by journalists and editorial boards on what to cover and how to cover AI. Gatekeeper studies cover the shed light on these editorial choices (Shoemaker & Vos, 2009). Gatekeeping – the editorial choices made by journalists and editorial boards – can be explained by the news values journalists adhere to. Galtung and Ruge (1965) identify news values for news in general, among others, proximity, unexpectedness, negativity, elite countries. Their original list of news values has been revised by several studies (Allern, 2002; Brighton & Foy, 2007; Gans, 1979; Harcup & O'Neill, 2001, 2017) conclude that the original list of news values needed to be revised. More specifically for science news, Badenschier and Wormer (2012) identify additional news values based on proximities between countries, with regard to (a) their political handling of science and research, (b) their language, religion, and culture, and (c) their scientific culture.

Rosen, Guenther, and Froehlich (2016) identify several domains that affect selection criteria for news, and as a result affect the publication of news, which ultimately build news agendas. Besides aforementioned news values, they identify personal interests, professional role conceptions, and communication routines. They also distinguish types of media organizations that discriminates between selection criteria. Specific characteristics of media organizations may affect how news is selected. Although Rosen, Guenther and Froehlich equate organizational influence to the role of the editor or editorial boards, the news organization is more than that. For instance, selection criteria may differ between television news programs and newspapers or magazines. Another organizational distinction is the targeted audience: whether newspapers specifically target adults or youngsters, or the general population, the higher educated or the financially interested people, it suggests that agendas of newspapers are not uniform across media organizations but differs across types of news media organizations. The current study thus focuses on the structural differences in choosing and thus reporting about AI developments in society.

Apart from framing AI by selecting topics, approaching AI from an evaluative perspective indicates the extent journalists present AI as being for the good or bad. Like other new technologies over the course of centuries (cf. printing press, automobiles, moving pictures, the Internet), AI received positive sentiments and negative sentiments alike. AI, as an assistive technology, seems very positive. However, as AI evolves, people tend to get scared the moment some entity can outperform, even outthink humans. This point in time, yet unspecified, is called singularity. It is quite understandable that people perceive singularity as a threat: not-living machines, able to outperform human beings. A similar occurrence is the so-called uncanny valley effect (Mori, MacDorman, & Kageki, 2012): robots that become more similar to human beings are more positively perceived, until a certain point when people perceive the robot as being too real. At that point, acceptance drops significantly. To understand the evaluation of AI in newspaper articles, the texts are analyzed in terms of positive and negative sentiments. Similar to the choice of AI-related issues, the evaluation of AI may differ across types of media organizations.

Types of Media Organizations

In order to compare AI news reports, the current study distinguishes four dimensions, each with a different religious or socio-economic profile. Some aspects of AI in popular perceptions are in sensationalist terms: either in terms of a Utopian ideal or a dystopian nightmare (Brennen, Howard, & Nielsen, 2018). Previous research shows that popular newspapers, distributed at the national level, often publish news in a more sensationalistic manner as compared to other types of newspapers (Schaap & Pleijter, 2012). Therefore the expectation is that popular newspapers are more likely to publish more about AI.

A second dimension refers to news reports in newspapers with a dedicated interest in finance and economics. AI may impact on the economy in terms of increasing wealth by increasing productivity. At the same time, increased use of AI in the industries may increase unemployment in the short run. Such topics would be expected to be published more likely in economy-focused newspapers, such as Het Financieele Dagblad (economic-financial) and NRC Handelsblad. The development of AI is intended to improve life by "taking the robot out of the human"(refs), either to unburden people from tedious tasks, or to prevent people from having to work in hazardous environments, either in heavy industry or in warzones (e.g., drones). In general, the implementation of AI is expected to increase economic productivity, efficiency, and economic growth. At the same time, concerns are raised about rising unemployment because AI machines "take over" (Makridakis, 2017). Given these assumptions, newspapers with an economic orientation are expected to publish more news reports about AI as compared to other newspapers.

A further distinction between newspapers and their news reports refers to their religious orientation (third dimension). Even though the Netherlands is increasingly becoming secular, more so for Catholics than for protestants (De Hart, 2018), the Netherlands still has several newspapers with a Christian worldview. These Christian newspapers publish national news using a religious perspective when reporting on socio-political issues. Some aspects of the debate on AI may be related to Christian viewpoints. Philosophical debates about mind and consciousness. For instance, the question of whether scientists can create an AI being that is humanlike or may even outperform humans (cf. singularity). Like the heart is merely a pump, computationalists claim consciousness ultimately can be represented in algorithms. Thus, computationalism suggests that AI having a conscious mind is possible to create. Others argue that computational algorithms cannot capture consciousness (Davenport, 2012; Swiatczak, 2011). This worldview contrasts with the Christian worldview, where mankind should not tamper with (the creation of) life (cf., discussions on abortion and euthanasia). Similar debates on other technological advances emerged (cf., medical vaccinations, nanotechnology) (Hussain, Ali, Ahmed, & Hussain, 2018; Toumey, 2011). Thus, newspapers with a Christian worldview are expected to differ from other newspapers in the choice of AI-related topics and terms of the evaluations of AI.

A third distinction focuses on the (inter)national versus regional orientation of newspapers. An important distinction in Dutch newspapers is national and regional newspapers. National newspapers intend to reach readers in the entire country, while so-called regional newspapers intend to reach readers in a smaller region, roughly coinciding with a province or a sub-region thereof, delineated by cultural identity or a socio-economic region. Whereas national newspapers mostly focus on national and international news, regional newspapers also focus on regional and local news. Previous research has shown that people's world view is related to the types of newspapers they read. For instance, people who display a more localistic orientation tend to read regional and local newspapers more often than they would national newspapers (Elvestad, 2009; Vergeer, 1993). As a result, the predominant orientation of regional newspapers is on local areas such as neighborhood, the city and its surrounding areas (Boukes & Vliegenthart, 2017), even though regional newspapers also publish national news. National newspapers, on the other hand, publish mostly about national and international affairs. Their outlook on the world is much more cosmopolitan. News about specific regionals issues and events is only published in national newspapers when the news is relevant for people across the entire nation. Applied to science news, previous research shows that national newspapers more often publish news stories about science than regional newspapers do. Regional newspapers prefer to publish smaller science articles than national newspapers (Hijmans, Pleijter, & Wester, 2003). We expect these differences between regional and national newspapers to appear for AI news as well.

Data, Measurements and Analysis

Data

Data were collected from Lexis Nexis, a comprehensive news database covering all national and regional newspapers from 2000 and further. Using the keywords "kunstmatige intelligentie" and "AI", the initial sample (N = 6592) was preprocessing by removing general announcements (e.g., TV guide articles). Within articles, three types of data cleaning were applied. First, metadata, such as LexisNexis labels (e.g.,"TITLE", "ABSTRACT"), were removed. Second, word stemming was applied: reducing words to the stem (base) of the words in order to remove conjugations (e.g., "walking" and "walked' become "walk") and thereby making verbs identical. Third, stop words were removed (stopwords R package; (Benoit, Muhr, & Watanabe, 2019)): stopwords are ubiquitous words in language with little meaning and too common to differentiate between texts (e.g., "the", "is", "and").

Some Dutch regional newspapers titles have local editions. Some local editions of a single regional newspaper title occasionally publish the same article. These duplicate articles were removed, and the local editions were consolidated under the heading of the main regional newspaper title. A similar approach was used for the national newspapers NCR Handelsblad and NRC.Next, which are two separate titles, but as of 2015, are produced by the same editorial board. The final sample consisted of 4224 news articles in 25 newspaper titles, with a total number of words of 2,935,663 (Mean = 695.00, SD = 539.48).

Measurements

Dependent Variables

The *monthly number of articles on AI in general and specific topics* for each newspaper title was calculated by aggregating the number of articles by month. Topics were measured using two approaches. The first approach used the Boolean search operator "OR" on extensive lists of smart assistants (N = 20), tech companies (N = 62), game consoles (N = 130), game developers (N = 595), and car manufacturers (N = 426), and science. Lists were scraped from Wikipedia pages (see Appendix). Measuring references to science, the Boolean search operator "OR" for the following list of stemmed keywords were used (the English translation of keywords between brackets): university", "wetenschap" (science), vakgroep (scientific department), "science", "scient", "hoogleraar" (professor), "professor", "promovend" (PhD student), " TU" (Dutch abbreviation of technical university). Whether news originated from different countries was measured using a complete list of all countries (N = 197). The second approach to identify topics in news articles was topic modeling (Blei, Ng, & Jordan, 2003), a statistical technique to uncover topics in large textual data (Puschmann & Scheffler, 2016). Topic modeling is an exploratory technique, enabling to find systematically co-occurring keywords. However, interpretation of these empirical topics still requires knowledge of the field. Also, some topics may emerge that defy interpretation. Using the measure perplexity (Blei et al., 2003) to find the optimal number of topics, 50 topics were uncovered producing the lowest perplexity score. A further selection of topics was made based on the interpretation of the topics and the gamma-parameter (gamma ≥.20). The gamma-parameter indicates the importance of topics for articles (see Table 1). Selecting articles with a higher gamma value ensured the topic is essential in the newspaper article, and not merely mentioned in a subordinate clause of the article.

The *monthly amount of sentiment* per article and newspaper title was calculated by taking the total sum per month per newspaper title. Sentiments in news articles were determined by using a precompiled NRC-lexicon of Dutch words reflecting degrees of sentiments (Jockers, 2017). This dictionary contains words that refer to dimensions of either positive or negative sentiments. A new difference scale was created by subtracting the negative sentiment score from the positive sentiment score: positive sentiment values indicated more positive sentiments, while negative values indicated negative sentiments.

Independent Variables

Newspaper titles were classified on four characteristics: *geographical orientation, popular newspapers, economic orientation, secular versus religious orientation*. Newspapers in the Netherlands are either intended for a national audience (national newspapers) or intended for an audience in a specific region within the Netherlands (regional newspapers). Newspapers were also classified as popular newspapers or not. Newspapers also differ concerning their religious orientation. The current study distinguished newspapers with a Christian orientation and newspapers with a secular orientation. Newspapers with an economic orientation were newspapers with a distinct economy section in the newspaper. For all four types of newspapers, dichotomous measurements (0 = no, 1 = yes) were created.

Date was measured by the publication date of the newspaper article. To account for a possible non-linear growth across time, the square of *date* was also included.

Table 1. Topics from LDA topic modeling.

Topic	Number of articles	Topic	Number of articles
robot football	127	health care	72
tech giants fake news	110	concerns AI warfare	71
smart assistants	94	humanity Turing test Blade Runner	52
deep learning Watson: chess, go	89	philosophy writers	47
singularity	82	chatbots apps	43
autonomous driving	82	mobile devices China	37
computer gaming	78	quantum computing	36
AI in Asia	74	consciousness philosophy	31

Analysis

To analyze the salience of AI articles, topics, and sentiments in different types of newspapers across time, Growth Curve Analysis was used (Mirman, 2014), a combination of longitudinal analysis and mixed models. All data were aggregated by month, year and main newspaper titles. Aggregation resulted in a sample size of 5700 observations (= 25 newspaper titles*12 months*19 years, see Table 2).

Aggregation per month was chosen to ensure that the average number of articles per time unit substantially deviates from zero, and the number of time unites with zero articles is limited. Furthermore, publication of AI-news is less time-critical than national political news or a major accident is. Editorial boards may more easily postpone AI-news to make room for more important news.

Because the number of articles (AI and specific topics) were non-negative, discrete numbers, growth curve analysis was performed by using negative binomial mixed models (R-package lme4; Bates et al., 2019). To analyze sentiments, linear mixed modeling was applied using lme4. Before the analysis, the independent variables were checked for multicollinearity (O'Brien, 2007), showing the maximum Variance Inflation Factor to be 20.0. Initially, the distinction between quality newspapers and other newspapers was to be included in further analyses. However, because all quality newspapers are also national newspapers, it led to severe multicollinearity (VIF = 66.1). Therefore, it was decided to exclude the distinction between quality newspapers and other newspapers for the statistical analysis.

Table 2. Descriptive measures of variables in the growth curve analyses.

	Mean	Standard deviation
Number of articles	0.74	2.24
Sentiments	7.61	27.15
Newspaper type		
popular	0.06	0.58
national	1.10	2.88
religious	1.45	4.43
economic	0.96	3.09
Topics		
singularity	0.01	0.11
robot football	0.02	0.14
deep learning	0.01	0.13
Asia and AI	0.01	0.11
consciousness philosophy	0.00	0.07
chatbots apps	0.01	0.08
mobile devices China	0.01	0.08
autonomous driving	0.01	0.11
quantum computing	0.01	0.07
tech giants and fake news	0.02	0.14
health care	0.01	0.10
Turing test	0.01	0.09
computer gaming	0.01	0.12
philosophy, writers, books	0.01	0.08
concerns about AI warfare	0.01	0.10
smart assistants	0.01	0.12

N = 5700

Findings

Descriptive Analyses

This section presents general descriptive analyses on how AI news articles are related to countries, types of newspapers, types of actors, objects, and general sentiments. Figure 1 shows the change over time for the top 10 most mentioned foreign countries, several objects, and actors in AI, articles by newspaper type, and positive or negative sentiments. From 2014 onward, attention for different countries related to AI increased. Salience specifically increased for China, and to a lesser extent, the USA and Germany. Interestingly, salience of Japan and AI showed an abrupt decrease in Dutch newspapers articles. India showed a rapid increase in salience in 2017. In terms of news values based on proximity (Badenschier & Wormer, 2012), these findings are inconclusive: China is in many ways quite dissimilar to the Netherlands, but the USA can be seen as an elite country (Galtung & Ruge, 1965), and Germany as being geographically in close proximity to the Netherlands.

The top actors and objects were tech giants (e.g., Google, Facebook, IBM, Microsoft) and science institutes (cf., universities, scientific institutes, professors), closely followed by car brands. The salience of car brands is related to autonomous driving that made its entry in the 2010 s on public roads. Smart assistants, game developers, and gaming consoles are much less often mentioned. As for types of newspapers, those with an economic orientation showed the sharpest increase over time for salience of AI, followed by national newspapers. Christian newspapers devoted the least attention to AI in general. In terms of positive and negative sentiments, these opposing sentiments show the same increase

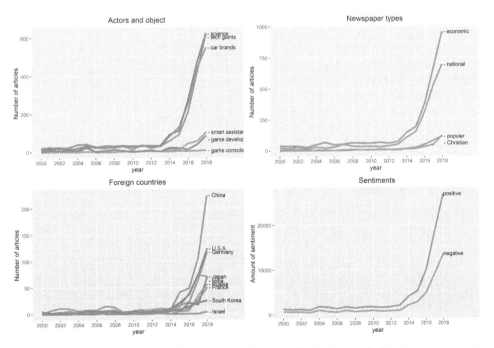

Figure 1. Attention for Artificial Intelligence related to specified actors and objects, newspaper type, countries and sentiments scores.

over time. Positive sentiments are, however, more prevalent in newspaper articles than negative sentiments.

Figure 2 shows that the topics vary extensively in the salience in newspapers. Reporting about tech giants and fake news shows the highest salience. This topic notably increased as a result of the 2016 US elections, reportedly showing much fake news. This topic also included the actions taken by Facebook, Google, and Twitter to battle fake news.

Explaining the Rise of Salience for AI and Its Topics

Table 3 shows the growth curve models of the number of articles in newspapers and the sentiments in these articles. The date parameters show a substantial linear increase over time in the number of articles (b = 63.94, p <.05), which showed to slow-down, given the negative quadratic date parameter(b = − 14.23, p <.05). Popular newspapers (b =.12, p <.05) and national newspapers (b =.39, p <.05) published more about AI, as compared to other newspapers. Newspapers with a religious orientation published slightly less about AI than other newspapers (b = −.11, p <.05). Newspapers with an economic orientation did not differ from other types of newspapers in terms of salience for AI.

Over time, the balance between positive and negative sentiments remained balanced: articles did not become more or less favorable. Popular newspapers (b = − 5.75, p <.05) and national newspapers (b = − 1.30, p <.05) showed to be more negative than other newspapers. Newspapers with a religious (b = 6.49, p <.05) or an economic orientation (b =.45, p <.05) were more positive than negative about AI.

Table 4 shows the growth curve analysis of salience of AI topics in newspaper articles. The singularity topic showed an increase over time (b = 165.10, p <.05). Popular

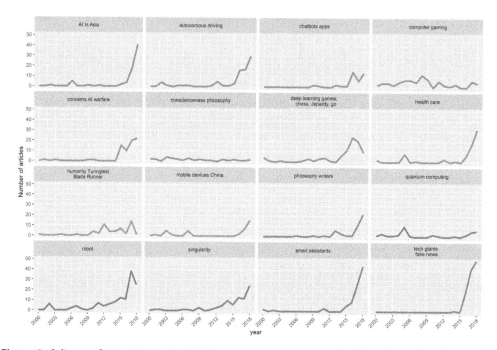

Figure 2. Salience of AI topics across time.

Table 3. Growth curve models of total number of articles and sentiments.

	Number of articles	Sentiments
Fixed effects		
Constant	−2.05*	−0.45
Date		
Linear	63.94*	−18.59
Squared	−14.23*	−11.45
Newspaper type		
Popular $_{(0=no,\ 1=yes)}$	0.12*	−5.75*
Geographical $_{(0=regional,\ 1=national)}$	0.39*	−1.30*
Religious $_{(0=secular,\ 1=Christian)}$	−0.11*	6.49*
Economic $_{(0=no,\ 1=yes)}$	−0.01	0.45*
Random effects		
Intercept	1.53	2.38
Date $_{(linear)}$	3374.26	19466.28
Date $_{(squared)}$	768.12	11762.73
Deviance	7515.00	40925.00

N = 5700, *p <.05

newspapers (b =.18, p <.05) published more news about the singularity topic than other newspapers, fitting the more sensationalistic profile of popular newspapers. National newspapers (b =.12, p <.05) reported more frequently about singularity as compared to regional newspapers. Religious newspapers (b = −.07, p <.05) published less about the topic singularity. Religious newspapers, not reporting more about this topic is a surprising finding, given that it involves machines surpassing mankind – God's creation – in performing tasks. Newspapers with an economic orientation did not report more about singularity than other newspapers. This finding is not surprising because there is no apparent economic aspect to singularity itself.

Robots and football, one of the most popular topics to write about, showed an increase over time (b = 100.60, p <.05), yet significantly slowing down (b = 26.76, p <.05). Popular newspapers (b =.17, p <.05) and those with an (inter)national orientation (b =.11, p <.05) published more about robots and football than other newspapers. Newspapers with a religious or economic orientation did not publish more about this topic than other newspapers.

Publishing articles about deep learning algorithms, AI playing games against humans showed a general increase over time (b = 51.76, p <.05). Popular newspapers, those with a religious outlook or an economic orientation, did not publish more articles about deep learning algorithms. However, national newspapers (b =.16, p <.05), as compared to other newspapers, published more reports about deep learning. It is notable to find little differences between types of newspapers. Either the topic is too complex to write about, too incidental, or "chess computers games" are too familiar to journalists and the general audience to write about. These were one of the first applications for general use. Figure 2 suggests that deep learning is relatively unpopular to write about, except when Google's AlphaGo beat the world champion Lee Sedol (4–1) in March 2016. The attention for deep learning subsequently quickly dissipated.

The relation between AI and Asia as a topic received increased attention over time in newspapers (b = 58.46 and b = 48.42, p <.05). It is a very general topic, unrelated to most newspaper characteristics. Popular newspapers (b =.13, p <.05)and those with an (inter)national orientation devoted more attention to this topic as compared to other newspapers (b =.14, p <.05). Newspapers with a religious or economic orientation showed no

Table 4. Growth curve analyses of salience for AI topics.

	singularity computer surpassing man	robot football	deep learning chess, go Jeopardy Watson	Asia and artificial intelligence	conscious-ness philosophy	chatbots apps	mobile devices China	autonomous driving
Fixed effects								
Intercept	-6.61*	-5.51*	-5.53*	-6.10*	-6.26*	-7.76*	-6.47*	-5.57*
Date								
Linear	165.10*	100.60*	51.76*	58.46*	-73.00*	197.80*	-39.51*	53.32*
Squared	-43.01	-26.76*	-19.66	48.42*	-44.25*	-59.77	8.61	20.15
Newspaper type								
Popular (0=no, 1=yes)	0.18*	0.17*	-0.002	0.13*	0.22	-13.79	0.23*	0.06
Geographical (0=regional, 1=national)	0.12*	0.11*	0.16*	0.14*	0.35*	0.14*	0.18*	0.18*
Religious (0=secular, 1=Christian)	-0.07*	0.01	-0.01	-0.04	-0.10	0.04	-0.07	-0.08*
Economic (0=no, 1=yes)	0.10*	< 0.01	0.04	0.04	0.05	-0.02	0.16*	0.05
Random effects								
Intercept	2.82	1.16	< 0.01	0.7209	0.4819	< 0.01	0.56	0.50
Date (linear)	14170.50	3721.76	5168.00	200.58	49.08	2128.00	330.66	2439.30
Date (squared)	3542.07	969.653	2180.00	1123.58	226.41	3427.00	410.73	362.68
Deviance	584.5	795.5	634.5	462.5	317.9	296	262.5	565.7

N=5700, *p < .05

	quantum computing	tech giants and fake news	health care	testing for humanity Turing test Blade Runner	computer gaming	philosophy writers books	concerns AI warfare	smart assistants
Fixed effects								
Intercept	-6.36*	-45.14*	-5.73*	-6.00*	-5.93*	-7.10*	-6.50*	-8.06*
Date								
Linear	-28.01	2,933.00*	27.19*	96.87*	-50.74	163.30*	137.20*	236.80*
Squared	-13.29	-872.60*	29.07*	-51.65*	-117.30*	-29.79	-2.49	-29.23
Newspaper type								
Popular (0=no, 1=yes)	0.08	0.15*	0.15*	0.12	1.00*	0.13*	0.02	0.07
Geographical (0=regional, 1=national)	0.50*	0.12*	0.13*	0.13*	0.40*	0.10*	0.07*	0.13*
Religious (0=secular, 1=Christian)	-0.24*	-0.05*	-0.05	-0.02	-0.19	-0.01	< 0.01	-0.02
Economic (0=no, 1=yes)	0.16*	0.07*	0.08*	0.01	0.05	0.03	0.02	0.04
Random effects								
Intercept	0.30	1.29	0.60	< 0.01	1.716	1.32	< 0.01	7.16
Date (linear)	708.61	426.06	499.38	2834.99	13507.55	1936.19	0.15	55886.64
Date (squared)	16.87	2285.26	111.53	3366.49	7591.29	4.09	0.11	8352.43
Deviance	311.2	526.3	443.2	449.9	709.9	363.8	453.0	486.0

N = 5700, *p <.05

differences to other types of newspapers in terms of salience. A plausible interpretation for the heightened attention for Asia and AI, in general, is the increased attention for Asia as an economic and technological powerhouse, one to be reckoned with. Notable is Alibaba's success and its significant investments in developing AI (Lucas, 2017). Also, China's controversial social credit system is partly AI-powered (Jiang & Fu, 2018; Matsakis, 2019).

Consciousnesses and a philosophical approach to AI, overall not very popular to publish about (see Figure 2), showed a decline in attention over time (b = 73.00, p <.05). This topic involved news articles about writers and their book publications. As such, it is mostly related to infrequent interviews, public talks, and publications. Only national newspapers (b =.35, p <.05) published more about this topic, while other types of newspapers (popular, religious, economic) showed no significant differences.

Publications about chatbots and messenger apps show an increase over time (b = 197.80, p <.05). Popular newspapers, those with a religious or economic orientation, however, did not publish more than other newspapers. Only newspapers with an (inter) national orientation (b =.14, p <.05) publish more frequently about chatbots and apps than all other newspapers.

The topic of mobile devices from China showed a decrease in attention over time (b = − 39.51, p <.05). Popular newspapers (b =.23, p <.05), those with an (inter)national orientation (b =.18, p <.05), as well as newspapers with an economic orientation (b = 16, p <.05) showed more salience of this topic: relatively cheap smartphones produced by newcomers to the western smartphone markets, such as Oppo and Huawei. These devices are often branded with using AI for photo image quality enhancements as well as assisting disabled people with smartphones (Sawers, 2018), while Oppo announced a considerable investment to develop AI for mobile devices further. While popular and national newspapers may address this topic from a public service perspective (which are the best smartphones), newspapers with an economic outlook may use the mobile phone industry's economic impact as a perspective.

The topic of autonomous driving, ranking 6th in popularity in newspapers, showed an increase over time in newspapers (b = 53.32, p <.05). Popular newspapers, which are quite automobile-minded, did not publish more about autonomous driving than other newspapers. Newspapers with an (inter)national focus (b =.18, p <.05) published more about autonomous driving as compared to other newspapers. Newspapers with a religious outlook (b = −.08, p <.05) published less about autonomous driving, compared to other newspapers. Those with an economic outlook did not publish more about autonomous driving. This finding is somewhat surprising because the development of autonomous driving is transforming the entire global automobile industry in the coming decades (Gao, Kaas, Mohr, & Wee, 2016).

Quantum computing showed stable salience over time. Popular newspapers did not publish more or less as compared to other newspapers. Those with an (inter)national (b =.50, p <.05) or economic outlook (b =.16, p <.05) published more frequently as compared to other newspapers, while religious newspapers (b = −.24, p <.05) published less frequently about quantum computing. Considering the small number of newspaper articles (see Figure 2), this topic is considered a niche topic.

The topic tech giants and fake news is, by far, the number 1 topic (see Figure 2). It showed a substantial increase (b = 2933.00, p <.05), but the increase in attention slowed down over time (b = − 872.60, p <.05). Popular newspapers (b =.15, p <.05), those with an (inter)national (b =.12, p <.05) or economic outlook (b =.07, p <.05) published slightly more about tech giants and fake news, as compared to religious newspapers (b = −.05, p <.05).

Attention for health care in the context of AI showed a steadily growing increase over time (b = 27.19 and b = 29.07, p <.05). Popular newspapers (b =.15, p <.05), those with an (inter)national (b =.13, p <.05) or economic outlook (b =.08, p <.05) published more frequently about AI-related health care. Religious newspapers' publication behavior, however, did not differ from the general publication pattern. Devoting more attention to health care and AI seems evident in a rapidly aging country. It is, therefore, the more surprising that religious newspapers, whose target audience consists mostly of older people (Schmeets, 2018), did not devote more attention to this topic.

Attention for the famous Turing test (and the movie Blade Runner and its version of the Turing test "Voight-Kampff test"), showed an increase (b = 96.87, p <.05) over time which, however, leveled off (b = − 51.65, p <.05). Popular newspapers and those with a religious or economic orientation did not pay more or less attention to this topic. However, newspapers with an (inter)national orientation published more frequently about Turing-test-related topics (b =.13, p <.05).

Attention to AI-related computer gaming a declining trend over time (b = − 117.30, p <.05). This topic was one of the first topics to receive more AI-related attention in the Dutch press (see Figure 2), but also one of the topics with the sharpest decline over time. Popular newspapers (b = 1.00, p <.05) and those with an (inter)national focus (b =.40, p <.05) published more frequently than other newspapers. Newspapers with a religious or economic orientation showed no differences with other newspapers.

Writers of philosophical books about AI received more attention over time (b = 163.30, p <.05), compared to other newspapers. Independently, they received more attention in popular newspapers (b =.13, p <.05) and newspaper with an (inter)national orientation (b =.10, p <.05). Newspapers with a religious or economic orientation showed no differences with other newspapers.

The topic of raised concerns about warfare using AI showed a steady increase over time (b = 137.20, p <.05). Popular newspapers and those with a religious or economic interest did not publish differently as compared to other newspapers. Newspapers with an (inter)national outlook, however, published slightly more as compared to other newspapers (b =.07, p <.05). ftableure 2 showed that journalists' interest in this topic is most likely triggered by the open letter of 2015 raising concerns about AI, later signed by prolific people from science and the tech industry, such as Stephen Hawkins, Elon Musk, and Bill Gates.

Smart assistants on mobile devices or home speakers showed a steady increase over time (b = 236.80, p <.05). Newspapers with an (inter)national orientation published significantly more articles (b =.13, p <.05) than other types of newspapers. Popular, religious, and economic newspapers did not publish more frequently about smart assistants.

Reflecting on these findings on topics found in newspaper articles on AI, we saw that salience for most topics increased over time, except for some exceptions for the topics quantum computing and computer gaming. While quantum computing is still in its infancy, it is also an abstract theme, being difficult to explain in laymen's terms. As for computer gaming, using the term AI has mostly been a marketing concept instead of real AI. For eight out of 16 topics, popular newspapers showed more salience than other newspapers. This finding suggests that popular newspapers are more interested in writing about AI-related topics to inform their audience. Newspapers with an (inter)national perspective show significantly more publications for all AI-related topics, as compared to other newspapers. This finding seems plausible because most advances in AI and applications of AI are from other countries than the Netherlands (cf. China, the US). As mentioned before, these (inter)national newspapers, are often also quality newspapers, besides providing factual news, also provide background stories about implications of developments for society writ large. Religious newspapers showed little differences in addressing AI-related topics. Moreover, religious newspapers showed less salience as compared to other newspapers for the following AI-related topics: singularity, autonomous driving, quantum computing, tech giants and fake news. Newspapers with an economic orientation, as compared to other newspapers, showed more salience for a small number of AI-related topics: singularity, Chinese mobile devices, quantum computing, and tech giants, and fake news.

Discussion

This study set out to understand news reporting about AI: what AI-related topics editorial boards chose and what sentiments they used. The current study also focused on how these topics and sentiments changed about AI changed over time. Looking at the amount of attention AI received in the Dutch press, AI has a tremendous extended summer (cf. Crevier, 1993). However, the attention is not all about the good AI brings to society and mankind. Topic modeling uncovered that some AI-related topics are about the dark side of AI (cf. IA warfare, fake news). Still, sentiments about AI in the press remain stable over time: positive and negative sentiments in articles cancel each other out.

The sharp increase of salience for AI in newspapers over time is confirmed by findings for US newspapers (Chuan, Tsai, & Cho, 2019): Dutch journalists showed remarkable similarity with US reporters who also increasingly to report about AI from 2015 onward. The question of why it took until 2014 for journalists to write more about AI-developments most likely lies in the relevance of AI for their readers. While scientific work on AI has been around for many decades, it was mostly conducted in the laboratory and available to a smaller group of experts. Recent advances made it possible to implement AI in handheld devices, making it available for the general public and, therefore, more relevant for journalists – as a service to its audience – to publish about.

Over the last few decades, Dutch Newspapers built a very diverse AI-agenda, which diverged for different types of newspapers. Topic modeling uncovered 50 topics, of which 16 were interpretable. The popular press, reportedly responsible for sensationalistic reporting (Schaap & Pleijter, 2012), showed a diverse range of topics: highbrow topics such as consciousness, philosophy writers and books. These newspapers did not choose to publish more about more sensation fitting topics such as AI warfare and autonomous driving. Overall, popular newspapers were more negative about AI. National newspapers published more about any AI-topic, as compared to regional newspapers. These national newspapers were also more negative about AI. Religious newspapers were the only newspapers that focused less on AI for several topics. Mainly ignoring the topic singularity is surprising, which seemed highly relevant for newspapers with a religious worldview. In contrast, AI-reports in religious newspapers seemed more favorable than those in other newspapers. Newspapers with an economic orientation looked beyond mere economic prospects of AI by reporting about singularity and fake news. Still, these economic newspapers were more favorable as compared to other types of newspapers.

Although diverging topics emerged from the data, one topic relevant to journalists themselves was surprisingly absent: robot-journalism (Lewis, Guzman, & Schmidt, 2019). Robot-journalism (a.k.a. algorithmic journalism) refers to software that, e.g., can write news articles based on structured input such as football matches results, earthquake information, or stock markets. Other applications are classifying large amounts of documents, for instance for investigative journalism. The absence does not mean journalists do not publish about robot-journalism, it means they do not write about it in the context of AI. However, reporting about these innovations in journalism may prove very insightful for readers to show what the impact of new technology such as AI and machine learning is in their daily work.

Future research might focus on the causes and consequences of reporting about AI. Given the differences found between types of newspapers, the question arises whether these differences in agendas can be traced back to differences in news values journalists subscribe to, whether male or female journalists differ in how they report about technology. As for the consequences of news reporting about AI, future research directions might focus on how the general population reacts to AI, based on what they read in the newspapers. How knowledgeable are people about AI, based on what they read? More importantly, to what extent do the pros and cons of AI in news reports affect people's acceptance of AI in their personal life?

Even though Crevier (1993) already wrote a "definitive" historical account of the search for AI in 1993, little did he know that research on AI would intensify rapidly in the mid-2010 s? Crevier's concluding chapter presents three possible scenarios: The Colossus scenario (AI takes over the world), the Big Brother scenario (AI spies on us), and the blissful scenario (peaceful coexistence with AI). Of these three scenarios, the Colossus and liftoff scenarios have not taken place yet. Today's societies do show some characteristics of the Big Brother scenario, but not as Crevier predicted. The 9/11 attacks on the WTC (New York), the Pentagon (Arlington), and Flight 92 (Shanksville, Pennsylvania) increased the NSA's activities to monitor people (Sinha, 2013), although mass surveillance is curtailed since 2015 (Volz, 2015). In the Netherlands, the General Intelligence and Security Service (AIVD) and the Dutch police (Brinkhoff, 2017) were granted more rights to spy on its people. However, maybe the biggest snoopers are tech giants such as Facebook and Google, monitoring our activities online and offline. Do these scenarios resemble any topics in the Dutch press? The Colossus scenario fits topic singularity, while the Big Brother scenario marginally fits tech giants and fake news. The blissful scenario seems to fit the news-topics best: smart assistants and chatbots on mobile devices, autonomous driving, deep learning. Predicting which scenario will prevail in the near and far future, Crevier concludes that, in the coming two decades (counting from 1993), the blissful scenario will prevail.

Further in the future, the Colossus or Big Brother scenario may become more dominant. However, it is up to society to let that happen or to take relevant countermeasures against these scenarios. Until then, it is essential to keep reading the newspapers to stay informed about AI, whether it is in plain sight, or any other guises. For journalists, this means becoming more knowledgeable about AI and its consequences is of crucial importance. Reporting about AI should avoid sensationalizing AI either in terms of Utopian ideals or dystopian nightmares. Reporting plain facts, for readers to decide whether they should embrace AI to assist them or not will become one of the challenges for journalists, considering the increasing number of publications about AI. Given that the Dutch government's moves forward with advancing AI in society (Ministry of Economic Affairs and Climate, 2019), the role of journalists is more needed than ever.

Disclosure Statement

No potential conflict of interest was reported by the author.

ORCID

Maurice Vergeer http://orcid.org/0000-0002-4802-4701

References

Allern, S. (2002). Journalistic and commercial news values. *Nordicom Review, 23*(1–2), 137–152. doi:10.1515/nor-2017-0327

Badenschier, F., & Wormer, H. (2012). Issue selection in science journalism: Towards a special theory of news values for science news?. In S. Rödder, M. Franzen, & P. Weingart (Eds.), *The sciences' media connection –Public communication and its repercussions* (Vol. 28, pp. 59–85). Dordrecht, the Netherlands: Springer. doi:10.1007/978-94-007-2085-5_4

Bates, D., Maechler, M., Bolker, B., Walker, S., Christensen, R. H. B., Singmann, H., ... Fox, J. (2019). *lme4: Linear mixed-effects models using "Eigen" and S4 (Version 1.1-21)*. Retrieved from https://CRAN.R-project.org/package=lme4

Bemelmans, R., Gelderblom, G. J., Jonker, P., & de Witte, L. (2012). Socially assistive robots in elderly care: A systematic review into effects and effectiveness. *Journal of the American Medical Directors Association, 13*(2), 114–120. doi:10.1016/j.jamda.2010.10.002

Benoit, K., Muhr, D., & Watanabe, K. (2019). *stopwords: Multilingual stopword lists (Version 1.0)*. Retrieved from https://CRAN.R-project.org/package=stopwords

Blei, D. M., Ng, A. Y., & Jordan, M. I. (2003). Latent Dirichlet allocation. *Journal of Machine Learning Research, 3*(Jan), 993–1022. http://www.jmlr.org/papers/v3/blei03a.html

Boukes, M., & Vliegenthart, R. (2017). A general pattern in the construction of economic newsworthiness? Analyzing news factors in popular, quality, regional, and financial newspapers. *Journalism: Theory, Practice & Criticism*. doi:10.1177/1464884917725989

Brennen, J. S., Howard, P. N., & Nielsen, R. K. (2018). *An industry-led debate: How UK media cover artificial intelligence*. Retrieved from https://web.archive.org/web/20191005195719/https://reutersinstitute.politics.ox.ac.uk/sites/default/files/2018-12/Brennen_UK_Media_Coverage_of_AI_FINAL.pdf

Brighton, P., & Foy, D. (2007). *News values*. London, UK: Sage.

Brinkhoff, S. (2017). Big data data mining by the Dutch police: Criteria for a future method of investigation. *European Journal for Security Research*, 2(1), 57–69. doi:10.1007/s41125-017-0012-x

Chuan, C.-H., Tsai, W.-H. S., & Cho, S. Y. (2019). *Framing artificial intelligence in American newspapers*. 6, Hawaii. Retrieved from https://web.archive.org/web/20190125202543/http://www.aies-conference.com/wp-content/papers/main/AIES-19_paper_162.pdf

Crevier, D. (1993). *AI: The tumultuous history of the search for artificial intelligence*. New York, NY: Basic Books, Inc.

Davenport, D. (2012). Computationalism: Still the only game in town: A reply to Swiatczak's "Conscious representations: An intractable problem for the computational theory of mind.". *Minds and Machines*, 22(3), 183–190. doi:10.1007/s11023-012-9271-5

De Hart, J. (2018). Developments in Christian faith [Ontwikkelingen in de christelijke gelovigheid]. In J. de Hart & P. van Houwelingen (Eds.), *Christians in the Netherlands: Church attendance and Christian faith [Christenen in Nederland: Kerkelijke deelname en christelijke gelovigheid]* (pp. 75–97). The Hague, the Netherlands: Institute for Social Research.

Elvestad, E. (2009). Introverted locals or world citizens?. *Nordicom Review*, 30(2), 105–123. doi:10.1515/nor-2017-0154

Entman, R. M. (1993). Framing: Toward clarification of a fractured paradigm. *Journal of Communication*, 43(4), 51–58. doi:10.1111/j.1460-2466.1993.tb01304.x

Forum, B. (2015, March 29). *Baidu CEO Robin Li interviews Bill Gates and Elon Musk at the Boao Forum*. Retrieved from https://www.youtube.com/watch?v=NG0ZjUfOBUs

Galtung, J., & Ruge, M. H. (1965). The structure of foreign news. The presentation of the Congo, Cuba and Cyprus crises in four Norwegian Newspapers. *Journal of Peace Research*, 2(1), 64–90. doi:10.1177/002234336500200104

Gans, H. J. (1979). *Deciding what's news: A study of CBS evening news, NBC nightly news, newsweek, and time*. New York, NY: Vintage.

Gao, P., Kaas, H.-W., Mohr, D., & Wee, D. (2016). *Disruptive trends that will transform the auto industry*. McKinsey website. Retrieved from https://web.archive.org/web/20200217175306/https://www.theprocurement.it/wp-content/uploads/2016/04/INTERNATIONAL-Disruptive_trends_that_will_transform_the_auto_industry__McKinsey__Company.pdf

Gomez-Uribe, C. A., & Hunt, N. (2015). The Netflix recommender system: Algorithms, business value, and innovation. *ACM Transactions on Management Information Systems*, 6(4), 1–19. doi:10.1145/2843948

Harcup, T., & O'Neill, D. (2001). What is news? Galtung and Ruge revisited. *Journalism Studies*, 2(2), 261–280. doi:10.1080/14616700118449

Harcup, T., & O'Neill, D. (2017). What is news?. *Journalism Studies*, 18(12), 1470–1488. doi:10.1080/1461670X.2016.1150193

Hijmans, E., Pleijter, A., & Wester, F. (2003). Covering scientific research in Dutch newspapers. *Science Communication*, 25(2), 153–176. doi:10.1177/1075547003259559

Hussain, A., Ali, S., Ahmed, M., & Hussain, S. (2018). The anti-vaccination movement: A regression in modern medicine. *Cureus*, 10(7), 1–8. doi:10.7759/cureus.2919

Jiang, M., & Fu, K.-W. (2018). Chinese social media and big data: Big data, Big Brother, big profit? *Policy & Internet*, 10(4), 372–392. doi:10.1002/poi3.187

Jockers, M. (2017). *syuzhet: Extracts sentiment and sentiment-derived plot arcs from text (Version 1.0.4)*. Retrieved from https://CRAN.R-project.org/package=syuzhet

Kubrick, S. (1968). *2001: A space odyssey*. Retrieved from https://web.archive.org/web/20200212165652/https://www.imdb.com/title/tt0062622/

Lewis, S. C., Guzman, A. L., & Schmidt, T. R. (2019). Automation, journalism, and human–machine communication: Rethinking roles and relationships of humans and machines in news. *Digital Journalism*, 7(4), 409–427. doi:10.1080/21670811.2019.1577147

Lucas, L. (2017, October 11). Alibaba to invest $15bn in R&D labs in push to become AI leader. *Financial Times Online*. Retrieved from https://web.archive.org/web/20171014065455/http://www.cnbc.com/2017/10/11/alibaba-says-will-pour-15-billion-into-global-research-program.html

Makridakis, S. (2017). The forthcoming artificial intelligence (AI) revolution: Its impact on society and firms. *Futures*, *90*, 46–60. doi:10.1016/j.futures.2017.03.006

Matsakis, L. (2019, July 29). How the West got China's social credit system wrong. *Wired*. Retrieved from https://web.archive.org/web/20200128223351/https://www.wired.com/story/china-social-credit-score-system/

McCombs, M. E., & Shaw, D. L. (1972). The agenda-setting function of mass media. *Public Opinion Quarterly*, *36*(2), 176–187. doi:10.1086/267990

Ministry of Economic Affairs and Climate. (2019). *Strategic action plan for artificial intelligence [Strategisch Actieplan voor Artificiële Intelligentie]*. Retrieved from https://web.archive.org/web/20200217191251/https://www.rijksoverheid.nl/documenten/beleidsnotas/2019/10/08/strategisch-actieplan-voor-artificiele-intelligentie

Mirman, D. (2014). *Growth curve analysis and visualization using R*. Boca Raton, FL: Chapman and Hall/CRC.

Mori, M., MacDorman, K. F., & Kageki, N. (2012). The uncanny valley [from the field]. *IEEE Robotics Automation Magazine*, *19*(2), 98–100. doi:10.1109/MRA.2012.2192811

O'Brien, R. M. (2007). A caution regarding rules of thumb for variance inflation factors. *Quality & Quantity*, *41*(5), 673–690. doi:10.1007/s11135-006-9018-6

Pleijter, A., Hermans, L., & Vergeer, M. (2012). Journalists and journalism in the Netherlands. In D. Weaver & L. Willnat (Eds.), *The Global Journalist in the 21st Century* (pp. 242–254). London, UK: Routledge.

Puschmann, C., & Scheffler, T. (2016). Topic modeling for media and communication research: A short primer. *SSRN Electronic Journal*. doi:10.2139/ssrn.2836478

Rosen, C., Guenther, L., & Froehlich, K. (2016). The question of newsworthiness: A cross-comparison among science journalists' selection criteria in Argentina, France, and Germany. *Science Communication*, *38*(3), 328–355. doi:10.1177/1075547016645585

Sawers, P. (2018, December 3). Huawei's StorySign app can translate kids' books into sign language. Retrieved from https://venturebeat.com/2018/12/03/huaweis-storysign-app-can-translate-kids-books-into-sign-language/

Schaap, G., & Pleijter, A. (2012). The level of sensation on frontpage pictures: A content analysis of popular and quality newspapers in the Netherlands [Het sensatiegehalte van voorpaginafoto's: Een inhoudsanalyse van populaire en kwaliteitskranten in Nederland]. *Tijdschrift Voor Communicatiewetenschap*, *40*(1), 71–86. https://web.archive.org/web/20190330093233/https://core.ac.uk/download/pdf/16187035.pdf

Schmeets, H. (2018). *Who is religious, and who isn't?[Wie is religieus, en wie niet?]* [Webpagina]. Retrieved from https://web.archive.org/web/20200215021323/https://www.cbs.nl/nl-nl/achtergrond/2018/43/wie-is-religieus-en-wie-niet-

Scott, R. (1982). *Blade runner*. Retrieved from http://www.imdb.com/title/tt0083658/

Searle, J. R. (1980). Minds, brains, and programs. *Behavioral and Brain Sciences*, *3*(3), 417–424. doi:10.1017/S0140525X00005756

Shoemaker, P. J., & Vos, T. P. (2009). *Gatekeeping theory*. New York, NY: Routledge.

Sinha, A. (2013). NSA surveillance since 9/11 and the human right to privacy. *Loyola Law Review*, *59*, 861–946. https://web.archive.org/web/20200217191442/https://dspace.loyno.edu/jspui/bitstream/123456789/121/1/Sinha.pdf

Swiatczak, B. (2011). Conscious representations: An intractable problem for the computational theory of mind. *Minds and Machines*, *21*(1), 19–32. doi:10.1007/s11023-010-9214-y

Toumey, C. (2011). Seven religious reactions to nanotechnology. *NanoEthics*, *5*(3), 251–267. doi:10.1007/s11569-011-0130-2

Turing, A. M. (1950). Computing machinery and intelligence. *Mind*, *49*, 433–460. doi:10.1093/mind/LIX.236.433

Vergeer, M. (1993). The dead from afar. Geographical reach of information and interests and the use of local media [De doden van ver. Geografische reikwijdte van informatie-interesse en het gebruik van lokale media]. *Massacommunicatie, 21*(2), 102–119. https://web.archive.org/web/20170306111247/http://mauricevergeer.nl/pdf/Vergeer_1993_De%20doden%20van%20ver.pdf

Volz, D. (2015, November 27). NSA to shut down bulk phone surveillance program by Sunday. *Reuters.* https://web.archive.org/web/20190210161215/https://www.reuters.com/article/us-usa-nsa-termination-idUSKBN0TG27120151127

I-It, I-Thou, I-Robot: The Perceived Humanness of AI in Human-Machine Communication

David Westerman ⓘ, Autumn P. Edwards ⓘ, Chad Edwards ⓘ, Zhenyang Luo ⓘ, and Patric R. Spence ⓘ

ABSTRACT
As artificial intelligence (AI) technologies become more common and capable interaction partners (human-machine communication; HMC), understanding how people perceive and interact with them becomes increasingly important to study. This essay argues that one important avenue for this study is the application of relevant interpersonal and computer-mediated communication (CMC) theories. The paper suggests that these theories are relevant because the Computers as Social Actors (CASA) approach has shown that people tend to respond to technologies as they do to other people. It summarizes some theories that may be especially useful for future study in this field. Finally, a case is made that the study of AI and HMC may also be important for greater understanding of the human-human communication process as well.

> Man wishes to be confirmed in his being by man, and wishes to have a presence in the being of the other.-Martin Buber

Buber (1923/1958) suggests that establishing relationships with others is the fundamental meaning of life, as suggested by the quote above. He discusses two perspectives: "I-It" and "I-Thou", and applied to interpersonal communication, "I-It" refers to treating another person as an object, whereas "I-Thou" involves relating to another person on a deeper level and treating the other person as a unique individual (Buber, 1923/1958); feeling truly present with another. Buber (1947/ 2002) argues that we are not truly aware of another's existence every time we interact with them. Authentic dialogue – communication not focused on objective tasks/goals/problems, but instead focused on truly experiencing the partner – is what leads the ongoing mutual interaction that typifies "I-Thou." relationships Buber suggests that authentic dialogue that establishes these kinds of relationships does not only happen between humans, but also can happen between humans and other parties who are perceived to have awareness.

Can we come to truly experience the partner when that partner is an artificial intelligence (AI)? As technology increasingly becomes a relational partner, and human-machine communication (HMC) becomes more possible (and probable), how we relate with robots

Figure 1. Social action is social action.

and other AI technologies becomes a more fundamental question to address (Spence, 2019). How do we confirm the being of robots, possibly moving toward "I-Thou" type relationships with AI? And perhaps more importantly, what does this tell us about ourselves? These are the central questions that this paper will address. These questions stem from the basic argument that: 1) AI is a Communication discipline, 2) we respond to technologies as we do people, and thus, 3) communication theories can likely help us understand how we develop relationships with AI (especially HMC).

Communication and AI

The development and use of communication technologies might productively be considered a series of presence workarounds, enabling communicators to share information and participate in social life while removing the requirement of being collocated in space and time. Communication technologies have progressively allowed more affordances, cues, and richness for enhancing social presence when interacting with distant human partners. However, even when those increased affordances are not there, people find ways to accomplish the goal of connection through technology (Walther, 1992). Importantly, technology is not just a medium, but can also be a participant in the communication process (Lombard & Ditton, 1997). Presently, communication technologies are culminating in artificial intelligence, which enables the technological social actors/messengers to be more intimate, proximate, variously embodied, and real. In other words, developments in AI have led to new communication contexts in which people talk not only *through* technologies, but also *to* and *with* them as if they are legitimate partners (Fortunati & Edwards, 2020; Guzman, 2018, 2020).

AI, a branch of computer science, studies the "automation of intelligent behavior" (Luger, 2002, p. 1). Through AI technologies, machines can be made to "think" (Garnham, 1987), or to at least appear to be thinking. Humans have taken decades to use AI to simulate human intelligence or the minds of humans (Dautenhahn, 2007). From classic AI focusing on the problem-solving aspect of human intelligence (general AI), to giving AI more humanlike bodies and levels of social intelligence (e.g., recognizing human facial expression and expressing emotions), developers have been continuing to make AI to appear more humanlike. Since people are increasingly interacting with AI systems on a daily basis (Riedl, 2019) and in the workplace (Bankins & Formosa, 2019), it is vital to understand what this technology means beyond a technical issue. The current challenges require interdisciplinary insights, especially the need to take humans' perceptions and behavioral responses into account (Shank et al., 2019). Bryson and Theodorou (2019) argue that we need to take a "human-centric" approach to AI to ensure that humans are able to have control.

Dating back to Alan Turing's (1950) classic test outlining the importance of the perceived nature of the communication partner, AI has always been a communication issue at heart. Turing suggested that computer intelligence would be indistinguishable from human intelligence when a human judge is unable to tell whether they were interacting with a computer or a human. Thus, for an AI to be perceived as intelligent, communication was central, as communication is what leads to the metal model of the other interactant as human or not. Thus, dating back to this foundational article of AI (Ein-Dor, 1999), AI was a social science. Gunkel (2012) has also argued that, "whether it is explicitly acknowledged or not, communication (and 'communication' as the concept is understood and mobilized in the discipline of communication studies) is fundamental to both the theory and practice of artificial intelligence (AI)" (p. 2). However, this connection seems to have been lost in the communication discipline, and we have instead focused almost entirely on computer-mediated communication (CMC), with technology only a medium through which human actors communicate with each other (interestingly, Turing was also at the forefront of CMC, as he suggested that a text-only channel would be the best for passing the Turing Test, focusing on how a reduction of certain cues in a communication channel might strategically be used to accomplish communication goals). The treatment of computers as fundamentally media through which humans communicate had worked quite well until the rise of social machines (Guzman, 2018). In such contexts, technologies "are not a medium through which human interact, but rather a medium with which humans interact" (Zhao, 2006, p. 402).

To pass the Turing test and be deemed capable of "intelligence," a program needs to be confirmed by human judges to be human based on its communication abilities. Indeed, we make judgments about the humanness (Thou-ness) of the entity with which we are interacting based in part on the words that entity uses (e.g., Westerman et al., 2019). Thus, as outlined by Turing, how an entity such as a social machine communicates largely is what drives our perceptions of that entity's intelligence and humanness or roboticness. But what aspects of communication matter in these judgments? To help answer that question, the Computers as Social Actors (CASA) paradigm provides direction and is discussed next.

Computers (Technologies) as Social Actors

In the HMC context, one of the most influential contributions for understanding perception is the CASA paradigm. Pioneered by Nass and colleagues (e.g., Reeves & Nass, 1996), CASA is a conceptual framework for a host of empirical investigations into the behavioral and social-cognitive tendencies of human beings' responses to computers. CASA has also been applied more recently to studies of human communication with more agentic and communicative AI interlocutors and social robots (e.g., C. Edwards et al., 2016; Edwards, Edwards, Westerman et al., 2019; K. J. Kim et al., 2013; Park et al., 2011; Spence et al., 2019; Xu, 2019). Xu and Lombard (2016) have expanded CASA to Media as Social Actors (MASA), and suggest that a variety of cues from technologies can trigger social responses and lead to a feeling of social presence from various forms of media, old and new. Overall, the CASA paradigm posits that people fundamentally understand and relate to technologies as if they were other people.

Nass and Moon (2000) highlighted that anthropomorphism (or this type of perception) of computers and the consequent application of social rules seem to be a mindless process. This mindlessness occurs because 1) we tend to overuse and rely on human social categories even when interacting with computers, 2) apply and engage in overlearned social behaviors, and 3) exhibit premature cognitive commitments. In general, if the computer's cues are sufficient for humans to attribute humanness to it, we then mindlessly apply scripts from human-human interaction to the human-computer interaction. Although other explanations have been offered for this process, there are many primary and secondary cues that are likely to trigger such mindless social responses (cf, Xu & Lombard, 2016). Then, once the trigger has occurred, and we respond with one of our overlearned scripts, we stop looking for more cues that might engage another script (we satisfice).

Similar to other heuristics, engaging in these social scripts is generally very useful. Except when it is not, and "sometimes they lead to severe and systematic errors" (Tversky & Kahneman, 1974). The representativeness and availability heuristics are very relevant to HMC and AI/Communication in this way. Triggering cues make the technology seem to represent a social entity, to which we then apply easily available overlearned social rules and scripts. As Gilbert (1991) pointed out, "People are credulous creatures who find it very easy to believe and very difficult to doubt" (p. 117). Gilbert thus suggested that people are Spinozan information processors (cf., Carpenter, 2018), with belief tied together with understanding, requiring an extra step and more effort to then doubt or disconfirm our beliefs. As Lee (2004) also pointed out, it may not be that we have to suspend disbelief willingly; our default is to believe unless something convinces us not to. These cognitive tendencies may help explain why it is quite common to relate to robots and other AI in a manner that we also logically understand is best suited to relating to other humans.

One script for interaction with AI is the human-human interaction script. People expect that an interaction partner will be another human, and thus they anticipate their communication with robots will a greater sense of uncertainty and lower anticipations of social presence and liking (C. Edwards et al., 2016; Spence et al., 2014). Yet, people's actual initial interactions with and subsequent perceptions of social robots versus human beings after such interaction do not match those initial perceptions (Edwards et al., 2019). It seems that the primary cue of interaction triggers an expectation of that partner being human, and then the cue of who that partner is (human or machine) leads to comparisons to that expectation. However, the experience of actual interaction with machines can help override these initial perceptions.

Overall, if a technology triggers our social scripts, we respond to the technology using those social scripts and rules. This "click, whirr" response (Cialdini, 2001) suggests that it might take only a few cues or pieces of information for something to seem social, and thus, engage our social responses to it. Deriving from the earlier Media Equation (media = real life; Reeves & Nass, 1996), there is strong empirical evidence that people apply the same social interaction rules to computers and machine communicators they use with human beings, despite logically knowing that the computer or robot is not a human (called ethopoeia by Nass & Moon, 2000). In other words, if we often respond to technologies as we do people, the theories explaining the interaction process with humans should be applicable to interactions with machines (HMC) as well. Therefore, interpersonal communication (IPC) theories and computer-mediated communication (CMC) theories are relevant to the study of HMC (Westerman et al., 2020; Xu & Lombard, 2016). What follows is not a complete list of such theories, as others have already suggested some possibilities as well, but instead, provides an overview of some that seem particularly applicable.

IPC Theories and AI

A key component in HMC will be how relationships form in interaction between humans and machine partners. When people interact with AI, they apply interpersonal and relational norms to these interactions (A. Kim et al., 2019). Baxter's (1988) relational dialectics theory (RDT) suggests that all relationships are characterized by the ongoing presence and communicative management of tensions and are full of negotiated meanings and contradictions (Baxter & Montgomery, 1996). There will likely be parallel tensions characterizing discourses of human and human-machine relationships. Because these tensions are competing discourses negotiated and constituted in communication, in our attempts to relate with AI or social robots, we will likely face pushes and pulls just as we do with other people (Sugiyama, 2013). The relational tension of *novelty and predictability*, for example, is a prominent one. A robot that has novel messages at times will potentially be exciting and more attractive than a robot that does not ever surprise us in its communication. For a social robot working on the factory floor, we will not want novelty but would need predictability for safety and security. Prokopenko (2014) argues that computational intelligence needs to be both predictable and stable but be "complex in creating innovations" (para. 5). Research in this area would be well served by applying Baxter's work to the study of AI. Just as with human relationships, the context and type of relationship will matter for how partners negotiate these tensions and transition in some cases from an "I-It" positionality to an "I-Thou" relationship.

Regarding the relational tension of *disclosure and privacy*, people balance their privacy concerns with the need to self-disclose in interpersonal relationships. In the HMC context, Amazon's Alexa needs to "listen" at all times to function, but there are substantial privacy concerns to address (Lau et al., 2018). What happens to our messages with Alexa when seeking health advice? Are these messages deleted or saved by Amazon? As HMC becomes commonplace, relational tensions/contradictions will emerge as they would in human-human relationships. Will the same RDT strategies that are useful in human-human communication work in AI and communication? Future research is necessary to examine RDT in this context to foster an understanding of the potential for "I-Thou" relationships between humans and machine partners. It could be that people have individual differences related to an "I-Thou" or "It-It" relational dialectic with communication and machine partners, much in the same way they might with a close friend or a stranger on the street.

Another approach that is relevant to the study of AI and communication is Grice's (1975) maxims. Grice's maxims are general expectations that people have about other people's communication, and thus, can be used to predict ways that will seem more human and confirming to people. The four maxims are 1) Quality, 2) Quantity, 3) Relation, and 4) Manner. Quality generally refers to the fact that we expect people to tell the truth and not to say things that they do not have evidence to support. Quantity refers to the notion that we expect people to give the right amount of information for a communicative purpose. Quantity is a Goldilocks maxim; we expect not too much but not too little. The maxim of relation suggests that what we say is expected to be relevant to the task at hand. Finally, manner suggests we should try to be clear in the way we communicate. When taken together, these maxims suggest ways in which our communication should meet the expectations for cooperation held by other people. These can be broken, of course, and often are to great strategic effect (we expect people to be honest, so when they break the maxim of quality, it can work well for the breaker), but people tend not to like it when they know others are not following the maxims.

Scholars have begun applying the work of Grice to AI. Interactional AI systems (spoken-dialogue systems) have been built based on Grice's cooperative principle (Nijholt, 2011; Schmidt, 2005). Baron (2015) writes, "While we are willing to countenance the fact that humans withhold information, do not always tell the truth, sometimes go off-topic, and can be wordy or obscure, it is hard to imagine anyone designing a robot with such less-than-felicitous conversational behavior. We would never be sure we could trust what the robot said to us (rendering it pragmatically unreliable)" (p. 262). As such, it is vital to understand if Grice's conversational maxims can be applied to AI in the same ways they are utilized in human-human communication. Are there differences in how we apply conversational maxims to machine partners and human partners? Moreover, do these differences contribute to our understanding of an "I-Thou" or "I-It" relational stance within the HMC context? These types of questions need to be addressed to further increase the communication competency of machine communication partners.

It seems that programming AI and other social robots to communicate in ways that are consistent with Grice's maxims would be advantageous, most of the time. This may also help our understanding of some of the struggles of AI and natural language, insofar as Grice's maxims articulate expectations that may not always seem natural. As mentioned above, Ein-

Dor (1999) suggested that one problem with AI is the need to understand commonsense knowledge, of which so much relies on defaults that are culturally and contextually specific. This means that such commonsense knowledge can always be changing, as culture and contexts change. Grice also refers to the notion of implicatures, wherein, something means something other than what is logically said. Language is not necessarily logical, and thus, the maxim of relation especially means that what makes sense today and can be easily understood by a person with the commonsense contextual and cultural knowledge, may not make sense tomorrow. Twenty years ago, Ein-Dor said, referring to a time span of 40 years in the future (so, by 2039): "The emergence of general purpose systems for processing natural language requires a solution to the commonsense knowledge problem; I doubt that this problem will be adequately solved within the time span of this forecast" (p. 196). Of course, people do not always follow these maxims, but those who do are more likely to be perceived as competent communicators.

The application of O'Keefe's (1988) theory of Message Design Logic demonstrates that the same communication pragmatics explaining human communication competence also apply to HRI. Message design logics (MDL) are working models of communication that lead to distinct ways of thinking about communication situations and reasoning from goals to messages. Mirroring earlier research in human communication that established an MDL sophistication advantage in communication dilemmas (O'Keefe & McCornack, 1987), Edwards, Edwards, Gambino (2019) showed that a social robot using a rhetorical MDL was evaluated most positively (compared to a robot using conventional or expressive messaging) in terms of competence, credibility, attractiveness, goal attainment (ability to motivate and provide face support), and predicted success. Also, participants inferred things about the robot's overall approach to communication and social others–its goals, strategies, and possibilities – based on the MDL it employed. For AI as well as for people, working definitions of communication may vary from simplistic (information transfer) to intermediate (social cooperation) to complex (meaning-making; identity-enactment), with important effects on the organization, content, and effectiveness of interpersonal communication messages.

These are but a few of the many IPC theories and concepts that seem relevant for understanding HMC. The paper next moves to considering theories more typically associated with mediated interpersonal communication, or CMC.

CMC Theories and AI

As mentioned above, dating back to Turing (1950), it seems that CMC is relevant to AI, and thus, CMC theories also seem applicable to considering AI and communication. Three theories/perspectives traditionally discussed in CMC literature that have relevance to HMC and can inform our understanding of humans interacting with such technologies are the Social Identity/Deindividuation Effect (SIDE) Model (Lea & Spears, 1992), Social Information Processing Theory (SIPT; Walther, 1992) and Hyperpersonal Model (Walther, 1996). Each theory will be described briefly, with a discussion of the relevance to AI/HMC following each.

Sometimes when we interact with others online, we do so at a role or group levels (perhaps more toward the "I-it" side of Buber's spectrum). SIDE model (Lea & Spears, 1992) suggests how and why this might happen. According to SIDE, visual anonymity is pervasive in CMC, and the lack of individuating nonverbal information leads to deindividuation of others. Deindividuation then leads to relating to others based more on group membership rather than getting to know others as individuals. Thus, CMC users may feel more similar and have higher social attraction when group identity is made more salient than individual identity, and so we relate to others as group members. As Walther and Carr (2010) pointed out, there is a good deal of evidence to support SIDE model; however, SIDE scholars have suggested that people do sometimes get to know each other as individuals over time online (e.g., Postmes et al., 2005).

How then does this all tie into HMC? First, again, if we respond to machines as we do humans, then human interaction theories are relevant to HMC. For example, drawing back upon past research that has identified a human-human interaction script (e.g., Edwards et al., 2019), people expect interactions to occur with humans. Leading people to believe they will interact with robots also leads to lower expectations of social presence and liking in the interaction (C. Edwards et al., 2016; Spence et al., 2014), but these differences did not appear in experiments involving a more human-like (anthropomorphic) social robot (Edwards et al., 2019). Perhaps this occurs because telling people they will interact with a robot highlights the group membership cues that the interactant is different from the person, in line with SIDE predictions. However, as social information processing theory (SIPT; Walther, 1992) would predict, actual interaction with the robot helps overcome those initial lower expectations (Edwards et al., 2019).

Can truly interpersonal relationships (moving toward "I-thou") develop online though? SIPT (Walther, 1992) is a theory that suggests that we can and do get to know people through electronic channels, even those that might be considered "lean," and thus, CMC can be interpersonal. SIPT is based on the assumption that communicators have similar goals, no matter the channels used to communicate with each other, and we adapt our behaviors to the limits and affordances of a channel in order to achieve those goals. One way we adapt our behavior is by encoding and decoding meanings conveyed typically through nonverbals into language, and such language cues can functionally interchange verbal and nonverbal cues (e.g., Walther et al., 2005). People also adapt by asking more and deeper questions and disclosing more deeply when they interact with strangers online (Tidwell & Walther, 2002; Westerman, 2007). CMC may take longer to accomplish goals, but given enough time, goals such as impression formation and relationship development can occur at equal levels using various channels (Walther et al., 1994), and people can develop true interpersonal knowledge of others (Walther, 2019). Overall, people must be willing and able to put in the work to build relationships (Walther & Parks, 2002), but SIPT is an agentic theory that suggests that people find ways to use channels to accomplish their goals (Walther et al., 2015).

SIPT has been criticized for being no longer relevant after CMC moved away from the text-only environment that existed when the theory was first formulated and into the multimodal one that exists today (cf, Walther et al., 2015). Although multimodality is an interesting question for SIPT, there is still much communication that takes place using only text. For example, chatbots would be an aspect of HMC that seems especially relevant for SIPT (Westerman et al., 2019). This would perhaps be especially true if a person was unaware that the social actor on the other side of the screen was a chatbot. SIPT suggests that we use the social information that is available, and if language is the only thing we have, it would be heavily relied upon to do interpersonal work such as impression formation and affinity seeking, and this process would likely be the same whether the source was a bot or a human. Of course, various linguistic cues would likely signal humanness more than others (Westerman et al., 2019), but future research can continue to examine this from a SIPT perspective.

SIPT suggests that given enough time people can achieve relational outcomes through CMC that are similar to those achieved through FtF interaction. It is also possible that people use technological channels to achieve even greater relational outcomes than those that might occur through face-to-face interaction. The Hyperpersonal model (Walther, 1996) suggests the conditions necessary for this to happen. In some circumstances, senders can more carefully select information to represent themselves, thus having more control over their self-presentation. This kind of selective self-presentation is especially pronounced in dating websites (Toma & Hancock, 2011). Receivers of that information see that carefully selected presentation, and respond to it, especially if they want to idealize the other person. These kinds of overattributions can come from language choices that people make when interacting online (Spottswood et al., 2013) and from stereotypes held by receivers (Walther, 2006). This is especially possible if/because the channel allows for disentrainment: a break from the norms and restrictions of face-to-face communication (FtF), and people thus have more time to edit their messages and are free from other distractions present in FtF. People do seem to adapt their messages based on the goals that have as well (Walther, 2007; Walther et al., 2010). Finally, feedback from a receiver to a sender can provide behavioral confirmation for the sender's selected presentation, actually helping the sender become the idealized presentation. Thus, this model overall suggests that under some circumstances, relational development can occur in a sort of hyper-state.

Hyperpersonal communication might be a particularly interesting one for HMC and AI scholars to consider. People may use more in-depth perception to move beyond simple stereotyping of a robot; however, people would seem to need appropriate motivation and skills to be able to do so. Perhaps if a robot is programmed to selectively self-present in a very positive way, and the receiver desires a relationship, then a hyperpersonal relationship with the robot would also be predicted. A social robot could record and store every single interaction with every single partner, and these interactions can be encoded for later analysis. Thus, a social robot can "learn" how to communicate individually with each human by drawing on this communication history, in a more detailed and accurate way. Individualized communication strategies can be thus programmed, stored and used automatically when needed with an individual user. This may increase the possibility that a selective self-presentation of a robot can help lead to hyperpersonal communication. Robots could also be designed to collect information (or indicators) about their human communication partner that is impossible for humans to collect, but potentially helpful for communication (e.g., heart rate, body temperature, Galvanic skin response). This information could be used by the robot to help decide which individualized strategies to use in a specific situation. The ethical concerns are obvious, but this could lead to a hyperpersonal situation, and lead the robot to respond to the person as a very unique individual (I-Thou).

Overall, these three CMC theories suggest is that we can use the information that is available in a situation toward relational goals, no matter the channel used for communicating, in various ways. Walther (2009) suggests that it might be more important to consider the conditions under which each of these theories is most applicable. More careful consideration of certain communication goals might be one important consideration, as different theories might be tied in with different goals. For example, if one's goal can only be accomplished by getting to know another social actor on a more intimate interpersonal level, then SIPT seems most applicable to explaining and predicting communication patterns, as people would be more motivated to overcome the possible limitations presented by the technology, in order to reach deeper levels of intimacy. However, if one's goal does not require increased intimacy or may be hindered by it, then interacting at a superficial level may be enough, and it may be under these conditions that SIDE processes are more likely to be applicable. For example, if one wants a cheeseburger at a drive-thru, getting to know the person at the other end of the speaker may get in the way of accomplishing that goal (and context might also suggest this is kind of creepy), and an impersonal interaction (Walther, 1996) might do the job. Goals like this seem especially relevant for initial interactions where the likelihood/desire for future interaction is nil. Alternatively, if someone simply wants a relationship, but does not necessarily want to get to know the other social actor truly, then the hyperpersonal model may be the most applicable. Whether or not all of these also apply when the technology is the communication partner, rather than the medium for social interaction, is a question for future research.

Applying HMC Back to Human-to-Human Communication?

Overall, as Edwards et al. (2019) pointed out, much of HMC relies on prototyping, or comparison to exemplar robots when considering our likely responses and our actual responses to robots. But these prototypes may not only apply to robots. The tendency for people to objectify and use one another as tools has been observed historically (e.g., Dewey, 1916), and attempts have been made to account for why people are treated as machines or tools in some situations and not in others. Postman (1992) suggested that we have a growing tendency to view humans as machines, and thus reconceptualize human problems and relationships as mechanistic, leading us to treat computers as humans, and humans as computers. An important avenue of investigation is identifying what aspects of agent or context may trigger the application of machine interaction scripts with people.

The study of HMC and AI and communication tends to focus on the artificiality of the machine and how the machine may appear more human. However, what if we are the "artificial" part of this equation? At the very least, we sometimes interact in a way that is not really "human." As the CASA approach suggests, we often respond to cues without really considering them in great detail. The idea of scriptedness in communication is perhaps an understudied part of human-human interaction, although much human communication is "scripted" and "programmed" (Kellerman, 1991). We also tend to follow a routine (Kellerman, 1991) and respond in very scripted and "robotic" ways when interacting with other people, especially in initial interactions. We rely a great deal on scripts and schema to help us interpret the information we get from other people. Put another way, "The ease with which we all engage in normal social discourse in itself suggests that much of our behavior is spontaneous rather than the planned outcome of some reflective process" (Fazio, 1990, p. 78).

Thus, do we have a programming for communication that underlies why and how we come to interact with others, including AI technologies such as robots, and if so, should we be surprised that we wish to be in the presence of them and confirm their being, even when their being is somewhat mechanical (like ours is)? Ein-Dor (1999) pointed out that one issue with

AI and communication is that understanding language requires "commonsense knowledge." When we interact with another person, there is a general knowledge base that we expect the other person to possess and understand. Ein-Dor presented three reasons that commonsense knowledge is so difficult to program: 1. There is so much of it, 2. It consists largely of defaults (heuristics?) when having complete knowledge would require both the rules and the exceptions to those defaults, and 3. So much of this commonsense knowledge is culturally and contextually specific. For the classic social robot Kismet, Breazeal (2003) reported programming the robot to use "rules of thumb" for figuring out responses. It would seem that we use these as well when interacting with other social actors. An interesting question to ponder is whether or not we know all the defaults and specifics of communication. We likely do not, and instead, we satisfice and make plenty of mistakes and faux pas when we interact in unfamiliar contexts and cultures.

Walther's (2019) definition of interpersonal communication is of use here as well. He "defines interpersonal knowledge as the impression one has about the way a specific target individual responds in a unique fashion to the information-seeker as distinct from the way that the target individual responds to anyone else" (p. 377). This process of gaining interpersonal knowledge occurs over time, as mentioned by SIPT, and through repeated interaction (Walther, 1992). Thus, each interpersonal relationship is unique and based upon the unique interactions that individuals in the relationship have with each other. Those interactions must be interactive and contingent in order to reach the level of interpersonal (and not merely "personal"). This also seems very much in line with the notion of interpersonal relationship as "I-Thou", in that one is treating the other person in a unique way as part of a unique relationship. Reliance on scripts and cues solely (the kind associated with CASA) seems more in line with the notion of "I-It," as there is an engagement with the other social actor as an object, albeit, in a social or "personal" way sometimes. This might make it sound like we do not treat machines as we do people, but much of our human-human communication relies on these very cues and scripts as well and is not very interpersonal according to this Walther (2019) definition. Things like stereotyping fall very much in line here. Perhaps all encounters, both human and robot, begin with some stereotypical first impressions (e.g., Mieczkowski et al., 2019; Oliveira et al., 2019; Packard et al., 2019), that might be based on what Walther (2019) called static information we learn about another social actor. These impressions may be used as part of a screening to determine if we want to put in the effort and time to move toward a more interpersonal, "I-Thou" relationship. Of course, our stereotypes of machines may be inaccurate, but this is true of interactions with people as well. Thus, it seems like we respond to machines and AI as we do people, but we may not always respond to people in a very interpersonal way. Might breaking away from "scripts" be the thing that helps get to "I-Thou" in both HMC and human-human communication? Future scholarship can consider this question more fully.

Thus, learning more about this aspect of HMC also holds promise for learning more about human-human interaction; not only can we apply human communication ideas to HMC, but we can also apply HMC ideas to human communication. Nass and Moon (2000) discussed the possibility of disaggregating things related to "being human" that cannot be separated in human-human communication. However, they can be separated and tested accordingly when replacing a human with technology. This seems especially potent when considering AI and HMC. Past studies of HMC often combine social cues of robots (cf, Westerman et al., 2020). However, as Westerman et al. (2020) also point out, doing more rigorous tests that do such disaggregation would be useful for learning more about the relative value of individual cues, and the combinatory power of them as well. Also, examining more about how we treat machines as humans also offers questions about treating humans as machines. As Ho et al. (2018) argue, "what matters most is not the partner's humanness, but what occurs in the interaction itself" (p. 726). Overall, whether the interlocutor is human or machine, we still have much to learn about Buber's notions of "I-it" and "I-thou" relating, but we have offered what we believe to be some useful thoughts to help guide that learning. As Christian (2012) states, in the digital age, "All communication is a Turing test" (p. 9), as all communication is likely processed similarly, as we cannot always be sure that we are interacting with a person when we interact with a social actor online. We may also say that perhaps, rather than considering each new technology that comes along and replacing the C in CASA with the first letter of the said newest technology, it might make more sense to simply say that social actors are social actors and social actions are social actions (please refer back to Figure 1).

Disclosure statement

No potential conflict of interest was reported by the authors.

ORCID

David Westerman http://orcid.org/0000-0001-9550-0304
Autumn P. Edwards http://orcid.org/0000-0002-5963-197X
Chad Edwards http://orcid.org/0000-0002-1053-6349
Zhenyang Luo http://orcid.org/0000-0002-3832-4452
Patric R. Spence http://orcid.org/0000-0002-1793-6871

References

Bankins, S., & Formosa, P. (2019). When AI meets PC: Exploring the implications of workplace social robots and a human-robot psychological contract. *European Journal of Work and Organizational Psychology*, 1–15. Advance online publication. https://doi.org/10.1080/1359432X.2019.1620328

Baron, N. S. (2015). Shall we talk? Conversing with humans and robots. *The Information Society*, 31(3), 257–264. https://doi.org/10.1080/01972243.2015.1020211

Baxter, L. A. (1988). A dialectical perspective of communication strategies in relationship development. In S. Duck (Ed.), *Handbook of personal relationships* (pp. 257–273). Wiley.

Baxter, L. A., & Montgomery, B. M. (1996). *Relating: Dialogues and dialectics*. Guilford Press.

Breazeal, C. (2003). Toward sociable robots. *Robotics and Autonomous Systems*, 42(3–4), 167–175. https://doi.org/10.1016/S0921-8890(02)00373-1

Bryson, J. J., & Theodorou, A. (2019). How society can maintain human-centric artificial intelligence. In M. Toivonen & E. Saari (Eds.), *Human-centered digitalization and services* (pp. 305–323). Springer Nature Singapore.

Buber, M. (1958). *I and Thou* (R. Gregor-Smith, Trans.; 2nd ed.). Continuum. (Original work published 1923)

Buber, M. (2002). *Between man and man* (R. Gregor-Smith, Trans.; 2nd ed.). Routledge. (Original work published 1947)

Carpenter, C. J. (2018). Using Spinozan processing theory to predict the perceived likelihood of persuasive message claims: When message recall matters. *Southern Communication Journal*, 83(1), 1–12. https://doi.org/10.1080/1041794X.2017.1373146

Christian, B. (2012). *The most human human: What artificial intelligence teaches us about being alive*. Anchor Books.

Cialdini, R. B. (2001). *Influence: Science and practice*. Allyn & Bacon.

Dautenhahn, K. (2007). Socially intelligent robots: Dimensions of human–robot interaction. *Philosophical Transactions of the Royal Society of London B: Biological Sciences*, 362(1480), 679–704. https://doi.org/10.1098/rstb.2006.2004

Dewey, J. (1916). *Democracy and education*. Free Press.

Edwards, A., Edwards, C., & Gambino, A. (2019). The social pragmatics of communication with social robots: Effects of robot message design logic in a regulative context. *International Journal of Social Robotics*. Advance online publication. https://doi.org/10.1007/s12369-019-00538-7

Edwards, A., Edwards, C., Westerman, D., & Spence, P. R. (2019). Initial expectations, interactions and beyond with social robots. *Computers in Human Behavior*, 90, 308–314. https://doi.org/10.1016/j.chb.2018.08.042

Edwards, C., Edwards, A., Spence, P. R., & Westerman, D. (2016). Initial interaction expectations with robots: Testing the human-to-human interaction script. *Communication Studies*, 67(2), 227–238. https://doi.org/10.1080/10510974.2015.1121899

Ein-Dor, P. (1999). Artificial intelligence: A short history and the next 40 years. In K. E. Kendall (Ed.), *Emerging information technologies: Improving decisions, cooperation and infrastructure* (pp. 117–140). Sage.

Fazio, R. H. (1990). Multiple processes by which attitudes guide behavior: The mode model as an integrative framework. *Advances in Experimental Social Psychology*, 23, 75–109. https://doi.org/10.1016/S0065-2601(08)60318-4

Fortunati, L., & Edwards, A. (2020, in press). Opening space for theoretical, methodological, and empirical issues in human-machine communication. *Human-Machine Communication*, 1, 7–18. https://doi.org/10.30658/hmc.1.1

Garnham, A. (1987). *Artificial intelligence: An introduction*. Routledge.

Gilbert, D. T. (1991). How mental systems believe. *American Psychologist*, 46(2), 107–119. https://doi.org/10.1037/0003-066X.46.2.107

Grice, H. P. (1975). Logic and conversation. In P. Cole & J. L. Morgan (Eds.), *Syntax and semantics, Vol. 3, speech acts* (pp. 41–58). Academic Press.

Gunkel, D. J. (2012). Communication and artificial intelligence: Opportunities and challenges for the 21st century. *Communication +1, 1*(1), 1–25. https://doi.org/10.7275/R5QJ7F7R

Guzman, A. L. (2018). What is human-machine communication, anyway? In A. L. Guzman (Ed.), *Human machine communication: Rethinking communication, technology, and ourselves* (pp. 1–28). Peter Lang.

Guzman, A. L. (2020, in press). Ontological boundaries between humans and computers and the implications for human-machine communication. *Human-Machine Communication, 1*, 37–54. https://doi.org/10.30658/hmc.1.3

Ho, A., Hancock, J., & Miner, A. S. (2018). Psychological, relational, and emotional effects of self-disclosure after conversations with a chatbot. *Journal of Communication, 68*(4), 712–733. https://doi.org/10.1093/joc/jqy026

Kellerman, K. (1991). The conversation MOP II. Progression through scenes in discourse. *Human Communication Research, 17*(3), 385–414. https://doi.org/10.1111/j.1468-2958.1991.tb00238.x

Kellerman, K. (1992). Communication: Inherently strategic and primarily automatic. *Communication Monographs, 59*(3), 288–300. https://doi.org/10.1080/03637759209376270

Kim, A., Cho, M., Ahn, J., & Sung, Y. (2019). Effects of gender and relationship type on the response to artificial intelligence. *Cyberpsychology, Behavior, and Social Networking, 22*(4), 249–253. https://doi.org/10.1089/cyber.2018.0581

Kim, K. J., Park, E., & Sundar, S. S. (2013). Caregiving role in human–robot interaction: A study of the mediating effects of perceived benefit and social presence. *Computers in Human Behavior, 29*(4), 1799–1806. https://doi.org/10.1016/j.chb.2013.02.009

Lau, J., Zimmerman, B., & Schaub, F. (2018). Alexa, are you listening?: Privacy perceptions, concerns and privacy-seeking behaviors with smart speakers. *Proceedings of the ACM on Human-Computer Interaction, 2*(CSCW), 102. https://doi.org/10.1145/3274371

Lea, M., & Spears, R. (1992). Paralanguage and social perception in computer-mediated communication. *Journal of Organizational Computing, 2*(3–4), 321–341. https://doi.org/10.1080/10919399209540190

Lee, K. M. (2004). Why presence occurs: Evolutionary psychology, media equation, and presence. *Presence, 13*(4), 494–505. https://doi.org/https;//doi.10.1162/1054746041944830

Lombard, M., & Ditton, T. (1997). At the heart of it all: The concept of presence. *Journal of Computer-Mediated Communication, 3*(2). https://doi.org/10.1111/j.1083-6101.1997.tb00072.x

Luger, G. F. (2002). *Artificial intelligence: Structures and strategies for complex problem solving* (4th ed.). Addison-Wesley Longman.

Mieczkowski, H., Liu, S. X., Hancock, J., & Reeves, B. (2019). Helping not hurting: Applying the stereotype content model and BIAS map to social robotics. *Proceedings of the ACM/IEEE international conference on human-robot interaction* (pp. 222–229), Daegu, Korea (South). https://doi.org/10.1109/HRI.2019.8673307

Nass, C., & Moon, Y. (2000). Machines and mindlessness: Social responses to computers. *Journal of Social Issues, 56*(1), 81–103. https://doi.org/10.1111/0022-4537.00153

Nijholt, A. (2011, January). No grice: Computers that lie, deceive and conceal. In L. R. Miyares & M. R. A. Silva (Eds.), *Proceedings of 12th international symposium on social communication* (pp. 889–895). Center for Applied Linguistics.

O'Keefe, B. J. (1988). The logic of message design: Individual differences in reasoning about communication. *Communications Monographs, 55*(1), 80–103. https://doi.org/10.1080/03637758809376159

O'Keefe, B. J., & McCornack, S. A. (1987). Message design logic and message goal structure effects on perceptions of message quality in regulative communication situations. *Human Communication Research, 14*(1), 68–92. https://doi.org/10.1111/j.1468-2958.1987.tb00122x

Oliveira, R., Arriaga, P., Correia, F., & Paiva, A. (2019). The stereotype content model applied to human-robot interaction in groups. *Proceedings of the ACM/IEEE international conference on human-robot interaction* (pp. 123–132), Daegu, Korea (South). https://doi.org/org/10/1109/HRI.2019.8673171

Packard, C., Boelk, T., Andres, J., Edwards, C., Edwards, A., & Spence, P. R. (2019). The pratfall effect and interpersonal impressions of a robot that forgets and apologizes. *Proceedings of the*

ACM/IEEE international conference on human-robot interaction (pp. 524–525), Daegu, Korea (South). https://doi.org/10.1109/HRI.2019.8673101

Park, E., Kim, K. J., & Del Pobil, A. P. (2011). The effects of a robot instructor's positive vs. negative feedbacks on attraction and acceptance towards the robot in classroom. In B. Mutlu, C. Bartneck, J. Ham, V. Evers, & T. Kanda (Eds.), *Social robotics. ICSR lecture notes in computer science* (pp. 135–141). Springer.

Postman, N. (1992). *Technopoly: The surrender of culture to technology.* Vintage Books.

Postmes, T., Spears, R., Lee, T., & Novak, R. (2005). Individuality and social influence in groups: Inductive and deductive routes to group identity. *Journal of Personality and Social Psychology, 89*(5), 747–763. https://doi.org/.10.1037/0022-3514.89.5.747

Prokopenko, M. (2014). Grand challenges for computational intelligence. *Frontiers in Robotics and AI, 1*(2), 1–3. https://doi.org/10.3389/frobt.2014.00002

Reeves, B., & Nass, C. (1996). *The media equation: How people treat computers, television, and new media like real people and places.* CSLI Publications.

Riedl, M. O. (2019). Human-centered artificial intelligence and machine learning. *Human Behavior and Emerging Technologies, 1*(1), 33–36. https://doi.org/10.1002/hbe2.117

Schmidt, C. T. A. (2005). Of robots and believing. *Minds and Machines, 15*(2), 195–205. https://doi.org/10.1007/s11023-005-4734-6

Shank, D. B., Graves, C., Gott, A., Gamez, P., & Rodriguez, S. (2019). Feeling our way to machine minds: People's emotions when perceiving mind in artificial intelligence. *Computers in Human Behavior, 98*, 256–266. https://.doi.org./10.1016/j.chb.2019.04.001

Spence, P. R. (2019). Searching for questions, original thoughts, or advancing theory: Human-machine communication. *Computers in Human Behavior, 90*, 285–287. https://doi.org/10.1016/j.chb.2018.09.014

Spence, P. R., Edwards, A., Edwards, C., & Jin, X. (2019). 'The bot predicted rain, grab an umbrella': Few perceived differences in communication quality of a weather Twitterbot versus professional and amateur meteorologists. *Behaviour & Information Technology, 38*(1), 101–109. https://doi.org/10.1080/0144929X.2018.1514425

Spence, P. R., Westerman, D., Edwards, C., & Edwards, A. (2014). Welcoming our robot overlords: Initial expectations about interaction with a robot. *Communication Research Reports, 31*(3), 272–280. https://doi.org/10.1080/08824096.2014.924337

Spottswood, E. L., Walther, J. B., Holmstrom, A. J., & Ellison, N. B. (2013). Person-centered emotional support and gender attributions in computer-mediated communication. *Human Communication Research, 39*(3), 295–316. https://doi.org/10.1111/hcre.12006

Sugiyama, S. (2013). Melding with the self, melding with relational partners, and turning into a quasi-social robot: A Japanese case study of people's experiences of emotion and mobile devices. *Intervalla, 1*(1), 71–84. Retrieved from https://www.fus.edu/intervalla/volume-1-social-robots-and-emotion-transcending-theboundary-between-humans-and-icts/melding-with-the-self-meldingwith-relational-partners-and-turning-into-a-quasi-social-robot-ajapanese-case-study-of-people-s-experiences-of-emotion-andmobile-devices

Tidwell, L. C., & Walther, J. B. (2002). Computer-mediated communication effects on disclosure, impressions, and interpersonal evaluations: Getting to know one another a bit at a time. *Human Communication Research, 28*(3), 317–348. https://doi.org/10.1111/j.1468-2958.2002.tb00811.x

Toma, C. L., & Hancock, J. T. (2011). A new twist on love's labor: Self-presentation in online dating profiles. In K. B. Wright & L. M. Webb (Eds.), *Computer-mediated communication in personal relationships* (pp. 41–55). Peter Lang.

Turing, A. M. (1950). Computing machinery and intelligence. *Mind, 49*(236), 433–460. https://doi.org/10.1093/mind.LIX.236.433

Tversky, A., & Kahneman, D. (1974). Judgment under uncertainty: Heuristics and biases. *Science, 185*(4157), 1124–1130. https://doi.org/10.1126/science.185.4157.1124

Walther, J. B. (1992). Interpersonal effects in computer-mediated interaction: A relational perspective. *Communication Research, 19*(1), 52–90. https://doi.org/10.1177/009365092019001003

Walther, J. B. (1996). Computer-mediated communication: Impersonal, interpersonal, and hyperpersonal interaction. *Communication Research, 23*(1), 3–43. https://doi.org/10.1177/009365096023001001

Walther, J. B. (2006). Nonverbal dynamics in computer-mediated communication, or :(and the net : ('s with you, :) and you :) alone. In V. Manusov & M. L. Patterson (Eds.), *Handbook of nonverbal communication* (pp.461–479). Sage.

Walther, J. B. (2007). Selective self-presentation in computer-mediated communication: Hyperpersonal dimensions of technology, language, and cognition. *Computers in Human Behavior, 23*(5), 2538–2557. https://doi.org/10.1016/j.chb.2006.05.002

Walther, J. B. (2009). Theories, boundaries, and all of the above. *Journal of Computer-Mediated Communication, 14*(3), 748–752. https://doi.org/10.1111/j.1083-6101.2009.01466.x

Walther, J. B., & Carr, C. T. (2010). Internet interaction and intergroup dynamics: Problems and solutions in computer-mediated communication. In H. Giles, S. Reid, & J. Harwood (Eds.), *The dynamics of intergroup communication* (pp. 209–220). Peter Lang.

Walther, J. B., Van Der Heide, B., Ramirez, A., Jr., Burgoon, J. K., & Pena, J. (2015). Interpersonal and hyperpersonal aspects of computer-mediated communication. In S. S. Sundar (Ed.), *The handbook of psychology and communication technology* (pp. 3–22). Wiley-Blackwell.

Walther, J. B. (2019). Interpersonal versus personal uncertainty and communication in traditional and mediated encounters: A theoretical reformulation. In S. R. Wilson & S. W. Smith (Eds.), *Reflections on interpersonal communication research* (pp. 375–393). Cognella Academic Publishing.

Walther, J. B., Anderson, J. F., & Park, D. (1994). Interpersonal effects in computer-mediated interaction: A meta-analysis of social and antisocial communication. *Communication Research, 21*(4), 460–487. https://doi.org/10.1177/009365094021004002

Walther, J. B., Loh, T., & Granka, L. (2005). Let me count the ways: The interchange of verbal and nonverbal cues in computer-mediated and face-to-face affinity. *Journal of Language and Social Psychology, 24*(1), 36–65. https://doi.org/10.1177/0261927X04273036

Walther, J. B., & Parks, M. R. (2002). Cues filtered out, cues filtered in; Computermediated communication and relationships. In M. L. Knapp & J. A. Daly (Eds.), *Handbook of interpersonal communication* (3rd ed., pp. 529–563). Sage.

Walther, J. B., Van Der Heide, B., Tong, S. T., Carr, C. T., & Atkin, C. K. (2010). The effects of interpersonal goals on inadvertent influence in computer-mediated communication. *Human Communication Research, 36*(3), 323–347. https://doi.org/10.1111/j.1468-2958.2010.01378.x

Westerman, D. (2007). *Comparing uncertainty reduction in face-to-face and computer-mediated communication: A social information processing theory perspective*. Michigan State University.

Westerman, D., Cross, A. C., & Lindmark, P. G. (2019). I believe in a thing called bot: Perceptions of the humanness of "chatbots,". *Communication Studies, 70*(3), 295–312. https://doi.org/10.1080/10510974.2018.1557233

Westerman, D., Edwards, A., Edwards, C., & Spence, P. R. (2020). Social robots and social presence: Interpersonally communicating with robots. *International Journal of Telepresence, 1*(2). https://ijtelepresence.org/1-2/

Xu, K. (2019). First encounter with robot Alpha: How individual differences interact with vocal and kinetic cues in users' social responses. *New Media & Society, 21*(11-12), 2522–2547. https://doi.org/10.1177/1461444819851479

Xu, K., & Lombard, M. (2016). *Media are social actors: Examining the CASA paradigm in the 21st century* [Paper presented]. 2016 international communication association annual conference, Fukuoka, Japan.

Zhao, S. (2006). Humanoid social robots as a medium of communication. *New Media & Society, 8*(3), 401–419. https://doi.org/10.1177/146144806061951

A Bot and a Smile: Interpersonal Impressions of Chatbots and Humans Using Emoji in Computer-mediated Communication

Austin Beattie, Autumn P. Edwards, and Chad Edwards

ABSTRACT
Artificially intelligent (AI) agents increasingly occupy roles once served by humans in computer-mediated communication (CMC). Technological affordances like emoji give interactants (humans or bots) the ability to partially overcome the limited nonverbal information in CMC. However, despite the growth of chatbots as conversational partners, few CMC and human-machine communication (HMC) studies have explored how bots' use of emoji impact perceptions of communicator quality. This study examined the relationship between emoji use and observers' impressions of interpersonal attractiveness, CMC competence, and source credibility; and whether impressions formed of human versus chatbot message sources were different. Results demonstrated that participants rated emoji-using chatbot message sources similarly to human message sources, and both humans and bots are significantly more socially attractive, CMC competent, and credible when compared to verbal-only message senders. Results are discussed with respect to the CASA paradigm and the human-to-human interaction script framework.

A significant portion of computer-mediated communication (CMC) occurs between humans and artificial intelligence (AI) – based chatbots (or bots). *Chatbots* are automated computer programs designed to communicate in human-like ways for task fulfillment (Morgan, 2017) and are increasingly populating a broad spectrum of CMC contexts. Chatbots are used as insurance agents (Huckstep, 2017), financial counselors (Hendricks, 2017), military recruiters (Maass, 2014), and mental health specialists (Molteni, 2017), to name just a few of many roles. Like human-human CMC, nonverbal messages present an interpretive challenge when talking to bots. This challenge is especially salient in the environments where most chatbots operate – texting and instant messaging (IM) (Huang, Yen, & Zhang, 2008).

Because nonverbal messages carry a substantial proportion of communicative information, which texting and IM channels typically limit the ability to facilitate, scholarly (Daft & Lengel, 1984; Kiesler & Sproull, 1992) and mainstream sources (e.g., Kravitz, 2018) have argued that greater aggression and misunderstanding and less person-centeredness may occur between CMC communicators. Despite these limitations, people use CMC each day for a variety of communicative purposes, including many which involve detail-oriented and outcome-based aspects (e.g., Blair, Fletcher, & Gaskin, 2015). To convey nonverbal cues in CMC, users often include emoji in their messages. *Emoji* are rich, small digital images that express emotions and ideas (Oxford, 2018). By providing CMC users with more options for expression and by working on many devices and platforms (Unicode, 2016; Warren, 2014), emoji may help to limit discrepancies between verbal and nonverbal messages inherent to many CMC contexts. Research on how emoji (and older symbolic representations of facial expressions such as emoticons, Walther & D'Addario, 2001) impact CMC stems from several disciplines representing critical (e.g., Stark & Crawford, 2015) to social scientific paradigms (Derks, Bos, & Von Grumbkow, 2007). Despite the popularity of emoji and their potential to enhance CMC communication quality, few studies have examined how emoji impact impressions of communicator quality and fewer studies have examined such factors in the context of human-machine communication (HMC). With consideration to affordances brought to CMC by advancing chatbot and emoji technologies across a wide spectrum of CMC contexts, this study explored whether emoji use impacted perceptions of source interpersonal attractiveness, CMC competence, and credibility; and whether perceptions of these variables difference between human and chatbot sources.

Chatbots in Computer-Mediated Communication

Chatbots increasingly are involved in online contexts previously handled by human agents (Bradford, 2017). Companies historically have used chatbots to perform basic tasks such as providing customer support (Hyken, 2017), booking appointments (Bradford, 2017), and giving restaurant recommendations (Orda, 2017). More recently, due to advances in AI learning, speech recognition, and natural language processing and generation (e.g., IBM's Watson, Google's DeepMind), current chatbots are more "conversational" in nature (Morgan, 2017). As a result, the deployment of chatbots has moved beyond basic customer service roles to a broad range of areas encompassing such places as personal banking (Nyguyn, 2017), insurance coverage (Huckstep, 2017), and military recruitment (i.e., the U.S. Army's Sgt. Star; Maass, 2014). Beyond their popularity in e-commerce, chatbots also fill emotional and social support roles, such as counseling Syrian refugees (Romeo, 2016) and assisting Australians with access to national disability benefits (Maack, 2016). "Woebot," a chatbot available via a smartphone application, provides free daily chat conversations, mood tracking, curated videos, and word games to help people manage their mental health in addition to other topics (Molteni, 2017). Research into Woebot's efficacy indicates users reported significantly lower symptoms of depression after two weeks of treatment when compared to those in an information-only control group (Fitzpatrick, Darcy, & Vierhile, 2017).

To test theoretical understandings with consideration to a wide variety of HMC settings, researchers have explored how chatbots impact human communication processes across a broad spectrum of environments. For instance, in the context of information seeking, Edwards, Edwards, Spence, and Shelton (2014) examined how agent type (Twitterbot vs. human) impacted impressions of communication quality on social media and found that participants viewed the bots as credible, attractive, and competent. A follow-up study by Edwards, Beattie, Edwards, and Spence (2016) found that participants responded to Twitterbots in terms of cognitive elaboration, information seeking, affective learning, and motivation to learn in similar ways as their human counterparts.

Ho, Hancock, and Miner (2018) explored informational and emotional disclosures with chatbots and found that participants experienced similar impressions of relational warmth, enjoyment, and comforting responses between chatbots and a human control condition. Although HMC research continues to determine the boundary conditions of interpersonal and CMC theory with respect to the varying forms in which AI appears in everyday life, limited HMC research has specifically explored chatbots versus humans in more typical conversations.

Emoji, CMC, and Nonverbal Communication

A critical area for CMC is understanding how online message qualities impact communication quality. Healthcare providers now text patients for HIV prevention and intervention support (Cornelius et al., 2012), tobacco cessation (Obermayer, Riley, Asif, & Jean-Mary, 2004), counseling and mental health (Ainsworth et al., 2013), and diabetes management (e.g., Franklin, Waller, Pagliari, & Greene, 2006). Furthermore, a longitudinal texting study found planning-type communication accounted for 31% of messages between participants (Battestini, Setlur, & Sohn, 2010; Church & de Oliveira, 2013).

Scholars and the mainstream media alike have expressed concern about communication online. An oft-cited reason to avoid CMC platforms (particularly texting) is the relative inability to facilitate nonverbal cues between users (e.g., Daft & Lengel, 1984; Kiesler & Sproull, 1992; Kravitz, 2018; O'Neill, 2010). This concern is not without grounding: nonverbal gestures serve several critical communicative functions: (a) *providing information*, (b) *regulating interaction*, and (c) *expressing intimacy* (Ekman & Friesen, 1969; Harrison, 1973). Nonverbal messages are vital to interpersonal processes such as conveying and interpreting feelings and attitudes (Duncan, 1969). Thus, by limiting people's nonverbal options, some CMC channels might impede interpersonal and group nonverbal processes, potentially leading to de-personalization and de-individuation effects among their users (e.g., Kiesler, Siegel, & McGuire, 1984; Sproull & Kiesler, 1986). Scholars argue these limitations become more relevant as tasks involve higher degrees of uncertainty or confusion (e.g., Daft & Lengel, 1986), suggesting that CMC could be a suboptimal choice for facilitating potentially intricate or detail-oriented conversations, which presents important practical considerations for chatbot designers.

Emoji afford CMC users possible ways to overcome nonverbal limitations in text-dominant CMC channels. Emoji are similar to ASCII (abbreviated from American Standard Code for Information Interchange, the code that represents text in computers and other devices) emoticons (e.g., ":-)") and graphical emoticons (e.g., "☺"), but with several significant improvements. Emoji sets include nonverbal elements found in previously established (i.e., ASCII and graphical) emoticon variants such as emotive facial displays (e.g., | |, | |), as well as hundreds of other symbols ranging from slices of pizza (| |) to office buildings (| |) (Unicode, 2016). Additionally, because emoji are written in Unicode, they are transmittable between most current devices and operating systems (although there are some platform-specific differences in how emoji are displayed, e.g., Miller et al., 2016). For sake of clarity, we refer to all emoticon technologies as "emoji."

Studies that have explored the impacts of emoji in CMC have ranged from critical essays that examined emoji as "conduits for affective labor in the social networks of informational capitalism" (e.g., Stark & Crawford, 2015, p. 1) to social-scientific experiments that examined empirical impacts of specific emotion-display choices on message interpretation (e.g., Walther & D'Addario, 2001). Prada et al. (2018) found that participants used emoji to be more expressive over CMC. Similarly, a study by Zhou, Hentschel, and Kumar (2017) reported participants described conversations without emoji as "boring, dry, and limited in the expressiveness they allowed" (p. 751). Derks et al. (2007) found that context predicted emoji use, such that people were more likely to use emoji in socio-emotional situations than task-oriented situations. Skovholt, Grønning, and Kankaanranta (2014) explored emoji as surrogates for nonverbal functions (e.g., Ekman & Friesen, 1969; Harrison, 1973) and argued emoji could be used as (a) *attitude markers* following signatures, as (b) *joke markers* following attempts at humor, and noted they served a (c) hedging function as *strengtheners* to person-centered messages and as *softeners* to task-oriented messages. Thus, using emoji may help fulfil nonverbal functions traditionally absent from text-based CMC (Skovholt et al., 2014) and make AI appear more socially present due to adding nonverbal behaviors (e.g., Goble & Edwards, 2018).

Theoretical Perspectives

Because chatbots are taking on more social roles, scholars are continuing to understand how humans interpret bot behaviors. The Computers are Social Actors paradigm (CASA; Reeves & Nass, 1996) suggests that people apply human social rules and expectations when interacting with media such as computers and robots (Nass & Moon, 2000; Xu & Lombard, 2016). For instance, individuals assign human personality characteristics to computers and artificially intelligent agents (Mou & Xu, 2017; Mou, Xu, & Xia, 2019; Nass, Moon, Fogg, Reeves, & Dryer, 1995; Purington, Taft, Sannon, Bazarova, & Taylor, 2017).

CASA contributes significantly to establishing knowledge regarding overall similarities in the behavioral patterns and norms people infer from computers. Recent frameworks have also begun to explore human-machine interactions with interpersonal communication theory. The human-to-human interaction script framework (Edwards, Edwards, Spence, & Westerman, 2016; Edwards, Edwards, Westerman, & Spence, 2019; Spence, Westerman, Edwards, & Edwards, 2014) addresses how people interact with social machines (e.g., AI, chatbots, social robots) and generally argues that due to the scripted and expectancy-laden quality of human interaction, people anticipate more uncertainty and less liking and social presence in human-robot (or chatbot) interactions and may judge identical message behavior differently when it is delivered by a person or social machine, especially when the machine has a less human-like form (e.g., Edwards et al., 2019). These interpersonal impression aspects are essential to consider in evaluating the potential utility of chatbots using technological affordances such as the emoji.

Understanding perceptions of chatbot message features are fundamental to determining human behavioral outcomes in HMC contexts. Communication scholars have long argued that perceptions of uncertainty (e.g., Berger & Calabrese, 1975; Knobloch & Solomon, 2005), liking (Heider, 1958; Miller, Downs, & Prentice, 1998; Tesser, 1988), and social attraction (e.g., Hesse & Floyd, 2011) are essential factors in processing relational information and forming social relationships. Thus, because chatbots are common in a variety of online social situations, this study explored interpersonal impressions and related variables of communication quality to determine the potential relational, interactional, and theoretical implications of emoji-using chatbots.

Social Attraction

The degree to which people are attracted to interactional partners significantly impacts communication quality. According to McCroskey and McCain (1974), interpersonal attraction predicts both the quality and quantity of communication between individuals. Perceptions of social attraction often accompany perceptions of persuasiveness and credibility (McCroskey, Hamilton, & Weiner, 1974). McCroskey et al. (1974) argued social attraction is a dimension of overall interpersonal attraction that concerns how much a person likes or wants to be around another. Because researchers have shown that emoji use facilitates higher degrees of nonverbal emotive affect and immediacy (e.g., Dresner & Herring, 2010; O'Neill, 2010; Prada et al., 2018; Skovholt et al., 2014), people might perceive emoji-sending bots to be more socially attractive. Research demonstrates a positive relationship between nonverbal immediacy and interpersonal attraction (Rocca & McCroskey, 1999). Furthermore, Ganster, Eimler, and Krämer (2012) showed that participants who viewed emoji reported significantly improved emotional states compared to those who received verbal-only messages, thus we believe similar impressions will hold for chatbots that send emoji. Because research suggests emoji facilitate higher degrees of nonverbal affect and immediacy, and can improve receivers' moods, emoji use should positively impact people's perceptions of the source's social attractiveness:

H1: Participants will rate message sources using emoji as more socially attractive than message sources using verbal-only messages.

CMC Competence

Competence refers to the ability to perform actions successfully and appropriately. Scholars have argued that communication competence is essential to maintaining healthy relationships (McCroskey, 1982; Rubin, Martin, Bruning, & Powers, 1993; Wiemann, 1977; Wrench & Punyanunt-Carter, 2007), and is a necessary factor toward collaborative behavior in CMC (Bubaš, 2001). Spitzberg (2006) argued that to be CMC competent, interactants must be motivated, skilled with the systems they use, and have learned the social conventions that underlie a given CMC interaction. Spitzberg argued competent CMC users (a) show attentiveness and concern for their interaction partners, (b) actively control the time and relevance of communication and are (c) emotionally expressive. Because research indicates that emoji use allows people to communicate with more nonverbal immediacy and regulatory function, (e.g., Shovholt et al., 2014) we argue that emoji-use by both humans and chatbots will contribute to the heightened perceptions of attentiveness, emotional expression, and regulatory-related qualities of competent CMC users. Therefore, we propose the following hypotheses:

H2: Participants will rate message sources using emoji as more CMC competent than message sources using verbal-only messages

Credibility

Credibility, the degree to which a person views a message source as believable, was our last variable. Scholars argue credibility directly affects communication quality and thus is a critical interpersonal impression to impart (e.g., Andersen & Clevenger, 1963; McCroskey & Young, 1981). McCroskey and Teven (1999) conceptualized credibility along three primary dimensions: *competence, goodwill*, and *trustworthiness*. Humans or bots using emoji in CMC may influence any or all three credibility dimensions. For instance, a bot sending emoji may impact impressions of source *competence* simply because they are demonstrating knowledge of CMC or topical conversational norms (e.g., the "bad" restaurant featured a frown face) that might feature emoji (e.g., Spitzberg, 2006). Chatbots sending emoji may also be perceived to be demonstrating human *goodwill* or *trustworthiness* by taking steps to convey relational information and keeping information "open" via giving more conversational cues. More so, because researchers have suggested emoji use can serve as a form of nonverbal online immediacy in contexts such as in business and education (e.g., Darics, 2017; Dixson, Greenwell, Rogers-Stacy, Weister, & Lauer, 2017; Lo, 2008), and have demonstrated a positive relationship between immediacy and credibility (e.g., Teven & Hanson, 2004); humans or chatbots that use emoji use may impart perceptions of *goodwill* or caring. Because of the multiples ways emoji use might impact credibility impressions, we pose a final hypothesis:

H3: Participants will rate message sources using emoji as more credible than message sources using verbal-only messages.

Finally, we are interested in a direct comparison of impressions formed of human versus chatbot using emoji and verbal-only messages. With chatbots becoming increasingly popular in contexts such as healthcare (e.g., Fitzpatrick et al., 2017), insurance (Huckstep, 2017), and finance (Hendricks, 2017); understanding how the use of emoji influences interpersonal perceptions outside of specific contextual boundaries presents significant theoretical and practical utility. In *Designing Bots: Creating Conversational Experiences*, Shevat (2017) argued conversational bots may use emoji to relay information, enrich a conversation, and to relay emotions; suggesting emoji use may make bots more effective interactants. Supporting Shevat's (2017) argument, Fadhil, Schiavo, Wang, and Yilma (2018) found that participants revealing medical information to a chatbot experienced higher enjoyment, positive attitude, and confidence when interacting with bots that used emoji versus those that used text-only message styles. Edwards et al. (2014) and Edwards et al. (2016) demonstrated that bots on Twitter can be viewed as effective on a host of interpersonal impression variables. Ho et al. (2018) showed that people can perceive warmth, enjoyment, and comforting messages from chatbots.

Although researchers have found interpersonal similarities between human-human and human-machine interaction, they have also demonstrated notable differences. For instance, Mou and Xu (2017) explored perceptions of HMC through a study in which several volunteers provided personal transcripts of human-human and human-chatbot message transcripts. Raters perceived the humans conversing with other humans as more open, agreeable, extroverted, conscientious, and self-disclosing than those interacting with AI. In a second study of similar design, Mou et al. (2019) had participants view transcripts and assign gender categories to message receivers in either human-human or human-AI interactions and found that participants' predictive ability was significantly higher in human-human transcripts (68.98%) than in human-AI transcripts (42.86%). Thus, because previous studies demonstrated that people form interpersonal impressions of human and machine communicators that are both similar and different, we pose the following research question:

> **RQ1**: Will there be differences in interpersonal impressions (interpersonal attractiveness, CMC competence, credibility) formed of a human versus chatbot message source?

Method

Participants

The sample consisted of 96 students enrolled in undergraduate courses at a large Midwestern research university. Of the participants, 62.50% ($n = 60$) identified as women and 37.50% ($n = 36$) identified as men. The majority (70.80%, $n = 68$) identified as White, followed by African-American (13.50%, $n = 13$), multi-racial (8.30%, $n = 8$), Hispanic/Latino (5.20%, $n = 5$), and Asian/Pacific Islander (2.10%, $n = 2$). Participant ages ranged from 18 to 37 years, with a mean age of 20.98 ($SD = 3.83$) and a median age of 20.00.

Procedure

Participants were randomly assigned to either the (a) human or (b) chatbot agent condition using either (a) verbal-only or (b) emoji-added messages.[1] Simulated conversations were created using fakeswhat.com (https://www.fakewhats.com), an online generator that creates screenshots modeled after the Whatsapp IM application (which can facilitate both IM and SMS). The conversation featured a message source asking for a restaurant recommendation. See Figure 1. The responding agent (human or chatbot) gave three recommendations. The recommendations emphasized whether a restaurant had good or bad reviews. The response messages shown in the verbal-only and emoji conditions were identical except for the incorporation of smiles (4) and frowns (1) in the latter. Emoji were chosen for their ability to serve the *providing information* function (e.g., Ekman & Friesen, 1969; Harrison, 1973) of nonverbal communication. Smiles accompanied expressions of positive affect for the interaction and positive restaurant recommendations. The frown was paired next to advice to avoid a restaurant with bad reviews.[2] A total of 10 conversational turns occurred between the recommendation seeker and the responding agent (chatbot or human).

Participants were instructed to read the conversation carefully and to consider the messages on the "sender" (or left) side of the screenshot message thread (similarly to Mou & Xu, 2017; Mou et al., 2019). The sender was described as a contact named "Alex" or "A. L.E.X. Chatbot," depending on the agent condition to which participants had been assigned. After participants read the conversations, they completed a survey questionnaire containing three standard measures, open-ended questions, and a brief demographic section.

Figure 1. Screenshots created for manipulation of verbal-only and emoji conditions.

Instruments

McCroskey and McCain's (1974) scale assessed participant impressions of attraction across the measure's *social attraction* dimension. Participants reported their answers across Likert-type scale items (five items) ranging from 1 ("strongly disagree") to 5 ("strongly agree"). A reliability coefficient of .82 (Item $M = 3.36$, $SD = .83$) demonstrated good reliability. Spitzberg's (2006) scale measured participant impressions of CMC competence along the appropriateness (4 items) and effectiveness (4 items) dimensions using Likert-type items ranging from 1 ("not at all true of the person") to 5 ("very true of the person"). Spitzberg's scale demonstrated a good reliability coefficient of .77 (Item $M = 3.67$, $SD = .61$). McCroskey and Teven's (1999) measure of source credibility determined participant impressions of credibility using 18 semantic differential items across three dimensions: *competence* (e.g., "trained" or "untrained"), *goodwill* ("has others' concerns at heart" or "does not have others' concerns at heart") and *trustworthiness* ("trustworthy" or "untrustworthy"). Because of the sample size, the multidimensional structure of the model was not tested. A reliability coefficient of .94 (Item $M = 5.24$, $SD = 0.99$) was attained for the entire instrument, demonstrating good reliability.

Results

A 2 × 2 between-subjects MANOVA was conducted to determine the effects of the manipulated independent variables of type of agent (human or chatbot) and message type (verbal-only or emoji) on the dependent variables of social attraction, CMC competence, and credibility (which were significantly positively correlated ranging from .45 to .55, $p < .01$). The assumption of equality of covariance matrices was satisfied, Box's $M = 11.99$, $F = .63$, $p = .88$. There was a significant main effect of type of message (verbal-only versus emoji) on the combined set of dependent variables [Wilks' $\lambda = .856$, $F(3, 90) = 5.03$, $p = .003$, $\eta^2 = .14$]. However, there was not a significant main effect for type of agent [Wilks' $\lambda = .958$, $F(3, 90) = 1.31$, $p > .05$, $\eta^2 = .04$] or an interaction effect of agent type and message type [Wilks' $\lambda = .983$, $F(3, 90) = .52$, $p > .05$, $\eta^2 = .02$] on the combined set of dependent variables. Therefore, in answer to RQ1, there were no significant differences in interpersonal impressions formed of a human versus chatbot message source. Table 1 contains the means and standard deviations on the dependent variables for the three message conditions.

To examine the differences between the message conditions, univariate follow-up procedures were conducted. Levene's tests indicated no violation of the assumption of homogeneity of variance: social attraction, $F(3, 92) = 1.578$, $p = .20$, CMC competence $F(3, 92) = .69$, $p = .56$, and credibility $F(3, 92) = .35$, $p = .79$. The ANOVAs for social attraction [$F(1, 92) = 12.22$, $p = .001$, $\eta^2 = .12$], CMC competence [$F(1, 92) = 9.01$, $p = .003$, $\eta^2 = .09$] and credibility [$F(1, 92) = 6.07$, $p = .016$, $\eta^2 = .06$] achieved significance. Pairwise comparisons revealed that the source of the message with emoji was rated significantly more positively on all three dependent variables than the source of the verbal-only message.

Results indicated that a human and chatbot source were rated as similarly socially attractive, CMC competent, and credible when delivering the same message content (whether verbal-only or emoji). However, both types of agents (human and chatbot)

Table 1. Means and standard deviations for the dependent variables.

Variable	Verbal-only M	(SD)	Emoji Total M	(SD)
Social Attraction				
Human	3.28$_a$	(0.62)	3.72$_a$	(0.82)
Chatbot	3.02$_a$	(0.55)	3.52$_a$	(0.56)
Total	3.15$_a$	(0.59)	3.62$_b$	(0.71)
CMC Competence				
Human	3.47$_a$	(0.65)	3.96$_b$	(0.61)
Chatbot	3.53$_a$	(0.53)	3.77$_a$	(0.55)
Total	3.50$_a$	(0.59)	3.87$_b$	(0.58)
Credibility				
Human	5.01$_a$	(.88)	5.52$_a$	(1.11)
Chatbot	5.01$_a$	(1.01)	5.50$_a$	(0.89)
Total	5.01$_a$	(0.94)	5.51$_b$	(1.00)

Means in a row with differing subscripts differed significantly at $p < .05$

garnered more favorable interpersonal impressions when their messages included emoji than when they were verbal only. Therefore, the hypotheses, which predicted a social attractiveness (H1), CMC competence (H2), and credibility (H3) advantage for emoji-added messages received support.

Discussion

This study examined the effect of emoji use on impressions of interpersonal attractiveness, CMC competence, and credibility in a computer-mediated context; and whether perceptions differed of human and chatbot message sources. Results demonstrated that participants rated emoji-featuring messages higher than verbal-only messages on all three dependent variables of social attraction (H1), CMC competence (H2), and credibility (H3).

Additionally, scores for the interpersonal impression variables did not vary significantly between human or chatbot message sources, suggesting participants evaluated chatbots similarly to humans, which is in line with the findings of earlier studies of perceptions of Twitterbots (e.g., Edwards et al., 2014; Edwards et al., 2016; Goble, Beattie, & Edwards, 2016).

Participants viewed emoji-using message sources as more socially attractive than message sources using verbal-only message strategies. In a related study, Ganster et al. (2012) found that participants viewing positive-valanced emoji were associated with higher levels of perceived mood. Although our experiment did not test valance, Ganster et al. (2012) argued that the act of adapting a smiling face to a digital medium, rather than the emoji symbol itself, led to more positive moods. Consistent with Ganster et al., participants rated emoji conditions higher on all dependent variables than verbal-only conditions echoing literature that emphasizes a relationship between CMC nonverbal immediacy behaviors like emoji (e.g., Darics, 2017; Lo, 2008) to social attraction (e.g., Rocca & McCroskey, 1999).

Participants experiencing higher amounts of social attraction for emoji-using messages (either with chatbots or humans) than those employing verbal-only strategies (H1) present significant practical implications. Scholars have noted the predictive and convergent validity (e.g., Ayres, 1989; Duran & Kelly, 1988) of McCroskey and McCain's (1974) interpersonal attraction scale on interaction quality. People are more likely to interact with partners to whom they are attracted. Thus, if chatbots are to become a viable conversational partner, for instance in supportive contexts (e.g., Molteni, 2017), it stands to reason the creators of chatbots and related technologies might incorporate message features that will make users more attracted to chatbots, and therefore more likely to engage them in initial and subsequent interactions.

Participants also rated emoji-senders as more CMC competent than sources of verbal-only message (H2). Participants may have felt emoji-using message sources were exerting effort to contextualize, clarify, and orient their messages toward the recipient, which are adaptive qualities of competent communicators (Spitzberg, 2006, p. 642). Furthermore, because people process nonverbal messages faster than verbal messages (e.g., Kuzmanovic et al., 2012), participants might have perceived emoji-using sources as mindful of time constraints and communication relevance. Echoing Spitzberg (2006), emoji use itself may have been interpreted as a CMC skill. Spitzberg (2006) argues "expressiveness skills can be displayed in CMC interactions through the use of emoticons and similar paralinguistic features of message content" (p. 643). Should emoji possess the capacity to convey attentiveness and expressiveness (a recent study by Prada et al., 2018 argued people use emoji to be more expressive), which are key CMC skills leading to perceptions of competence, chatbot designers may wish to consider incorporating emoji or other similar behaviors when perceptions of expression and competence are key to users' needs and satisfaction.

Lastly, results demonstrated that participants rated emoji-using message sources as more credible than verbal-only message sources (H3). Scholars over decades of communication research have argued that credibility, the degree to someone views another as competent, trustworthy, and caring (McCroskey & Teven, 1999) is one of the most important interpersonal impressions. Westerman, Spence, and Van Der Heide (2012) established a positive relationship between online cues and impression of credibility, the higher ratings of credibility for emoji sources in this study may have been a result of message sources providing their targets with more information. For instance, participants may have felt that emoji-using messages possessed a degree of applied knowledge or skill with the CMC context (e.g., Spitzberg, 2006). Second, participants may have interpreted the higher immediacy and affect associated with nonverbal gestures (Dresner & Herring, 2010) as a sign of goodwill or caring on behalf of the sender. For instance, if participants perceived emoji use as source attempts to clarify, contextualize, or further express the meaning of their messages (e.g., Prada et al., 2018; Spitzberg, 2006); participants may have felt the message sender cared for conversation, the information exchanged, or the message recipient.

The perception that a chatbot can be credible presents important implications for several potential interaction contexts. This is meaningful is contexts like social support where perceptions of personal characteristics impact future behaviors such as support seeking (e.g., Mortenson, 2009), especially among stigmatized individuals (Williams & Mickelson, 2008, p. 507). Many stressors are stigmatizing (e.g., infertility, depression), which may cause people to withdraw from social situations entirely (Goffman, 1963). According to Dovidio, Major, and Crocker (2000) "the psychological and social consequences of stigma involve the responses both of the perceivers and of stigmatized people themselves" (p. 5), suggesting support seeker perceptions will be necessary for chatbot designers to understand, as perceptions of a person's network influence support quality (Williams & Mickelson, 2008). Thus, careful consideration of what CMC behaviors influence perceptions of credibility could be a critical quality of successfully implementing chatbot technologies. Pan, Feng, and Windgate (2018) argued self-disclosure and openness lead to higher impressions of interpersonal trust in online support forums. Thus, if participants saw emoji-use as a means toward self-disclosure, openness, or expression (e.g., Prada et al., 2018) emoji use might be associated with trustworthiness, and thus potentially making CMC users appear more credible, and will be more likely to interact with them.

Results also suggest interpersonal impressions did not vary between human or chatbot conditions in terms of the source's perceived social attractiveness, CMC competence, or credibility. This finding is consistent with the CASA paradigm (Reeves & Nass, 1996) and related studies (e.g., Mou & Xu, 2017; Mou et al., 2019) which found similar perceptions between bots and humans. Our results further extend the primary findings of the CASA paradigm into chatbot communication. People seemed to evaluate chatbots, like other people, as social actors in CMC.

Limitations and Future Direction

The most significant limitation of this study is the experimental manipulation. Using manipulated screen-shot images of conversations between fictional interactants enabled strong experimental control. However, we did not use actual AI chatbots due to the available technology at the time of data collection and concerns of internal validity. Although researchers have utilized screenshots in other studies examining perceptions of human versus AI agency (e.g., Edwards et al., 2016; Edwards et al., 2014; Spence, Edwards, Edwards, & Jin, 2019), the emergent nature of AI technology may provide more realistic manipulation materials in the future and should be explored. Future studies could explore the potential of a live experiment in which participants engage in an actual texting exchange, or perhaps computer-animated SMS or IM conversations as a stimulus.

Interpersonal elements and context also limit the applications of this study. This experiment used a relatively common CMC/SMS interaction (picking a restaurant) between two unknown (to the participants) interactants. However, individuals use CMC for conversations ranging from trivial (picking a restaurant) to more serious (healthcare) (e.g., Fitzpatrick et al., 2017). These contextual-based limitations grow when accounting for different interaction partners. People might perceive emoji use as appropriate or useful in the context of planning a social event with a longtime friend but might not be receptive of emoji from less familiar or professional acquaintances in conversations that impact long-term health or wellbeing. The countless combinations of context and partner underscore why future research should continue exploring the interplay of partner, context, and message features to better understand how these factors impact interpersonal impressions.

Operating system variations (e.g., Apple iOS or Android) also present limitations. Although Unicode standardizes the name and general facial expressions for each emoji symbol, inconsistencies exist between different operating systems (Blagdon, 2013). A recent study (Miller et al., 2016) measuring emoji interpretation determined that both sender and receiver perceptions regarding a given symbol differed significantly both between users of the different platforms, as well as within users of the same platforms. Interpretive variance and ecological considerations suggest significant challenges, and further questions, toward understanding the impacts of emoji use in CMC contexts.

Conclusion

Recalling Spitzberg (2006), the act of sending a symbol alone may demonstrate a message sender's care and attention to detail in relation to the conversation. This study's results are congruent with literature that demonstrates person-centered message qualities leads to higher evaluations of communicative partners (see review by High & Dillard, 2012) and Spitzberg's (2006) predications and explanations of CMC competence, and extends them to the context of HMC. While the implications for this study may seem overly theoretical and unbound by specific context (e.g., healthcare or financial settings), our focus is on impressions of bots untouched by potential mediating variables related to context, and appropriateness for our available sample. Thus, we used a casual scenario (picking a restaurant) for sake of experiential scope of the sample (mostly college students unlikely to have extensive experience interacting with healthcare professionals) to determine effects of AI behavior on impressions that predict future willingness to interact. Understanding the potential benefits of a "smile" to a CMC or HMC message is an essential step to further understanding emoji use until future research addresses experimental design, contextual, and display-related limitations.

This study is among others attempting to better understand how AI behaviors influence interpersonal impressions in CMC. There are numerous directions for continued research into nonverbal CMC in many contexts between humans and automated agents. Studying specific cues (or the lack thereof) in HMC is vital to the development of more sophisticated understandings, and better interfaces for HMC users. This study contributes an important understanding to the human-human interaction script theory (Spence et al., 2014) and future study on chatbots: emoji-using chatbots are perceived similarly to humans on variables of communication quality. Chatbot designers ought to incorporate nonverbal expressive features like emoji into their design, as users may form more positive impressions about chatbot technologies. In human-human applications, appearing a more competent CMC communication could be as simple as adding a smile (or frown) to SMS conversations, or following up a task-oriented business e-mail with a "thumbs up" sign. Understanding how emoji use by people and chatbots will impact interpersonal impressions will be a growing concern for competent communicators in an increasingly technological and automated world.

Notes

1. Originally, there was another condition in the study examining emoticons. This condition was dropped for clarity due to the suggestion of a reviewer. The overall argument and findings did not change as a result and the design is clearer. Thank you to the reviewer for this idea.
2. We did not manipulate varying numbers of smiles or frowns or attempt to tease out the effects of emojis expressing positive versus negative affect. The affect valence, number, and placement of emojis reflected our attempt at experimental realism. Our choices were based on scans of similar chat conversations available online.

Disclosure statement

No potential conflict of interest was reported by the authors.

ORCID

Austin Beattie http://orcid.org/0000-0003-2667-4321
Autumn P. Edwards http://orcid.org/0000-0002-5963-197X
Chad Edwards http://orcid.org/0000-0002-1053-6349

References

Ainsworth, J., Palmier-Claus, J. E., Machin, M., Barrowclough, C., Dunn, G., Rogers, A., & Hopkins, R. S. (2013). A comparison of two delivery modalities of a mobile phone-based assessment for serious mental illness: Native smartphone application vs text-messaging only implementations. *Journal of Medical Internet Research, 15,* e60. doi:10.2196/JMIR.2328

Andersen, K., & Clevenger, J. T. (1963). A summary of experimental research in ethos. *Communication Monographs, 30,* 59–78. doi:10.1080/03637756309375361

Ayres, J. (1989). The impact of communication apprehension and interaction structure on initial interactions. *Communication Monographs, 56,* 75–88. doi:10.1080/03637758909390251

Battestini, A., Setlur, V., & Sohn, T. (2010). A large scale study of text-messaging use. In *Proceedings of the 12th international conference on human computer interaction with mobile devices and services* (pp. 229–238). ACM. doi:10.1145/1851600.1851638

Berger, C. R., & Calabrese, R. J. (1975). Some explorations in initial interaction and beyond: Toward a developmental theory of interpersonal communication. *Human Communication Research, 1,* 99–112. doi:10.1111/j.1468-2958.1975.tb00258.x

Blagdon, J. (2013). How emoji conquered the world: The story of the smiley face from the man who invented it. *The Verge.* Retrieved from https://www.theverge.com/2013/3/4/3966140/how-emoji-conquered-the-world

Blair, B. L., Fletcher, A. C., & Gaskin, E. R. (2015). Cell phone decision making: Adolescents' perceptions of how and why they make the choice to text or call. *Youth & Society, 47,* 395–411. doi:10.1177/0044118X13499594

Bradford, L. (2017). How chatbots are about to change communication. *Forbes.* Retrieved from https://www.forbes.com/sites/laurencebradford/2017/07/24/how-chatbots-are-about-to-change-communication/#4922f33f4aa8

Bubas, G. (2001). *Computer mediated communication theories and phenomena: Factors that influence collaboration over the internet*. Paper presented at the 3rd meeting of the CARNet Users Conference, Zagreb, Croatia.

Church, K., & de Oliveira, R. (2013). What's up with whatsapp?: Comparing mobile instant messaging behaviors with traditional SMS. In *Proceedings of the 15th international conference on human-computer interaction with mobile devices and services* (pp. 352–361). doi:10.1145/2493190.2493225

Cornelius, J. B., Lawrence, J. S. S., Howard, J. C., Shah, D., Poka, A., McDonald, D., & White, A. C. (2012). Adolescents' perceptions of a mobile cell phone text messaging-enhanced intervention and development of a mobile cell phone-based HIV prevention intervention. *Journal for Specialists in Pediatric Nursing, 17*, 61–69. doi:10.1111/j.1744-6155.2011.00308.x

Daft, R. L., & Lengel, R. H. (1984). Information richness: A new approach to managerial behavior and organizational design. *Research in Organizational Behavior, 6*, 191–233. doi:10.21236/ada128980

Daft, R. L., & Lengel, R. H. (1986). Organizational information requirements, media richness and structural design. *Management Science, 32*, 554–571. doi:10.1287/mnsc.32.5.554

Darics, E. (2017). E-leadership or "How to be boss in Instant Messaging?" The role of nonverbal communication. *International Journal of Business Communication, X*, 1–27. doi:org/2329488416685068

Derks, D., Bos, A. E., & Von Grumbkow, J. (2007). Emoticons and social interaction on the Internet: The importance of social context. *Computers in Human Behavior, 23*, 842–849. doi:10.1016/j.chb.2004.11.013

Dixson, M. D., Greenwell, M. R., Rogers-Stacy, C., Weister, T., & Lauer, S. (2017). Nonverbal immediacy behaviors and online student engagement: Bringing past instructional research into the present virtual classroom. *Communication Education, 66*, 37–53. doi:10.1080/03634523.2016.1209222

Dovidio, J. F., Major, B., & Crocker, J. (2000). Stigma: Introduction and overview. In T. F. Heatherton, R. E. Kleck, M. R. Hebl, & J. G. Hull (Eds.), *The social psychology of stigma* (pp. 1–28). New York, NY: Guilford.

Dresner, E., & Herring, S. C. (2010). Functions of the nonverbal in CMC: Emoticons and illocutionary force. *Communication Theory, 20*, 249–268. doi:10.1111/j.1468-2885.2010.01362.X

Duncan, S. (1969). Nonverbal communication. *Psychological Bulletin, 72*, 118–137. doi:10.1037/h0027795

Duran, R. L., & Kelly, L. (1988). The influence of communicative competence on perceived task, social, and physical attraction. *Communication Quarterly, 36*, 41–49. doi:10.1080/01463378809369706

Edwards, A., Edwards, C., Westerman, D., & Spence, P. R. (2019). Initial expectations, interactions, and beyond with social robots. *Computers in Human Behavior, 90*, 308–314. doi:10.1016/j.chb.2018.08.042

Edwards, C., Beattie, A. J., Edwards, A., & Spence, P. R. (2016). Differences in perceptions of communication quality between a Twitterbot and human agent for information seeking and learning. *Computers in Human Behavior, 65*, 666–671. doi:10.1016/j.chb.2016.07.003

Edwards, C., Edwards, A., & Omilion-Hodges, L. (2018). Receiving medical treatment plans from a robot: Evaluations of presence, credibility, and attraction. In *Companion of the 2018 ACM/IEEE international conference on human-robot interaction* (pp. 101–102). ACM. doi:10.1145/3173386.3177050

Edwards, C., Edwards, A., Spence, P., & Westerman, D. (2016). Initial interaction expectations with robots: Testing the human-to-human interaction script. *Communication Studies, 67*, 227–238. doi:10.1080/10510974.2015.1121899

Edwards, C., Edwards, A., Spence, P. R., & Shelton, A. K. (2014). Is that a bot running the social media feed? Testing the differences in perceptions of communication quality for a human agent and a bot agent on Twitter. *Computers in Human Behavior, 33*, 372–376. doi:10.1016/j.chb.2013.08.013

Ekman, P., & Friesen, W. V. (1969). The repertoire of nonverbal behavior: Categories, origins, usage and codings. *Semiotica, 1*, 49–97. doi:10.1515/semi.1969.1.1.49

Fadhil, A., Schiavo, G., Wang, Y., & Yilma, B. A. (2018, May). The effect of emojis when interacting with conversational interface assisted health coaching system. In *Proceedings of the 12th EAI international conference on pervasive computing technologies for healthcare* (pp. 378–383). ACM. doi:10.1145/3240925.3240965

Fitzpatrick, K. K., Darcy, A., & Vierhile, M. (2017). Delivering cognitive behavior therapy to young adults with symptoms of depression and anxiety using a fully automated conversational agent (Woebot): A randomized controlled trial. *JMIR Ment Health, 4*, e19. doi:10.2196/mental.7785

Franklin, V. L., Waller, A., Pagliari, C., & Greene, S. A. (2006). A randomized controlled trial of Sweet Talk, a text-messaging system to support young people with diabetes. *Diabetic Medicine, 23*, 1332–1338. doi:10.1111/j.1464-5491.2006.01989.x

Ganster, T., Eimler, S. C., & Kramer, N. C. (2012). Same same but different!? The differential influence of smilies and emoticons on person perception. *Cyberpsychology, Behavior, and Social Networking, 15*, 226–230. doi:10.1089/cyber.2011.0179

Ganster, T., Eimler, S. C., & Krämer, N. C. (2012). Same but different!? The differential influence of smilies and emoticons on person perception. *Cyberpsychology, Behavior, and Social Networking, 15*, 226–230. doi:org/0.1089/CYBER.2011.0179

Goble, H., Beattie, A. J., & Edwards, C. (2016). The impact of Twitterbot race on interpersonal impressions. *Iowa Journal of Communication, 48*, 23–36.

Goble, H., & Edwards, C. (2018). A robot that communicates with vocal fillers has ... uhhh ... greater social presence. *Communication Research Reports, 35*, 256–260. doi:10.1080/08824096.2018.1447454

Goffman, E. (1963). *Stigma: Notes on the management of spoiled identity*. New York, NY: Simon & Schuster.

Harrison, R. P. (1973). Nonverbal communication. In I. S. Pool, W. Schramm, N. Maccoby, F. Fry, E. Parker, & J. L. Fern (Eds.), *Handbook of communication* (pp. 93–115). Chicago, IL: Rand McNally.

Heider, F. (1958). *The psychology of interpersonal relations*. New York, NY: Wiley.

Hendricks, D. (2017). Chatbots are changing the entire world of tech. *Inc*. Retrieved from https://www.inc.com/drew-hendricks/how-the-bot-revolution-will-change-commerce-and-business.html

Hesse, C., & Floyd, K. (2011). Affection mediates the impact of alexithymia on relationships. *Personality and Individual Differences, 50*, 451–456. doi:10.1016/j.paid.2010.11.004

High, A. C., & Dillard, J. P. (2012). A review and meta-analysis of person-centered messages and social support outcomes. *Communication Studies, 63*, 99–118. doi:10.1080/10510974.2011.598208

Ho, A., Hancock, J., & Miner, A. S. (2018). Psychological, relational, and emotional effects of self-disclosure after conversations with a chatbot. *Journal of Communication, 68*, 712–733. doi:org10.1093/joc/jqy026

Huang, A. H., Yen, D. C., & Zhang, X. (2008). Exploring the potential effects of emoticons. *Information & Management, 45*, 466–473. doi:10.1016/j.im.2008.07.001

Huckstep, R. (2017). Chatbot & the rise of the automated insurance agent. *The Digital Insurer*. Retrieved from https://www.the-digital-insurer.com/blog/insurtech-the-rise-of-the-automated-insurance-agent-aka-the-insurtech-chatbot/

Hyken, S. (2017). AI and chatbots are transforming the customer experience. *Forbes*. Retrieved from https://www.forbes.com/sites/shephyken/2017/07/15/ai-and-chatbots-are-transforming-the-customer-experience/#373fc61a41f7

Kiesler, S., Siegel, J., & McGuire, T. (1984). Social psychological aspects of computer-mediated communications. *American Psychologist, 39*, 1123–1134. doi:10.1037/0003-066X.39.10.1123

Kiesler, S., & Sproull, L. S. (1992). Group decision making and communication technology. *Organizational Behavior and Human Decision Processes, 52*, 96–123. doi:10.1016/0749-5978(92)90047-B

Knobloch, L. K., & Solomon, D. H. (2005). Relational uncertainty and relational information processing. *Communication Research, 32*, 349–388. doi:10.1177/0093650205275384

Kravitz, J. (2018). If your boyfriend of girlfriend is bad at communicating, here's how to talk to them about it. *Elite Daily*. Retrieved from https://www.elitedaily.com/p/if-your-boyfriend-girlfriend-is-bad-at-communicating-this-is-how-to-talk-to-them-about-it-11468655

Kuzmanovic, B., Bente, G., von Cramon, D. Y., Schilbach, L., Tittgemeyer, M., & Vogeley, K. (2012). Imaging first impressions: Distinct neural processing of verbal and nonverbal social information. *Neuroimage, 60*, 179–188. doi:10.1016/j.neuroimage.2011.12.046

Lo, S. K. (2008). The nonverbal communication functions of emoticons in computer-mediated communication. *CyberPsychology & Behavior, 11*, 595–597. doi:10.1089/cpb.2007.0132

Maack, M. (2016). Meet Nadia, the scaringly 'human' chatbot who can read your emotions. *The Next Web*. Retrieved from https://thenextweb.com/artificial-intelligence/2017/03/24/say-hello-to-nadia-the-terrifyingly-human-chatbot-with-emotional-intelligence/

Maass, D. (2014). Answers and questions about military, law enforcement, and intelligence agency chatbots. *Electronic Frontier Foundation*. Retrieved from https://www.eff.org/deeplinks/2014/04/answers-questions-about-military-law-enforcement-and-intelligence-agency-chatbots

McCroskey, J. (1982). Oral Communication Apprehension: A Reconceptualization. *Annals of the International Communication Association, 6*, 136–170. doi:10.1080/23808985.1982.11678497

McCroskey, J. C., Hamilton, P. R., & Weiner, A. N. (1974). The effect of interaction behavior on source credibility, homophily, and interpersonal attraction. *Human Communication Research, 1*, 42–52. doi:10.1111/j.1468-2958.1974.tb00252.x

McCroskey, J. C., & McCain, T. A. (1974). The measurement of interpersonal attraction. *Speech Monographs, 41*, 261–266. doi:10.1080/03637757409375845

McCroskey, J. C., & Teven, J. J. (1999). Goodwill: A reexamination of the construct and its measurement. *Communication Monographs, 66*, 90–103. doi:10.1080/03637759909376464

McCroskey, J. C., & Young, T. J. (1981). Ethos and credibility: The construct and its measurement after three decades. *Communication Studies, 32*(1), 24–34. doi:10.1080/10510978109368075

Miller, D. T., Downs, J. S., & Prentice, D. A. (1998). Minimal conditions for the creation of a unit relationship: The social bond between birthmates. *European Journal of Social Psychology, 28*, 475–481. doi:10.1002/(SICI)1099-0992(199805/06)28:3<475::AID-EJSP881>3.0.CO;2-M

Miller, H., Thebault-Spieker, J., Chang, S., Johnson, I., Terveen, L., & Hecht, B. (2016). "Blissfully happy" or "ready to fight": Varying interpretations of emoji. Proceedings of ICWSM 2016, Cologne, Germany.

Molteni, M. (2017). The chatbot therapist will see you now. *Wired*. Retrieved from https://www.wired.com/2017/06/facebook-messenger-woebot-chatbot-therapist/

Morgan, B. (2017). 5 ways chatbots can improve customer service in banking. *Forbes*. Retrieved from https://www.forbes.com/sites/blakemorgan/2017/08/06/5-ways-chatbots-can-improve-customer-experience-in-banking/#6be945a57148

Mortenson, S. T. (2009). Interpersonal trust and social skill in seeking social support among Chinese and Americans. *Communication Research, 36*, 32–53. doi:10.1177/0093650208326460

Mou, Y., & Xu, K. (2017). The media inequality: Comparing the initial human-human and human-AI social interactions. *Computers in Human Behavior, 72*, 432–440. doi:10.1016/j.chb.2017.02.067

Mou, Y., Xu, K., & Xia, K. (2019). Unpacking the black box: Examining the (de) Gender categorization effect in human-machine communication. *Computers in Human Behavior, 90*, 380–387. doi:10.1016/j.chb.2018.08.049

Nass, C., & Moon, Y. (2000). Machines and mindlessness: Social responses to computers. *Journal of Social Issues, 56*, 81–103. doi:10.1111/0022-4537.00153

Nass, C., Moon, Y., Fogg, B. J., Reeves, B., & Dryer, D. C. (1995). Can computer personalities be human personalities? *International Journal of Human-Computer Studies, 43*, 223–239. doi:10.1006/ijhc.1995.1042

Nyguyn, M. H. (2017) How chatbots and artificial intelligence will save banks and the finance industry billions. *Business Insider*. Retrieved from http://www.businessinsider.com/chatbots-banking-ai-robots-finance-2017-10

O'Neill, B. (2010). LOL! (laughing online): An investigation of non-verbal communication in computer mediated exchanges. *Working Papers of the Linguistics Circle, 20*, 117–123.

Obermayer, J. L., Riley, W. T., Asif, O., & Jean-Mary, J. (2004). College smoking-cessation using cell phone text messaging. *Journal of American College Health, 53*, 71–78. doi:10.3200/JACH.53.2.71-78

Orda, O. (2017). The five food and restaurant AI chatbots you should definitely know about. *Chatbots Life.com*. Retrieved from https://chatbotslife.com/the-five-food-and-restaurant-ai-chatbots-you-should-know-about-393c870b0ca5

Oxford. (2018). emoji. *The Oxford English Dictionary Online*. Retrieved from https://en.oxforddictionaries.com/definition/emoji

Pan, W., Feng, B., & Skye Wingate, V. (2018). What you say is what you get: How self-disclosure in support seeking affects language use in support provision in online support forums. *Journal of Language and Social Psychology, 37*(1), 3–27. doi:10.1177/0261927X17706983

Prada, M., Rodrigues, D. L., Garrido, M. V., Lopes, D., Cavalheiro, B., & Gaspar, R. (2018). Motives, frequency and attitudes toward emoji and emoticon use. *Telematics and Informatics, 35*(7), 1925–1934. doi:10.1016/j.tele.2018.06.005

Purington, A., Taft, J. G., Sannon, S., Bazarova, N. N., & Taylor, S. H. (2017). Alexa is my new BFF: Social roles, user satisfaction, and personification of the Amazon Echo. In *Proceedings of the 2017 CHI conference extended abstracts on human factors in computing systems* (pp. 2853–2859). ACM. doi:10.1145/3027063.3053246

Reeves, B., & Nass, C. (1996). *The media equation: How people treat computers, television, and new media like real people and places*. New York, NY: Cambridge University Press.

Rocca, K. A., & McCroskey, J. C. (1999). The interrelationship of student ratings of instructors' immediacy, verbal aggressiveness, homophily, and interpersonal attraction. *Communication Education, 48*, 308–316. doi:10.1080/03634529909379181

Romeo, N. (2016). The chatbot will see you now. *The New Yorker*. Retrieved from https://www.newyorker.com/tech/elements/the-chatbot-will-see-you-now

Rubin, R. B., Martin, M. M., Bruning, S. S., & Powers, D. E. (1993). Test of a self-efficacy model of interpersonal communication competence. *Communication Quarterly, 41*, 210–220. doi:10.1080/01463379309369880

Shevat, A. (2017). *Designing bots: Creating conversational experiences*. Boston, MA: O'Reilly Media.

Skovholt, K., Grønning, A., & Kankaanranta, A. (2014). The communicative functions of emoticons in workplace e-mails::-). *Journal of Computer-Mediated Communication, 19*, 780–797. doi:10.1111/jcc4.12063

Spence, P. R., Edwards, A., Edwards, C., & Jin, X. (2019). 'The bot predicted rain, grab an umbrella': Few perceived differences in communication quality of a weather Twitterbot versus professional and amateur meteorologists. *Behaviour & Information Technology, 38*, 101–109. doi:10.1080/0144929X.2018.1514425

Spence, P. R., Westerman, D., Edwards, C., & Edwards, A. (2014). Welcoming our robot overlords: Initial expectations about interaction with a robot. *Communication Research Reports, 31*, 272–280. doi:10.1080/08824096.2014.924337

Spitzberg, B. H. (2006). Preliminary development of a model and measure of computer-mediated communication (CMC) competence. *Journal of Computer-Mediated Communication, 11*, 629–666. doi:10.1111/j.1083-6101.2006.00030.x

Sproull, L., & Kiesler, S. (1986). Reducing social context cues: Electronic mail in organizational communications. *Management Science, 32*, 1492–1512. doi:10.1287/mnsc.32.11.1492

Stark, L., & Crawford, K. (2015). The conservatism of emoji: Work, affect, and communication. *Social Media+ Society, 1*, 1–11. doi:10.1177/2056305115604853

Tesser, A. (1988). Toward a self-evaluation maintenance model of social behavior. *Advances in Experimental Social Psychology, 21*, 181–227. doi:10.1016/S0065-2601(08)60227-0

Teven, J. J., & Hanson, T. L. (2004). The impact of teacher immediacy and perceived caring on teacher competence and trustworthiness. *Communication Quarterly, 52*, 39–53. doi:10.1080/01463370409370177

Unicode. (2016). The Unicode standard: A technical introduction. *The Unicode Standard*. Retrieved from http://www.unicode.org/standard/principles.html

Walther, J. B., & D'Addario, K. P. (2001). The impacts of emoticons on message interpretation in computer-mediated communication. *Social Science Computer Review, 19*, 324–347. doi:10.1177/089443930101900307

Warren, C. (2014) Who controls emoji anyway? *Mashable*. Retrieved from http://mashable.com/2014/06/18/so-who-controls-emoji-anyway/#cr7CMzCY5kqR

Westerman, D., Spence, P. R., & Van Der Heide, B. (2012). A social network as information: The effect of system generated reports of connectedness on credibility on Twitter. *Computers in Human Behavior, 28*(1), 199–206. doi:10.1111/jcc4.12041

Wiemann, J. M. (1977). Explication and test of a model of communicative competence. *Human Communication Research, 3*, 195–213. doi:10.1111/j.1468-2958.1977.tb00518.x

Williams, S. L., & Mickelson, K. D. (2008). A paradox of support seeking and rejection among the stigmatized. *Personal Relationships, 15*, 493–509. doi:10.1111/j.1475-6811.2008.00212.x

Wrench, J. S., & Punyanunt-Carter, N. M. (2007). The relationship between computer-mediated-communication competence, apprehension, self-efficacy, perceived confidence, and social presence. *Southern Communication Journal, 72*, 355–378. doi:10.1080/10417940701667696

Xu, K., & Lombard, M. (2016). *Media are social actors: Expanding the CASA paradigm in the 21st Century*. Presented at the Annual Conference of the International Communication Association, Fukuoka, Japan.

Zhou, R., Hentschel, J., & Kumar, N. (2017). Goodbye text, hello emoji: Mobile communication on wechat in China. In *Proceedings of the 2017 CHI conference on human factors in computing systems* (pp. 748–759). ACM. doi:10.1145/3025453.3025800

Predicting AI News Credibility: Communicative or Social Capital or Both?

Sangwon Lee , Seungahn Nah , Deborah S. Chung , and Junghwan Kim

ABSTRACT

News credibility as an essential democratic value has been at the forefront of scholarly endeavors over the last several decades. Despite prolific research in this area, scholarship on the credibility of algorithm-based and automated news has yet to offer empirical findings in regards to the causes and their impacts. In line with prior studies concerning news credibility, this study examines the driving forces in predicting the level of credibility on artificial intelligence (AI) news. Specially, this study unveils the effects of communicative capital, such as media use and public discussion, among audiences, as well as social capital, such as social trust, on AI news credibility. Data collected through a nationwide online survey reveals that media use through television, social network sites, and online news sites, as well as public discussion yielded a positive association with AI news credibility. Of particular interest is that social trust moderated the effect of public discussion on credibility, indicating that the relationship between discussion and credibility was even stronger for those who have a higher level of trust in others. Implications are further discussed.

Research on algorithm-based, automated, or AI (artificial intelligence) news has recently attracted much attention due largely to its innovative transformation of news production and consumption. Despite the increasing volume of studies, an examination of the credibility of AI news among news audiences has remained relatively unexplored in the digitally saturated media environment. News credibility has been at the center of scholarly endeavors over many decades (e.g., Addington, 1971; Berlo et al., 1969; Carr et al., 2014; Fico et al., 2004; Hovland & Weiss, 1951; Metzger et al., 2003; Slater & Rouner, 1996; Whitehead, 1968) as news plays a significant role in delivering information, facilitating public discussion, forming public opinion, and promoting civic participation. News credibility serves as a necessary condition for public communication processes and outcomes, thereby contributing to a vibrant civil community for a healthier democracy to function in a given society.

The extant literature demonstrates that underlying factors driving news credibility stems mostly from reliance on media, such as newspaper, television, radio, and the Internet (e.g., Johnson & Kaye, 1998, 2004, 2009, 2014, 2016; Knobloch et al., 2003). This media centric research tradition suffers from lack of a theorized model to predict the social contexts and conditions by which news audiences perceive news – especially algorithm and automation-based news. Thus, a theorized model should offer why and under what circumstances the public may perceive AI-based news as credible for community building.

Unlike previous studies, the current study theorizes an AI news credibility model from the social capital perspective (Bourdieu, 1986; Nah, 2010; Nah & Chung, 2012; Portes, 1998; Putnam, 1995, 2000). On the one hand, social trust as a major component of social capital offers the driving force for audiences to evaluate AI-based news contributing to their communities. On the other hand, social trust offers a necessary condition for audiences to evaluate AI news credibility moderating public conversation. Combining the social capital perspective with particular emphasis on social trust, this study underscores not only the effects of media use and public discussion but also the roles of social capital in tandem with communication factors. Specifically, the theorized model focuses on how public discussion interacts with social capital in predicting AI news credibility. To test the theorized model toward AI news credibility, the current study conducts a nation-wide survey in South Korea and offers theoretical, methodological, and practical implications.

News Credibility Research

Media credibility has been and continues to function as an important concept in the understanding of news media practices. It is a multifaceted and multidimensional concept that is central to the work of journalists. A renewed consideration for news media credibility is paramount in the present media environment that is transforming rapidly with multiple storytellers sharing their views on the news.

The discussion of media credibility, which is associated to the broader concept of trust, focuses on the communicative dimension (Bentele & Seidenglanz, 2008; Strömbäck et al., 2020). Media credibility has been defined in various ways, including believability (Tseng & Fogg, 1999), accuracy, fairness, completeness, and trustworthiness (Metzger et al., 2003). Within the discipline of communication studies, credibility is discussed in terms of the message source, message content, and the medium itself (Carr et al., 2014; Sundar & Nass, 2001).

Initially, media credibility research focused on the dimensions of source credibility (Nah & Chung, 2012), examining how various characteristics of communicators, such as an individual, group or organization (Kiousis, 2001), may influence message processing (Addington, 1971; O'Keefe, 1990). Hovland and Weiss (1951) early research on source credibility underscored that the trustworthiness of a source had an influence on the acknowledgment of messages and on one's potential change of opinion regarding a source. Fairness and justifiability were identified as other related concepts. Various dimensions have since been uncovered pointing to source credibility as a multidimensional construct (Berlo et al., 1969; Whitehead, 1968) although little agreement exists on the key dimensions (see Kiousis, 2001). The scholarship on source credibility has expanded over the years to include studies on audiences' perceptions of credibility regarding journalists, political candidates, and online sources (Kiousis, 2001). Additionally, related to source credibility is the area of research on message credibility, where the characteristics related to the message shape credibility perceptions (Fico et al., 2004; Slater & Rouner, 1996).

Unlike source credibility that focuses on the sender of the content, medium credibility, on the other hand, focuses on the channel in which the content is communicated (Kiousis, 2001). One of the first studies to examine medium credibility was Westley and Severin (1964). Among their key findings was the impact of demographic variables (e.g., age, gender, and education) on one's perceived credibility. They also found that television news was considered to be more credible than newspapers. Further, they distinguished between media credibility and media preference. Gaziano and McGrath (1986) used a 12-item credibility measure to examine credibility perceptions on television news and daily newspapers. This measure included dimensions of being fair, unbiased, complete, factual, and accurate. Using this scale, they found that television and newspaper scores were correlated with each other pointing to the public's similar assessment of the two news sources.

More recently, the changing media environment has further complicated the understanding on news credibility (Metzger & Flanagin, 2013; Sundar & Nass, 2001) with interactive platforms and new storytellers joining information dissemination practices. Thus, studies on news credibility have shifted their focus on examining perceived credibility of a variety of media platforms (Rimmer & Weaver, 1987). Although earlier studies demonstrated the dominance traditional media had on audiences' perceptions toward news media credibility (Abel & Wirth, 1977; Flanagin & Metzger, 2000; Gaziano & McGrath, 1986), more recent investigations on emerging media channels have presented contradictory findings pointing toward the increasing acceptance of alternative media as suitable sources for credible information.

Much research on media credibility assessments point to associations with content consumption, such as exposure, reliance, attention, and dependence (Atkin, 1973; Johnson & Kaye, 1998, 2000, 2004, 2009; T. Johnson & Kaye, 2010; Johnson & Kaye, 2014, 2016; Knobloch et al., 2003; Sweetser et al., 2008). For example, media use has been found to be an important component in credibility assessments across all media platforms (Greenberg, 1966; Johnson & Kaye, 2004; Shaw, 1973; Westley & Severin, 1964). Additionally, research has found that people ascribe the highest credibility ratings to their preferred media choices (Carter & Greenberg, 1965; Rimmer & Weaver, 1987).

An important aspect related to media use and exposure is media reliance – a variable that has repeatedly emerged as a predictor for evaluations on credibility. There is a robust body of scholarship on the relationship between media reliance and credibility assessments (Flanagin & Metzger, 2000; Greenberg, 1966; Kiousis, 2001; Wanta & Hu, 1994; Westley & Severin, 1964). In Johnson and Kaye (1998, 2000, 2004, 2009; T. Johnson & Kaye, 2010; Johnson & Kaye, 2014, 2016) have examined this issue systematically over a period of two decades and provide a solid overview of the changing notions of credibility assessments across various media channels. Their work has primarily examined the views of politically-interested individuals on their credibility assessments of television, newspapers, and also the Internet, including blogs. Their various studies have consistently supported the importance of media reliance.

For example, Johnson and Kaye (2000) investigated the extent to which traditional and online source reliance predicted the credibility of online newspapers, television news, news-magazines, candidate literature, and also political issue-oriented sites. They found media reliance to be the strongest predictor for online source credibility where study participants rated the Web as the most credible. Similalry, Johnson and Kaye (2004) found blog users to rate blogs as higher in credibility than traditional media sources where reliance on blogs was a strong predictor of blog credibility. In their longitudinal study on views toward online media credibility, T. Johnson and Kaye (2010) examined three presidential campaigns, again finding high credibility assessments for online issue sources and low assessments for television news. Further, Johnson and Kaye (2016) examined media reliance of political content on social media, including Twitter, social networking sites and mobile device applications. They found participants ranked social media to be moderate to high in credibility with reliance on media platform again a strong predictor of social media credibility.

Thus, Johnson and Kaye have contributed a significant amount of work in support of the criticality of media reliance on the credibility assessments of various news sources and have also traced the evolving notions of perceived credibility of various media platforms. Further support is also provided by Cassidy (2007) who examined credibility perceptions of daily print and online newspaper journalists. His study found journalists rated online news as moderately credible and that online newspaper journalists rated online news as significantly more credible than did print journalists, pointing to Internet reliance as a predictor of credibility assessments. From a non-U.S. context, Kim and Johnson (2009) explored politically interested online users' views on traditional media, their online counterparts, and independent online newspapers during the 2004 South Korean general election. They found independent online newspapers were viewed as the most credible source for political information. Further, reliance on online and traditional media sources were found to be strong credibility predictors for online sources. Political variables, including interest in the campaign, political involvement and voting, also emerged as significant predictors for online credibility assessments.

Increasingly, newsrooms around the globe are experimenting with AI and machine learning (ML) although with limited autonomy and through basic tasks, with automation and bots rarely being integrated into the process of producing news (Jones & Jones, 2019). Studies examining audiences' perception of AI-based news (i.e., automated news/robot journalism) credibility are also on the rise. Most research on this topic has found that AI-based news is considered to be more objective compared to news content authored by human journalists. Even though people often fail to distinguish AI-based and automated news content from that written by human journalists (e.g., Clerwall, 2014; Jung et al., 2017; Wölker & Powell, 2018), respondents tend to rate automated news content to be more objective and credible than the latter when the source is manipulated (human journalist vs robot/AI) (e.g., Clerwall, 2014; Liu & Wei, 2018; Van der Kaa & Krahmer, 2014).

For example, using an experiment, Clerwall (2014) examined people's perceptions of software-generated content verses content written by journalists. He found that even though the software-generated content was deemed "descriptive" and "boring," it was also perceived to be "objective." Similarly, Graefe et al. (2018) found that people tend to perceive computer-written news as more credible than human-written news, and such perceptions did not differ across topics. Liu and Wei (2018) also examined readers' news and source credibility perceptions on news stories written by humans vs. robots. Participants who held machine heuristics, or perceived them to be intention free, were found to experience less emotional involvement when news stories were attributed to news writing algorithms, thus resulting in lower perceptions of bias and slant.

These positive perceptions toward AI-generated news over human-authored news were even more pronounced in a study by Jung et al. (2017) in the South Korean context, where human journalists tend not to be trusted. The public gave higher scores (i.e., had a more positive perception) to AI-generated content – but only when it was conveyed to the users as AI-generated. Interestingly, when the same content was manipulated to say it was authored by human journalists, the scores were lower. On the other hand, the public gave lower scores to journalists' articles when they were noted to be written by humans and higher scores to purported AI-generated content that was actually written by humans.

Similarly, in a study about perceptions regarding Twitterbots and human Twitter agents, Edwards et al. (2014) found that Twitterbots were perceived as a credible source for information. Further, Twitterbots were rated similarly to human Twitter agents for credibility, communication competence, and intent to interact although the human agents were evaluated higher for social attraction and task attraction. In another study examining, perceptual differences between Twitterbots and human Twitter agents, Edwards et al. (2016) found that learning outcomes were the same for participants who learned from a Twitterbot or a human agent. These include information seeking, cognitive elaboration, affective learning, and motivational behaviors.

Yet, some studies have found different results. Spence et al. (2014) found that people were more uncertain about interacting with robots, anticipated less social attraction, or liking, to robots, and also expected less social presence when interacting with robots in lieu of human agents. For another example, Waddell (2018) employed two experiments to examine how machine authorship influences perceptions of news credibility. Both studies found negative associations with machine-based authorship. Specifically, in the first study, he found participants rated news attributed to a machine as less credible than news attributed to a human journalist. In the second study, he also found negative effects of stories attributed to a machine by source anthropomorphism and negative expectancy violations.

Liu and Wei (2019) suggest a more complex picture with regard to how human vs. machine news writers influence the evaluations of the news author and the news content. Findings reveal that machine-based news was viewed as being more objective but less expert when compared to human-written stories. When comparing specifically selected issues (e.g., refugee admission), news organizations with high credibility (e.g., the *New York Times*) were found to have enhanced perceived news objectivity when using machined-written news. For all other cases, use of machine-based stories reduced the perceptions on the trustworthiness and expertise of a source. Importantly, when complex stories that require a higher level of information processing were written by machines, they were found to enhance perceived news credibility more prominently.

While studies investigating the source credibility of AI news exist, however, studies that examine AI news in relation to other news media platforms are still rare. Thus, based on the above review of the literature, we build on these perspectives and propose the following research question about media use and reliance and the relationship between AI news credibility:

RQ: To what extent does media use (i.e., newspaper news use, TV news use, online news site news use, and SNS news use) predict AI news credibility?

Social Capital and News Credibility

The social capital perspective, stemming from works by Bourdieu and Coleman (Portes, 1998), emphasizes community networks, resources, and relationships that lead to mutually profitable outcomes through collective action. Some scholars have focused on institutionalized relationships and the benefits accrued from group membership within those solidarities (e.g., Bourdieu, 1986). Others have underscored the importance of its function through social structures, which facilitate particular actions by actors (e.g., Coleman, 1988). Both conceptualizations of social capital emphasize the criticality of strong tie relationships between social structures and their actors. Putnam (1995, 2000), who has widely popularized the notion of social capital, refers to social capital as the core elements of community life, including "networks, norms, and social trust" (Putnam, 1995, p. 67) that provide the methods for which citizens can collaborate on community issues to reach common goals. While Bourdieu and Coleman's definitions of social capital focus on strong ties, such as institutional memberships, Putnam's (2000) definition is more inclusive by finding weak ties formed through informal social meetings and organizations as being meaningful as well. Bonding similar individuals, such as those from intimate family relations, and bridging between diverse individuals, such as relations formed outside of one's local network, with mutual respect and reciprocity, is an essential part of Putnam's conceptualization of social capital.

Social capital has been measured in various ways, including organizational membership, neighborliness, public attendance, sociability, and civic engagement (Kikuchi & Coleman, 2012). Social trust, contentment, and civic engagement were used as indicators of social capital, for example, in measuring the relationship between traditional media use and online media use and that of social capital (Shah et al., 2001). In addition, mass media use has also been found to be positively related to social capital measures of neighborliness, social networks, and social trust (e.g., Beaudoin, 2009; Beaudoin & Thorson, 2004, 2006; Shah et al., 2001).

As online environments offer various news ways to interact with other individuals, research on how individuals may acquire social capital in online environments have been of particular interest. However, varying results exist (Ellison et al., 2010) with some finding online habitats to help generate new social capital (Rheingold, 1993), diminish social capital (Nie, 2001), or reinforce real-world relationships and supplement the development of social capital (Uslaner, 2000). In particular, Ellison et al. (2007) explored the formation and maintenance of social capital on Facebook and found strongest associations with bridging social capital. Kim and Lowrey (2015) examined Twitter and Facebook to identify predictors for producing citizen journalism. While they found bridging capital to be a strong positive predictor of citizen journalism activities on Facebook, bonding capital proved to be a strong negative predictor. Further, personal characteristics of users, such as social media use and civic skills, were the strongest predictors on Twitter-related citizen journalism activities.

Trust is a major component of social capital (Fukuyama, 1995; Putnam, 2000; Uslaner, 1998, 2004) and emerges from interpersonal relationships and social networks, and such ties influence the cultivation of views about community groups and, further, impact political and civic behaviors (Cappella & Jamieson, 1997; Uslaner, 1998, 2004). In fact, trust has been found to intervene in various aspects of individuals' social lives

(Tsfati & Cappella, 2003). Trust in fellow citizens and community members may function as valuable resources for individuals that may help to bond and bridge relationships and collectively achieve community objectives. For example, much like offline and online communities (Norris, 2002; Putnam, 2000; Williams, 2006), online news sites may also function as online social communities. Thus, in similar ways as physical networks, so can online news sites help to bond and bridge social capital leading to the formation of trust through news production and consumption (Nah & Chung, 2012).

A sub-phenomenon of trust is credibility. However, the concept of trust is broader, including a discussion on agents, social institutions, geographical settings and social systems while, as noted previously, the general discussion of credibility is focused on the communicative dimension (Bentele & Seidenglanz, 2008). Various definitions of trust highlight the condition of uncertainty on the part of the trustor (Gambetta, 1988; Tsfati, 2010). Thus, at the center of trust is the expectation that the relationship between trustee and trustor will lead to benefits and gains (Coleman, 1990). Given such a scenario, credibility is central to the concept of trust. Bringing social trust and media credibility together, Nah and Chung (2012) examined online community news audiences' perceptions of the roles of both professional and citizen journalists in the context of social capital. Their study revealed that media credibility was positively related to the public's understanding of professional journalists' role conceptions only. Social trust, on the other hand, was positively associated with the role conceptions of both professional and citizen journalists. Social trust in particular appears to play a critical role when citizen journalists interact with ordinary citizens. These findings point to the vital role social capital plays in influencing how online community news audiences perceive the importance of journalistic functions. Levy and Gvili (2015) explored the credibility of e-world of mouth across digital marketing channels in relation to social capital, information richness and interactivity. They found information richness to enhance channel credibility. Interactivity and credibility were positively associated, but this relationship was indirect and mediated by information richness and social capital. In terms of social capital, both bonding and bridging were identified as being correlated with e-WOM channel credibility. However, social capital bridging only had a direct relationship, and social capital bonding, which indicates close and trustful relationships among parties, was mediated by social capital bridging. In sum, social capital includes an understanding of the importance of social trust and social networks among individuals, groups, organizations, and institutions (Nah & Yamamoto, 2019).

Public Discussion, Social Trust, and AI News Credibility

Based on the literature cited above, the current study investigates how interpersonal discussion and social trust influence AI news credibility. In other words, this study considers extending AI-based news production systems not just as a mediator between machines and humans but as a social actor who communicates with news audiences (Lewis et al., 2019). In this regard, the study assumes that social capital in general and social trust in particular plays a vital role in influencing how news consumers perceive AI-based news regarding common issues and public affairs, thereby contributing to building civic community. Thus, the proposed theorized model predicts how social trust can moderate public discussion about community issues and public affairs, resulting in credibility in AI-based news as a communicator/producer.

This approach clearly advances previous research in this area. While previous news credibility research has mainly taken a media-centric approach where most studies have focused on media consumption patterns (e.g., media reliance) as underlying factors that drive news credibility (e.g., Beaudoin & Thorson, 2005; Johnson & Kaye, 1998, 2010, 2014), this research combines communicative capital and social capital approaches in order to gain a holistic understanding of why and under what contexts the public may perceive AI-based news to be credible. The logic behind our integrated approach is built on the assumption that human judgment is comparative in nature (Mussweiler, 2003). That is, the judgments we make depend on the context in which the judgments are made (e.g., Herr, 1986; Mussweiler, 2003). Thus, individuals' judgment toward the credibility of AI news does not merely depend on how one consumes news or how one thinks about AI news systems *per se*. Rather, people's judgments about news credibility is largely affected by non-technological factors, such as the social contexts under which news is consumed (Thorson et al., 2010).

For instance, the extent to which individuals engage in interpersonal discussions about public affairs can be an important factor that influences an individual's perception toward news credibility. When people engage in a discussion about public affairs, they will likely exchange information, thoughts, and perceptions about social norms (Ardèvol-Abreu et al., 2018; Kincaid, 2004). Such activity not only spurs further civic/political engagement (e.g., Cho et al., 2009; Nah & Yamamoto, 2019; Shah et al., 2005) but also plays a crucial role in building social capital, such as trust to individuals, organizations, and institutions such that these entities will cooperate in the pursuit of the common good for society (Ardèvol-Abreu et al., 2018).

Another important context under which the public may perceive AI-based news as credible for community building is the general level of trust that individuals have toward fellow citizens. Scholars have found that trust in fellow citizens is an important predictor of the degree to which people trust the media (Lee, 2005, 2010) because trust in any institution or system can be "conceptualized as interpersonal trust and individual actors are trusted as carriers of shared and accepted norms" (Fuchs et al., 2002, p. 430). In a similar vein, a number of scholars have found that an uncivil tone of discussion – whose activity may negatively affect an individual's trust toward the public sphere – led people to perceive the content as less credible (Anderson et al., 2018; Brooks & Geer, 2007; Ng & Detenber, 2005). On the other hand, if individuals engage in a public sphere where other fellow citizens are trusted (that these citizens are also doing their best to improve their community), then they are more likely to believe that the news covering their community can also be trustworthy; in other words, that the news is also presenting content in a way that contributes to the betterment of the community. As such, these studies overall suggest that people do not solely make credibility judgments on news content *per se* but rather within a broad social context under which such news is consumed, where individuals make sense of news through interaction with others and trust of fellow citizens in general.

Thus, we propose that discussion frequency and social trust are not just, respectively, important predictors of AI news credibility but that they also have joint interaction effects such that social capital among humans serves as a driving force for the credibility of machine or technology-based news, especially when they interact with public discussion concerning community issues or public affairs. Building on these theoretical rationales, we formulate the following hypotheses:

H1. Public discussion will be positively related to AI news credibility.

H2. Social trust will be positively related to AI news credibility.

H3. The relationship between political discussion and AI news credibility will be stronger for those who hold a higher level of trust in others.

Methods

Data Collection

To test the theorized model, the study conducted an online survey using online panels registered with Macromill Embrain, one of the largest survey agencies in South Korea. The study drew the samples to match the distribution of demographic features (gender, age, educational level, and income) across the regions. The online survey lasted between April 4 and April 9, 2019. The survey company sent out a total of 7,436 invitations with a hyperlink where online panels can fill out the survey questionnaire. Out of 2,395 panels who received the e-mail invitations, 2,109 participated in the survey. In the end, the survey had 1,502 respondents who completed the questionnaire, resulting in a final sample of 1,294 for analysis after excluding incomplete responses. This yielded a 28% response rate, which is similar to previous online surveys. Additionally, the study contains a table of zero-order Pearson's correlations to show the relationship among all the variables used for the theorized model. Zero-order correlations indicate that key theoretical variables of the model – social capital variables (i.e., social trust and AI news credibility) and communicative capital variables (i.e., media use and public discussion) – were all positively correlated (for further details, see Appendix).

Measures

Newspaper News Use
To measure the frequency of newspaper news consumption, respondents were asked on a 7-point scale (1 = not at all; 7 = very frequently) to respond to two questions: how often they use print news to gather information on (1) local issues and (2) national issues. To assess overall newspaper news consumption, we took the mean score of the two items (Spearman-Brown =.94; M= 3.40, SD = 1.77).

TV News Use
To measure the frequency of televised news consumption, respondents were asked on a 7-point scale (1 = not at all; 7 = very frequently) to respond to two questions: how often they use TV news to gather information about (1) local issues and (2) national issues. To assess overall TV news consumption, we took the mean score of the two items (Spearman-Brown = .89; M= 4.63, SD = 1.52).

Online News Site News Use
To measure the frequency of gathering news information through the use of websites of print news publications, respondents were asked on a 7-point scale (1 = not at all; 7 = very frequently) to respond to two questions: how often they use online news websites to gather information about (1) local issues and (2) national issues. To assess overall news sites news consumption, we took the mean score of the two items (Spearman-Brown = .96; M= 3.49, SD = 1.73)

SNS News Use
To measure the frequency of gathering news through SNS use, respondents were asked on a 7-point scale (1 = not at all; 7 = very frequently) to respond to two questions: how often they use SNS to gather information about (1) local issues and (2) national issues. To assess overall SNS news consumption, we took the mean score of the two items (Spearman-Brown = .97; M = 3.54, SD = 1.85).

Public Discussion
Respondents were asked on a 10-point scale (1 = not at all; 10 = always) to indicate how often they talked about current issues with others (M = 4.0, SD = 2.42).

Social Trust
To measure social trust, respondents were asked on a 7-point scale (1 = strongly disagree; 7 = strongly agree) to indicate to what extent they agree or disagree with the following three statements: (1) Community members seek out ways to make their community better, (2) People tend to cooperate to make a better community, and (3) I believe that people do their best to make a better community (Cronbach's α = .92, M= 3.78, SD = 1.33).

AI News Credibility
We built upon previous research on media credibility (e.g., Cassidy, 2007; Johnson & Kaye, 1998) to measure to what extent people trust AI news. We asked the respondents how much they agreed that AI news provides: (1) fair, (2) accurate, (3) believable, and (4) comprehensive information. Respondents were asked to respond to these questions on a 7-point scale (1 = strongly disagree; 7 = strongly agree; Cronbach's α = .95, M= 3.65, SD = 1.23).

Control Variables
In order to adjust for potential confounds, we controlled for demographic variables, including gender (Female: 49.3%), age (M = 42.43, SD = 12.79), education level (68.6% with college diploma or more), and income (median = KRW 30,000,000–45,000,000, approximately 25 USD,000-$40,000). In addition to demographic factors, we also controlled for efficacy and ideology. Efficacy was measured on a 7-point scale (1 = strongly disagree; 7 = strongly agree), where respondents were asked to indicate to what extent they agree or disagree with the following statements: (1) Public officials care about what people like me think, (2) Voting can influence governmental decision-making, (3) Ordinary citizens can influence their community's decision making process, and (4) There are many ways that citizens can participate in their community's decision making process (Cronbach's α = .79, M = 3.85, SD = 1.21). Ideology was measured by asking respondents'

stances on political, social, and economic issues using a 7-point scale (1 = very conservative; 7 = very liberal; Cronbach's α = .92, M = 4.24, SD = 1.20).

Analytical Procedure

To explore the proposed series of hypotheses, hierarchical ordinary least squares regression was used for the analysis. The independent variables were entered in separate blocks based on their presumed causal order to assess the relative contribution of each block of variables in explaining the variance in the dependent variable (i.e., AI news credibility). The demographic variables of gender, age, education, and income were entered in the first block, followed by ideology and efficacy in the second block. The variables measuring the frequency of use of news sources (newspaper news use, TV news use, online news site use, and SNS news use) were entered in the third block. Discussion frequency was entered in the fourth block, and social trust was entered in the fifth block. For the final block, the interaction variable (i.e., discussion X social trust) was created and added, allowing us to assess the moderating effect of social trust on the relationship between discussion and AI news credibility. The interaction term was created by multiplying the standardized values of the key main effect variables (i.e., discussion frequency and social trust) to avoid possible problems of multicollinearity (Cohen & Cohen, 1983). We plotted the interaction patterns using values of the interaction predictor one standard deviation below the mean, at the mean, and one standard deviation above the mean.

Results

RQ explored the association between media use and AI news credibility. Specifically, we examined the relationships between newspaper news use, TV news use, online news site news use, and SNS news use in the context of AI news credibility. Table 1 presents the results of hierarchical regression analysis. As shown in Table 1, news consumption via TV, online news sites, and SNS are positively related to AI news credibility (TV news: B = .15, p < .001; online news sites news: B = .17, p < .001; SNS news: B = .13, p < .001), while news consumption via newspaper is not significantly related to AI news credibility (B = .00, p > .05).

H1 predicted that discussion is positively associated with AI news credibility. Consistent with our expectation, the results in Table 1 show that discussion frequency is positively associated with AI news credibility (B = .08, p = .009). Thus, H1 is supported.

H2 predicted that social trust is positively associated with AI news credibility. Also consistent with our expectation, the results in Table 1 show that social trust is positively associated with AI news credibility (B = .21, p < .001). Thus, H2 is supported.

H3 predicted the interaction effect between discussion and social trust on AI news credibility. Consistent with our expectation, the results in Table 1 show that discussion significantly interacts with social trust in predicting AI news credibility (B = .07, p = .004). For better interpretation of the interaction term, the interaction plot is presented in Figure 1. Figure 1 shows that the relationship between discussion frequency and AI news credibility is stronger as levels of social trust increase. Thus, H3 is supported.

Table 1. Predicting AI credibility.

Predictors	Model 1	Model 2	Model 3	Model 4	Model 5	Model 6
Gender	.00	.01	.03	.03	.02	.02
Age	.06#	.05#	.03	.03	.02	.01
Education	−.01	−.05#	−.07**	−.07**	−.07**	−.07**
Income	.09**	.07*	.03	.02	.02	.02
Efficacy		.28***	.18***	.15***	.03	.02
Ideology		.05#	.02	.02	.00	.00
TV news			.16***	.16***	.15***	.15***
Newspaper news			.01	−.00	.01	.00
Online news sites			.19***	.18***	.17***	.17***
SNS news			.15***	.14***	.13***	.13***
Discussion				.09**	.08**	.08**
Social trust					.19***	.21***
Discussion X social trust						.07**
Total R^2 (%)	1.3	10.2	22.6	23.2	25.0	25.5

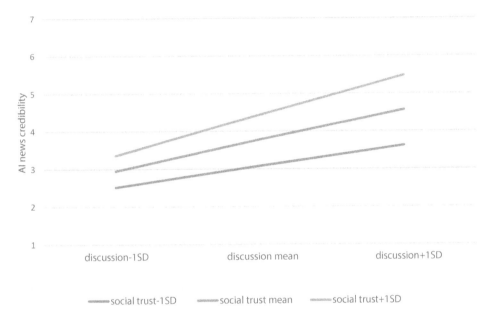

Figure 1. Interaction effects between discussion frequency and social trust on AI news credibility.

Discussion

The findings demonstrate that media use yielded significant positive effects on AI news credibility except for newspaper use. Given online news sites and news across social network sites (SNSs) produce more algorithm-based news production and alignments (Carlson, 2015; Clerwall, 2014), it is not surprising that the more news audiences consume content from online news sites and social network sites, the more likely news audiences are to perceive AI news as accurate, unbiased, comprehensive, and trustworthy in serving their communities. These results reaffirm findings from prior studies that media use and reliance lead to positive outcomes of media credibility over the decades (e.g., Cassidy, 2007; Johnson & Kaye, 2009, 2014). Further, sub-group analysis among news users has yet to offer a more complete picture of how different types of news use may lead to the varying degrees of AI news credibility across the diverse news channels and platforms.

Of particular interest is the positive relationship between political discussion and AI news credibility, indicating that citizens tend to attribute higher levels of credibility on AI news when discussing community issues or public affairs more frequently. That is, public conversation among citizens tends to build more favorable views toward AI news. As predicted, political talk plays a vital role in predicting AI news credibility. Equally important, social trust had a positive association with AI news credibility and proved to be an essential human-based factor leading to machine-based news credibility.

It is also noteworthy that social trust proves to be a necessary condition in a way that it moderates political discussion on AI news credibility. In other words, the relationship between political discussion and AI news credibility is even stronger for those who hold a higher level of trust in others. In the current study, social capital among humans serves as a driving force for credibility on machine or technology-based news especially when they interact with public discussion concerning community issues or public affairs.

With these findings, the current study offers several implications. On a theoretical level, it provides a testable theory for AI news credibility research from the social capital perspective. While adapting the communication approach from prior studies, the theory also provides an analytical framework to examine not only communicative capital, such as media use and public discussion, but also social capital as social contexts and conditions in which news audiences increasingly receive and perceive AI-based news content. While a more sophisticated model with moderating and mediating paths seems to be necessary to examine AI news credibility, these theoretical and analytical contributions carry noteworthy practical implications. In a nutshell, AI news credibility depends mainly on public talk and trust among and in others. Therefore, building trustful relationships with audiences is crucial for professional journalists to maintain higher levels of credibility on machine-based news, leading to a healthier democracy.

The current study focused on credibility of AI-based news with regard to community issues and public affairs. Prior studies (e.g., Jung et al., 2017), however, also compared AI produced news with human created news and found that the public and professional journalists alike rated automated news higher than journalists' written news stories. Therefore, a comparative study in the future will be worthy of consideration to see how social capital and public discussion work in tandem for both types of news.

Notwithstanding these implications, the current study has limitations and suggestions for future scholarship accordingly. Future studies need a probability sample while the nation-wide survey, through an online panel registered with a survey company, offers high quality data that draws a matching sample of demographic features. This way, future studies can increase the power of generalizability. Furthermore, a more elaborated model on moderating and mediating paths should be warranted to provide a more holistic picture of AI news credibility and its underlying mechanism.

Nevertheless, this study is one of the first of its kind, built on a theorized model reaffirming the roles of communicative capital and proving the roles of social capital as necessary conditions and social contexts predicting AI news credibility (e.g., Nah & Chung, 2012; Yamamoto & Nah, 2018). Future scholarship should test the theorized model through a more elaborated model to continue to examine this important research domain in the rapidly digitalized news media environment. In doing so, given that this study relied on data collected from a particular country, future research should also conduct comparative studies across diverse countries and cultures. In conclusion, the current study situated in South Korea should serve as a starting point for subsequent investigations in this area.

Disclosure Statement

No potential conflict of interest was reported by the authors.

ORCID

Sangwon Lee http://orcid.org/0000-0003-2471-8079
Seungahn Nah http://orcid.org/0000-0002-7182-2015
Deborah S. Chung http://orcid.org/0000-0002-5672-7124
Junghwan Kim http://orcid.org/0000-0001-5360-0059

References

Abel, J. D., & Wirth, M. O. (1977). Newspaper vs. TV credibility for local news. *Journalism Quarterly, 54*(2), 371–375. https://doi.org/10.1177/107769907705400223

Addington, D. W. (1971). The effect of vocal variations on ratings of source credibility. *Speech Monographs, 38*(3), 242–247. https://doi.org/10.1080/03637757109375716

Anderson, A. A., Yeo, S. K., Brossard, D., Scheufele, D. A., & Xenos, M. A. (2018). Toxic talk: How online incivility can undermine perceptions of media. *International Journal of Public Opinion Research, 30*(1), 156–168. https://doi.org/10.1093/ijpor/edw022

Ardèvol-Abreu, A., Diehl, T., & Gil de Zúñiga, H. (2018). Building social capital. How the news and the strength of the ties in the political discussion foster reciprocity. *Revista Internacional de Sociología, 76*(1), e083. https://doi.org/10.3989/ris.2018.76.1.16.147

Atkin, C. (1973). Instrumental utilities and information seeking. In P. Clark (Ed.), *New models of communication research* (pp. 205–242). Sage.

Beaudoin, C. E. (2009). Exploring the association between news exposure and social capital: Evidence of variance by ethnicity and medium. *Communication Research, 35*(5), 611–636. https://doi.org/10.1177/0093650209338905

Beaudoin, C. E., & Thorson, E. (2004). Social capital in rural and urban communities: Testing differences in media effects and models. *Journalism & Mass Communication Quarterly, 81*(2), 378–399. https://doi.org/10.1177/107769900408100210

Beaudoin, C. E., & Thorson, E. (2005). Credibility perceptions of news coverage of ethnic groups: The predictive roles of race and news use. *The Howard Journal of Communications, 16*(1), 33–48. https://doi.org/10.1080/10646170590915844

Beaudoin, C. E., & Thorson, E. (2006). The social capital of blacks and whites: Differing effects of the mass media in the United States. *Human Communication Research, 32*(2), 157–177. https://doi.org/10.1111/j.1468-2958.2006.00007.x

Bentele, G., & Seidenglanz, R. (2008). Trust and credibility—Prerequisites for communication management. In A. Zerfass, B. Van Ruler, & K. Sriramesh (Eds.), *Public relations research: European and International Perspectives and Innovations* (pp. 49–62). Wiesbaden: VS Verlag für Sozialwissenschaften.

Berlo, D. K., Lemert, J. B., & Mertz, R. J. (1969). Dimensions for evaluating the acceptability of message sources. *Public Opinion Quarterly, 33*(4), 563–576. https://doi.org/10.1086/267745

Bourdieu, P. (1986). The forms of capital. In J. G. Richardson (Ed.), *Handbook of theory and research for the sociology of education* (pp. 241–258). Greenwood Press.

Brooks, D. J., & Geer, J. G. (2007). Beyond negativity: The effects of incivility on the electorate. *American Journal of Political Science, 51*(1), 1–16. https://doi.org/10.1111/j.1540-5907.2007.00233.x

Cappella, J. N., & Jamieson, K. H. (1997). *Spiral of cynicism: The press and the public good*. Oxford University Press.

Carlson, M. (2015). The robotic reporter: Automated journalism and the redefinition of labor, compositional forms, and journalistic authority. *Digital Journalism, 3*(3), 416–431. https://doi.org/10.1080/21670811.2014.976412

Carr, D. J., Barnidge, M., Lee, B. G., & Tsang, S. J. (2014). Cynics and skeptics: Evaluating the credibility of mainstream and citizen journalism. *Journalism & Mass Communication Quarterly, 91*(3), 452–470. https://doi.org/10.1177/1077699014538828

Carter, R. F., & Greenberg, B. S. (1965). Newspapers or television: Which do you believe? *Journalism Quarterly, 42*(1), 29–34. https://doi.org/10.1177/107769906504200104

Cassidy, W. P. (2007). Online news credibility: An examination of the perceptions of newspaper journalists. *Journal of Computer-Mediated Communication, 12*(2), 478–498. https://doi.org/10.1111/j.1083-6101.2007.00334.x

Cho, J., Shah, D. V., McLeod, J. M., McLeod, D. M., Scholl, R. M., & Gotlieb, M. R. (2009). Campaigns, reflection, and deliberation: Advancing an OSROR model of communication effects. *Communication Theory, 19*(1), 66–88. https://doi.org/10.1111/j.1468-2885.2008.01333.x

Clerwall, C. (2014). Enter the robot journalist: Users' perceptions of automated content. *Journalism Practice, 8*(5), 519–531. https://doi.org/10.1080/17512786.2014.883116

Cohen, J., & Cohen, P. (1983). *Applied multiple regression/correlation analysis for the behavioral sciences.* Lawrence Erlbaum.

Coleman, J. (1988). Social capital in the creation of human capital. *The American Journal of Sociology, 94*, S95–S120. https://doi.org/10.1086/228943

Coleman, J. S. (1990). *Foundations of social theory.* Belknap Press.

Edwards, C., Beattie, A. J., Edwards, A., & Spence, P. R. (2016). Differences in perceptions of communication quality between a Twitterbot and human agent for information seeking and learning. *Computers in Human Behavior, 65*, 666–671. https://doi.org/10.1016/j.chb.2016.07.003

Edwards, C., Edwards, A., Spence, P. R., & Shelton, A. K. (2014). Is that a bot running the social media feed? Testing the differences in perceptions of communication quality for a human agent and a bot agent on Twitter. *Computers in Human Behavior, 33*, 372–376. https://doi.org/10.1016/j.chb.2013.08.013

Ellison, N., Lampe, C., Steinfield, C., & Vitak, J. (2010). With a little help from my friends: How social network sites affect social capital processes. In Z. Papacharissi (Ed.), *The networked self: Identity, community, and culture on social network sites* (pp. 124–145). Routledge.

Ellison, N. B., Steinfield, C., & Lampe, C. (2007). The benefits of Facebook "friends:" Social capital and college students' use of online social network sites. *Journal of Computer-Mediated Communication, 12*(4), 1143–1168. https://doi.org/10.1111/j.1083-6101.2007.00367.x

Fico, F., Richardson, J. D., & Edwards, S. M. (2004). Influence of story structure on perceived story bias and news organization credibility. *Mass Communication & Society, 7*(3), 301–318. https://doi.org/10.1207/s15327825mcs0703_3

Flanagin, A. J., & Metzger, M. J. (2000). Perceptions of Internet information credibility. *Journalism & Mass Communication Quarterly, 77*(3), 515–540. https://doi.org/10.1177/107769900007700304

Fuchs, D., Gabriel, O. W., & Völkl, K. (2002). Vertrauen in politische Institutionen und politische Unterstützung [Trust in Political Institutions and Political Sup- port]. *Österreichische Zeitschrift für Politikwissenschaft, 31*(4), 427–450.

Fukuyama, F. (1995). *Trust: The social virtues and the creation of prosperity.* Free Press.

Gambetta, D. (1988). Can we trust trust? In D. Gambetta (Ed.), *Trust: Making or breaking cooperative relations* (pp. 213-237). New York: Blackwell.

Gaziano, C., & McGrath, K. (1986). Measuring the concept of credibility. *Journalism Quarterly, 63*(3), 451–462. https://doi.org/10.1177/107769908606300301

Graefe, A., Haim, M., Haarmann, B., & Brosius, H. B. (2018). Readers' perception of computer-generated news: Credibility, expertise, and readability. *Journalism, 19*(5), 595–610. https://doi.org/10.1177/1464884916641269

Greenberg, B. S. (1966). Media use and believability: Some multiple correlates. *Journalism Quarterly, 43*(4), 665–670. https://doi.org/10.1177/107769906604300405

Herr, P. M. (1986). Consequences of priming: Judgment and behavior. *Journal of Personality and Social Psychology, 51*(6), 1106–1115. https://doi.org/10.1037/0022-3514.51.6.1106

Hovland, C. I., & Weiss, W. (1951). The influence of source credibility on communication effectiveness. *Public Opinion Quarterly, 15*(4), 635–650. https://doi.org/10.1086/266350

Johnson, T., & Kaye, B. (2010). Choosing is believing? How Web gratifications and reliance affect Internet credibility among politically interested users. *Atlantic Journal of Communication, 18*(1), 1–21. https://doi.org/10.1080/15456870903340431

Johnson, T. J., & Kaye, B. K. (1998). Cruising is believing?: Comparing Internet and traditional sources on media credibility measures. *Journalism & Mass Communication Quarterly, 75*(2), 325–340. https://doi.org/10.1177/107769909807500208

Johnson, T. J., & Kaye, B. K. (2000). Using is believing: The influence of reliance on the credibility of online political information among politically interested Internet users. *Journalism & Mass Communication Quarterly, 77*(4), 865–879. https://doi.org/10.1177/107769900007700409

Johnson, T. J., & Kaye, B. K. (2004). Wag the blog: How reliance on traditional media and the Internet influence credibility perceptions of weblogs among blog users. *Journalism & Mass Communication Quarterly, 81*(3), 622–642. https://doi.org/10.1177/107769900408100310

Johnson, T. J., & Kaye, B. K. (2009). In blog we trust? Deciphering credibility of components of the internet among politically interested internet users. *Computers in Human Behavior, 25*(1), 175–182. https://doi.org/10.1016/j.chb.2008.08.004

Johnson, T. J., & Kaye, B. K. (2010). Still cruising and believing? An analysis of online credibility across three presidential campaigns. *American Behavioral Scientist, 54*(1), 57–77. https://doi.org/10.1177/0002764210376311

Johnson, T. J., & Kaye, B. K. (2014). Credibility of social network sites for political information among politically interested Internet users. *Journal of Computer-mediated Communication, 19*(4), 957–974. https://doi.org/10.1111/jcc4.12084

Johnson, T. J., & Kaye, B. K. (2016). Some like it lots: The influence of interactivity and reliance on credibility. *Computers in Human Behavior, 61*, 136–145. https://doi.org/10.1016/j.chb.2016.03.012

Jones, B., & Jones, R. (2019). Public service chatbots: Automating conversation with BBC News. *Digital Journalism, 7*(8), 1032–1053. https://doi.org/10.1080/21670811.2019.1609371

Jung, J., Song, H., Kim, Y., Im, H., & Oh, S. (2017). Intrusion of software robots into journalism: The public's and journalists' perceptions of news written by algorithms and human journalists. *Computers in Human Behavior, 71*, 291–298. https://doi.org/10.1016/j.chb.2017.02.022

Kikuchi, M., & Coleman, C.-L. (2012). Explicating and measuring social relationships in social capital research. *Communication Theory, 22*(2), 187–203. https://doi.org/10.1111/j.1468-2885.2012.01401.x

Kim, D., & Johnson, T. J. (2009). A shift in media credibility: Comparing Internet and traditional news sources in South Korea. *International Communication Gazette, 71*(4), 283–302. https://doi.org/10.1177/1748048509102182

Kim, Y., & Lowrey, W. (2015). Who are citizen journalists in the social media environment? Personal and social determinants of citizen journalism activities. *Digital Journalism, 3*(2), 298–314. https://doi.org/10.1080/21670811.2014.930245

Kincaid, D. L. (2004). From innovation to social norm: Bounded normative influence. *Journal of Health Communication, 9*(sup1), 37–57. https://doi.org/10.1080/10810730490271511

Kiousis, S. (2001). Public trust or mistrust? Perceptions of media credibility in the information age. *Mass Communication & Society, 4*(4), 381–403. https://doi.org/10.1207/S15327825MCS0404_4

Knobloch, S., Dillman Carpentier, F., & Zillmann, D. (2003). Effects of salience dimensions of informational utility on selective exposure to online news. *Journalism & Mass Communication Quarterly, 80*(1), 91–108. https://doi.org/10.1177/107769900308000107

Lee, T. T. (2005). The liberal media myth revisited: An examination of factors influencing perceptions of media bias. *Journal of Broadcasting & Electronic Media, 49*(1), 43–64. https://doi.org/10.1207/s15506878jobem4901_4

Lee, T. T. (2010). Why they don't trust the media: An examination of factors predicting trust. *American Behavioral Scientist, 54*(1), 8–21. https://doi.org/10.1177/0002764210376308

Levy, S., & Gvili, Y. (2015). How credible is e-word of mouth across digital-marketing channels?: The roles of social capital, information richness, and interactivity. *Journal of Advertising Research, 55*(1), 95–109. https://doi.org/10.2501/JAR-55-1-095-109

Lewis, S. C., Guzman, A. L., & Schmidt, T. R. (2019). Automation, journalism, and human–machine communication: Rethinking roles and relationships of humans and machines in news. *Digital Journalism, 7*(4), 409–427. https://doi.org/10.1080/21670811.2019.1577147

Liu, B., & Wei, L. (2018, July). Reading machine-written news: Effect of machine heuristic and novelty on hostile media perception. In M. Kurosu (Ed.), *Human-Computer Interaction. Theories, Methods, and Human Issues* (pp. 307–324). Springer, Cham.

Liu, B., & Wei, L. (2019). Machine authorship In Situ: Effect of news organization and news genre on news credibility. *Digital Journalism, 7*(5), 635–657. https://doi.org/10.1080/21670811.2018.1510740

Metzger, M. J., Flanagin, A. J., Eyal, K., Lemus, D. R., & McCann, R. (2003). Credibility for the 21st century: Integrating perspectives on source, message and media credibility in the contemporary media environment. In P. J. Kalfleisch (Ed.), *Communication Yearbook* (Vol. 27, pp. 293–335). Lawrence Erlbaum.

Metzger, M. J., & Flanagin, A. J. (2013). Credibility and trust of information in online environments: The use of cognitive heuristics. *Journal of Pragmatics, 59*, 210–220. https://doi.org/10.1016/j.pragma.2013.07.012

Mussweiler, T. (2003). Comparison processes in social judgment: Mechanisms and consequences. *Psychological Review, 110*(3), 472–489. https://doi.org/10.1037/0033-295X.110.3.472

Nah, S. (2010). A theoretical and analytical framework toward networked communities: A case of the electronic community information commons. *Javnost-The Public, 17*(1), 23–36. https://doi.org/10.1080/13183222.2010.11009024

Nah, S., & Chung, D. S. (2012). When citizens meet both professional and citizen journalists: Social trust, media credibility, and perceived journalistic roles among online community news readers. *Journalism, 13*(6), 714–730. https://doi.org/10.1177/1464884911431381

Nah, S., & Yamamoto, M. (2019). Communication and citizenship revisited: Theorizing communication and citizen journalism practice as civic participation. *Communication Theory, 29*(1), 24–45. https://doi.org/10.1093/ct/qty019

Ng, E. & Detenber, B. H. (2005). The impact of synchronicity and civility in online political discussions on perceptions and intentions to participate. *Journal of Computer-Mediated Communication, 10*(3). https://doi.org/http://doi.10.1111/j.1083-6101.2005.tb00252.x

Nie, N. H. (2001). Sociability, interpersonal relations, and the Internet. *American Behavioral Scientist, 45*(3), 420–435. https://doi.org/10.1177/00027640121957277

Norris, P. (2002). Social capital and the news media. *Harvard International Journal of Press-Politics, 7*(2), 3–8. https://doi.org/10.1177/1081180X0200700301

O'Keefe, D. J. (1990). *Persuasion theory and research*. Sage.

Portes, A. (1998). Social capital: Its origins and applications in modern sociology. *American Review of Sociology, 24*(1), 1–24. https://doi.org/10.1146/annurev.soc.24.1.1

Putnam, R. D. (1995). Bowling alone: America's declining social capital. *Journal of Democracy, 6*, 65–78. https://doi.org/10.1353/jod.1995.0002

Putnam, R. D. (2000). *Bowling alone: The collapse and revival of American community*. Simon & Schuster.

Rheingold, H. (1993). *The virtual community: Homesteading on the electronic frontier*. MIT Press.

Rimmer, T., & Weaver, D. (1987). Different questions, different answers? Media use and media credibility. *Journalism Quarterly, 64*(1), 28–44. https://doi.org/10.1177/107769908706400104

Shah, D. V., Cho, J., Eveland, J. W., & Kwak, N. (2005). Information and expression in a digital age: Modeling Internet effects on civic participation. *Communication Research, 32*(5), 531–565. https://doi.org/10.1177/0093650205279209

Shah, D. V., Kwak, N., & Holbert, R. L. (2001). "Connecting" and "disconnecting" with civic life: Patterns of Internet use and the production of social capital. *Political Communication, 18*(2), 141–162. https://doi.org/10.1080/105846001750322952

Shaw, E. F. (1973). Media credibility: Taking the measure of a measure. *Journalism Quarterly, 50*(2), 306–311. https://doi.org/10.1177/107769907305000213

Slater, M. D., & Rouner, D. (1996). How message evaluation and source attributes may influence credibility assessment and belief change. *Journalism & Mass Communication Quarterly, 73*(4), 974–991. https://doi.org/10.1177/107769909607300415

Spence, P. R., Westerman, D., Edwards, C., & Edwards, A. (2014). Welcoming our robot overlords: Initial expectations about interaction with a robot. *Communication Research Reports, 31*(3), 272–280. https://doi.org/10.1080/08824096.2014.924337

Strömbäck, J., Tsfati, Y., Boomgaarden, H., Damstra, A., Lindgren, E., Vliegenthart, R., & Lindholm, T. (2020). News media trust and its impact on media use: Toward a framework for future research. *Annals of the International Communication Association*, 1–18. https://doi.org/10.1080/23808985.2020.1755338

Sundar, S. S., & Nass, C. (2001). Conceptualizing sources in online news. *Journal of Communication*, 51(1), 52–72. https://doi.org/10.1111/j.1460-2466.2001.tb02872.x

Sweetser, K. D., Porter, L. V., Chung, D. S., & Kim, E. (2008). Credibility and the use of blogs among professionals in the communication industry. *Journalism & Mass Communication Quarterly*, 85(1), 169–185. https://doi.org/10.1177/107769900808500111

Thorson, K., Vraga, E., & Ekdale, B. (2010). Credibility in context: How uncivil online commentary affects news credibility. *Mass Communication and Society*, 13(3), 289–313. https://doi.org/10.1080/15205430903225571

Tseng, S., & Fogg, B. J. (1999). Credibility and computing technology. *Communications of the ACM*, 42(5), 39–44. https://doi.org/10.1145/301353.301402

Tsfati, Y. (2010). Online news exposure and trust in the mainstream media: Exploring possible associations. *American Behavioral Scientist*, 54(1), 22–42. https://doi.org/10.1177/0002764210376309

Tsfati, Y., & Cappella, J. N. (2003). Do people watch what they do not trust? Exploring the association between news media skepticism and exposure. *Communication Research*, 30(5), 504–529. https://doi.org/10.1177/0093650203253371

Uslaner, E. M. (1998). Social capital, television, and the "mean world": Trust, optimism, and civic participation. *Political Psychology*, 19(3), 441–467. https://doi.org/10.1111/0162-895X.00113

Uslaner, E. M. (2000). Social capital and the net. *Communications of the ACM*, 43(12), 60–64. https://doi.org/10.1145/355112.355125

Uslaner, E. M. (2004). Trust, civic engagement, and the Internet. *Political Communication*, 21(2), 223–242. https://doi.org/10.1080/10584600490443895

Van der Kaa, H. A. J., & Krahmer, E. J. (2014). Journalist versus news consumer: The perceived credibility of machine written news. In *Paper presented at the Computation+Journalism symposium*. New York City: Columbia University. http://web.archive.org/web/20151006164247/http://compute-cuj.org/cj-2014/cj2014_session4_paper2.pdf.

Waddell, T. F. (2018). A robot wrote this? How perceived machine authorship affects news credibility. *Digital Journalism*, 6(2), 236–255. https://doi.org/10.1080/21670811.2017.1384319

Wanta, W., & Hu, Y. W. (1994). The effects of credibility, reliance, and exposure on media agenda-setting: A path analysis model. *Journalism Quarterly*, 71(1), 90–98. https://doi.org/10.1177/107769909407100109

Westley, B. H., & Severin, W. J. (1964). Some correlates of media credibility. *Journalism Quarterly*, 41(3), 325–335. https://doi.org/10.1177/107769906404100301

Whitehead Jr, J. L. (1968). Factors of source credibility. *Quarterly Journal of Speech*, 54(1), 59–63. https://doi.org/10.1080/00335636809382870

Williams, D. (2006). On and off the 'Net: Scales for social capital in an online era. *Journal of Computer-Mediated Communication*, 11(2), 593–628. https://doi.org/10.1111/j.1083-6101.2006.00029.x

Wölker, A., & Powell, T. E. (2018). Algorithms in the newsroom? News readers' perceived credibility and selection of automated journalism. *Journalism: Theory, Practice & Criticism*, 146488491875707. https://doi.org/10.1177/1464884918757072

Yamamoto, M., & Nah, S. (2018). A multilevel examination of local newspaper credibility. *Journalism & Mass Communication Quarterly*, 95(1), 76–95. https://doi.org/10.1177/1077699017721486

Appendix A. Zero-order correlations among the variables in the model

Variables	1	2	3	4	5	6	7	8	9	10	11	12	13
1. Gender	–												
2. Age	−.01	–											
3. Education	−.11***	−.10***	–										
4. Income	−.17***	.36***	.18***	–									
5. Efficacy	−.04	.05#	.12***	.08**	–								
6. Ideology	.04	−.07*	.09**	.03	.28***	–							
7. TV news	−.07**	.28***	.06*	.22***	.27***	.12***	–						
8. Newspaper news	−.15***	.20***	.14***	.25***	.23***	.05#	.52***	–					
9. Online news sites	−.08**	.10***	.09**	.12***	.22***	.10***	.38***	.50***	–				
10. SNS news	−.03	−.19***	.09**	.03	.22***	.15***	.20***	.28***	.34***	–			
11. Discussion	−.13***	.05	.13***	.19***	.40***	.13***	.32***	.37***	.38***	.33***	–		
12. Social trust	.01	.10***	.11***	.10**	.70***	.28***	.26***	.21***	.23***	.20***	.35***	–	
13. AI news credibility	−.01	.09**	−.00	.10***	.30***	.12***	.33***	.27***	.35***	.28***	.31***	.35***	–

Privacy, Values and Machines: Predicting Opposition to Artificial Intelligence

Josep Lobera, Carlos J. Fernández Rodríguez, and Cristóbal Torres-Albero

ABSTRACT
In this study we identify, for the first time, social determinants of opposition to artificial intelligence, based on the assessment of its benefits and risks. Using a national survey in Spain (n = 5200) and linear regression models, we show that common explanations regarding opposition to artificial intelligence, such as competition and relative vulnerability theories, are not confirmed or have limited explanatory power. Stronger effects are shown by social values and general attitudes to science. Those expressing egalitarian values and privacy concerns, as well as those less predisposed to innovation in a general sense, are more prone to oppose both technological applications. Lastly, we found evidence that, as in other complex technological applications, a new cognitive shortcut is produced. In this case, we found a strong correlation (0.652, $p < .001$) between public attitudes toward robotization in the workplace and toward artificial intelligence. We discuss the implications of this new cognitive schema, the "intelligent machine", as a new threatening or beneficial element.

A few years ago, Artificial Intelligence (AI) was just one more argument with which filmmakers used to make science fiction movies. However, today AI has become a reality, leading a great portion of the technological innovations that reach the market. The presence of the AI in our lives has been accompanied by a growing public debate about the risks and benefits that these technologies can bring to questions as wide ranging as privacy, national sovereignty and the health of democratic electoral processes (e.g. Brexit), and even new types of interactions in the workforce.

A person's attitude toward AI will determine human-AI interaction, and whether they will accept AI-based technology without criticism, with caution, or not at all. Similarly, public debate about how to regulate AI in fields such as the workplace or electoral campaigns is heavily conditioned by people's attitudes toward this new technology. Thus, our findings are of particular interest to the field of human-AI communication, as well as to those leveraging AI-based technologies in areas such as digital platforms, political communication, workforce organization and collaboration, commercial advertising, and those advancing the public debate around AI regulation.

At present, there are no empirical works that show what factors may mediate the opposition to artificial intelligence. In response, this study is the first to identify the factors affecting people's attitudes toward AI. We formulated the hypothesis based on two strands of work. First, we did a general literature review of the current understanding around opposition to controversial technologies. Hypothesis H1 through H4 and H7 arose from this review. The second approach was AI-specific, focusing on the main critical positions about the risks that may be involved in the introduction of technologies based on artificial intelligence. Hypothesis H5 and H6 resulted from this line of query.

Theoretical Framework

In contemporary societies, social representations of technoscience have become more complex, moving away from traditional optimistic representations (Allum, Sturgis, Tabourazi, & Brunton-Smith, 2008; Leiserowitz, Maibach, Roser-Renouf, Smith & Dawson, 2012). Certainly, a large majority of the population expresses a positive attitude toward the central body of science and technology, but there are certain controversial issues that are criticized by broad sectors of society (Torres-Albero & Lobera, 2017; Lobera, 2008).

The interest in understanding the critical positions toward controversial technologies has been expressed in different theoretical approaches. The theory of "cognitive deficit" has traditionally been the predominant explanation (Sturgis & Allum, 2004), producing a vibrant debate and disagreement among scholars, particularly in their assumption that the so-called "irrational" fears toward science and technology among some sectors of public opinion are based on their lack of scientific knowledge. At one end of the spectrum are those who believe in a purely "cognitive deficit" model and argue that this lack of knowledge explains critical positions toward science and technology (Bodmer, 1985; Ziman, 1991); at the other end are those who argue that there are other factors that explain this lack of support, as well as those who argue that scientific knowledge is a social construction and is difficult to quantify (Johnson, 1993). Recent studies show that the effect of knowledge on acceptance cannot be generalized wholesale from one application, or method, to others (Mielby, Sandøe, & Lassen, 2013). Since this is the first study specific to AI, we will test the validity of the cognitive deficit model. We hypothesize that the opposition to artificial intelligence will be higher among those with lower level of scientific knowledge of the individual (**H1**).

In recent decades, other explanations have been developed that emphasize the pressure of new technological risks (Beck, 1986) as key factors in explaining critical attitudes, encompassing a growing social demand for transformation of how science and technology are socially managed (Scheufele, 2014; Todt, 2011). Some studies suggest that the effect of social trust (Priest, 2001; Siegrist et al., 2000) and the level of confidence in scientists, regulators, and industry (Priest 2001) surpass the influence of the level of scientific knowledge on the perception of novel and potentially dangerous technologies. Thus, we expect a higher opposition to artificial intelligence among those with distrustful toward the appropriate functioning of science and technology (**H2**).

On the other hand, it may be argued that some individuals may characteristically resist change, i.e. be less innovative (Barak, 2018; Sheth & Stellner, 1979). This trait has been identified as a factor inhibiting the consumption of new products, as well as the adoption of new technologies in organizations (Jones, 2013). In this vein, we expect that the opposition to artificial intelligence will be higher among those less prone to innovation (**H3**).

Cultural theory points out that fears about new technologies are related to values and the maintenance of certain cultural dynamics (Douglas & Wildavsky, 1983). According to this perspective, it is not the technology that is resisted but the changes caused by it (Schein, 1985).

Each social group selects what constitutes a risk, protecting certain patterns of social interaction against others. Thus, there would be a relationship between the value systems and the selection of risks manifested by different social groups.

While a small number of works have tested cultural theory, those works have shown evidence supporting its validity, particularly when flagging up the influence of egalitarian values (Carlisle & Smith, 2005). In this vein, Grendstad and Selle (1997), Ellis and Thompson (1997), and Marris, Langford, and O'Riordan (1998) found that egalitarian values are associated with a greater concern about environmental issues of controversial technologies than individualist values. Thus, we expect a higher opposition to artificial intelligence among those expressing egalitarian values (**H4**).

Specific Public Concerns on AI

We have identified two main groupings of critical positions about the risks that may be involved in the introduction of technologies based on artificial intelligence. The first set of concerns addresses to the perceived link between artificial intelligence (AI) and its everlasting effects on work and employment. There is a consensus, particularly among experts, that AI will likely outperform humans in many activities and tasks in the following years (Grace, Salvatier, Dafoe, Zhang, & Evans, 2018). Nevertheless, there are differing views regarding the overall impact of AI on human life, which oscillate from celebrating its positive outcomes to apocalyptic gazes that see it as an existential threat to humanity (Madridakis, 2017; Sturken, Thomas, & Ball-Rokeach, 2004), highlighting the risks of an attack against humans (individually or collectively) by technology with artificial intelligence.[1] The issue of employment here is critical once the fast development of robotics and the growing automation of processes should put into risk a significant number of jobs, especially among the least skilled. This has led to a media hype about the challenges of a jobless future, supported to some extent by scholarly work.

Some experts have been emphasizing the disruption these new developments may involve, pointing at a future with fewer jobs available and smaller payrolls for most of the workforce (Brynjolfsson & McAfee, 2014; Frey & Osborne, 2017), while increasing the interest for basic income policies and robot taxation (Oberson, 2017; Standing, 2009 & 2017). Key institutions such as the World Economic Forum or the prestigious consulting firm PwC have stated in their reports that the net effect of robotics and AI will likely create mass technological unemployment (see Upchurch, 2018). This obviously poses important challenges for the future, although the determinism of technology in this narrative should not be overlooked (Edwards & Ramirez, 2016).

Another concern has to do with the quality of jobs created in the context of an AI-based economy. So far, the labor market in the new economy is quite polarized: while AI is boosting high-skilled jobs related to computing or robotics, a new layer of low-skilled jobs and low-paid jobs linked to different app-connected and "crowd-work platforms" tasks such as delivery, customer feedback and support, transport, storage and other services has emerged (Howcroft & Bergvall-Kåreborn, 2019). New forms of work mediated by algorithms have proliferated, degrading in many cases the quality of labor (Bergvall-Kåreborn & Howcroft, 2014; Fleming, 2017).

Some researchers have suggested that while a future without work is very unlikely, as proved by previous experiences (see Upchurch, 2018), the degradation of labor conditions should be considered as a major challenge in Western economies (Spencer, 2018). In this context of labor competition, we hypothesize that higher levels of opposition to AI will be linked to higher negative impacts on employment that individuals may experience due to AI-based innovations. Thus, we expect a lower opposition to artificial intelligence among those less exposed to negative effects on work and employment: those with college education, higher household income and economically inactive (**H5**).

The second strand of worries have to do with fears about privacy in a world mediated by the World Wide Web, the rise of e-commerce and the popularity of different social networks sites (Goldfarb & Tucker, 2012). Recently, new concerns have emerged about the use of personal information in electoral processes (Raab, 2019; Ward, 2018), particularly as a means for psychological targeting in political persuasion campaigns. Certainly, the interest on the power of watching and classifying information is already present in classic authors such as Foucault (1977), and the development of new forms of *post-panopticism* has attracted since then the interest of scholars (see Ball, Haggerty, & Lyon, 2012).

However, the increasing forms of surveillance developed in the context of the "War on Terror" (Lyon, 2007) and the rise of new-tech giants whose business models rely on the exploitation of personal data have ignited a public debate about how personal data is obtained and managed. The rapid expansion of the big data market is the result of the development of various technologies linked to the capture and storage of personal information from the internet, and may provide valuable information for consumer and social profiling. Regarding the State, the disclosure of mass surveillance leaked by Edward Snowden, the growing influence of State cyberpolicing capacities or the profiling of its citizens by the Chinese authorities are just some examples that show a discomforting revelation about the dangerous collusion of new forms of governance and IT applications (Lyon, 2014).

Furthermore, the scandals related to the usage of data without permission in the realm of business have gained as much attention in the media. The sales of personal information without explicit permission from the users – Facebook and Cambridge Analytica – and the risk of leaking such data as the result of hacking – Ashley Madison, Facebook again – have caused outrage among the public opinion, turning the attention to the issue of privacy in a context of widespread use of personal data in the markets.

This has led to a raising awareness about personal data and the need to protect it, acknowledging that there are important risks. The application of big data problem solving to a variety of areas, from geo-localization, health monitoring through wearable devices, online shopping or banking services helps to create new business niches, but also offers potential harms to users (Baruh & Popescu, 2017; Morozov, 2011). Security breaches may end up in stolen passwords, hacked e-mail and bank accounts, industrial piracy and other dangerous outcomes.

The issue of privacy is particularly salient among online consumers, and several studies have stated that negative perceptions about how personal data is treated may affect the frequency of online transactions (Akhter, 2014). Moreover, the use of images and personal information in a context where the individual voluntarily provides that information to a corporation might lead to future disputes about copyright, data protection and ownership. All this has raised apprehension about the potential misuse of such data and growing concerns about online privacy (Cecere, Le Guel, & Soulié, 2015), plus further fears that the interconnection of different data sets from both State and industry might increase the levels of surveillance in society (Lyon, 2014).

All these concerns have led to different discussions about how to tackle the problem of privacy aside from pushing certain regulations in national and supranational levels. Baruh and Popescu (2017) suggest that the collective dimension of privacy should be acknowledged in the public sphere, which in turn would provide alternatives for privacy protection that would go beyond the current "take it or leave it" neoliberal scenario. However, it seems difficult to give clear responses given the complexity of regulating internet and the different levels of concern that individuals express. A number of investigations have actually highlighted the importance of societal factors in the apparent variances among internet privacy concerns (Cecere et al., 2015; Thomson, Yuki, & Ito, 2015), and therefore not all of social groupings share equal views on how privacy should be protected, with different views regarding cultural background, gender and age. Following this vein, we expect that opposition to artificial intelligence will be higher among those more concerned about negative effects on privacy (**H6**).

Additionally, recent studies emphasize the importance of cognitive schemas or shortcuts in the positioning on controversial technological applications (Brossard et al., 2009; Ho, Brossard, & Scheufele, 2008; Scheufele, Corley, Shih, Dalrymple, & Ho, 2009). These schemas can be understood as "prior organized knowledge, abstracted from concrete experience", which orientate the responses of individuals to complex situations (Fiske & Linville, 1980, p. 543), and they are organized around semantic categories of high significance (Kumlin, 2001). These approaches are in line with Dake (1991), when he emphasized the importance of *Weltanschauungen* or worldviews as "guiding dispositions" that guide the responses of individuals in complex situations. Thus, we test an eventual cognitive shortcut with benefits and risks of robotization: we expect perceptions of AI to be associated with perceptions of robotization in the workplace (**H7**).

Methods

Our experimental design seeks to test hypotheses raised in the scientific literature on opposition to controversial technologies and those derived from critical positions toward artificial intelligence, presented above. We use data from the 9th National Survey on the Social Perception of Science and Technology in Spain 2018. As scientific coordinators of this survey, we included questions that allow us to relate the attitudes toward artificial intelligence with individual and contextual sociodemographic variables, as well as with factors related to knowledge and opinions about science and technology. The dependent variables of our analysis have been extracted from the 15th question of the questionnaire, which asks about the degree of identification, utilizing different phrases from a scale of 1 to 5.[2] In the 2018 survey, a total of 5,200 personal interviews (face to face) were carried out on people who had been residents in Spain for five or more years and were 15 years of age or older (the sample size in previous editions is similar). The sampling procedure was multistaged and stratified, with selection of primary units (municipality) and secondary units (census tracts) conducted through proportional random sampling and the last units (individuals) by random routes and quotas for gender and age. The sampling error for the total sample is ±1.25% for a confidence level of 95.5%, with the assumption of simple random sampling, calculated considering non-proportional samples.

Our dependent variable (opposition toward artificial intelligence) is built as the balance between the assessment of the perception of risks and the perception of the benefits of artificial intelligence. The analyzed phrases are the following: "*Using a scale of 1 to 5, where 1 means 'no risk' and 5 means 'many risks', to what extent do you think there are risks in Artificial Intelligence?*"; "*And now considering the benefits and using a scale of 1 to 5, where 1 means 'no benefit' and 5 means 'many benefits', to what extent do you think Artificial Intelligence has benefits?*". Thus, the dependent variable is constructed with the value of the risk assessment less the value of the assessment of the benefits. The distribution of this variable has a low skewness (0.066) and standard error of kurtosis (0.068), with a kurtosis value of −0,314, primarily due to a high concentration of people who consider that risks and benefits are balanced (see Appendices A–D).

The independent variables of sociodemographic character, chosen from a review of the literature, were the following: *gender, age, college education, work status* (economically active or inactive), and *household income*. Also, the *level of scientific knowledge*, as pointed out by the cognitive deficit model (Bodmer, 1985; Ziman, 1991) was included. This variable was constructed from the items of question 24 in the survey, in which it asks the respondent to choose the correct phrase for six pairs of statements: (1) the Sun revolves around the Earth/the Earth revolves around the Sun, (2) antibiotics cure infections caused by both viruses and bacteria/antibiotics cure infections caused by bacteria, (3) the first humans lived at the same time as dinosaurs/humans never co-existed with dinosaurs, (4) eating a genetically modified fruit changes the genes of the person who eats it/eating a genetically modified fruit does not change the genes of the person who eats it, (5) current climate change is a consequence of the hole in the ozone layer/current climate change is mainly due to the accumulation of greenhouse gases, (6) the number pi (π) is often used, among other things, in the manufacture of tires/the number pi (π) is the relationship between the legs and the hypotenuse of a triangle. The resulting variable is continuous and takes six values, from 0 to 6 successful answers.

A second set of variables related with values and attitudes was included:

- *Egalitarianism*. We have built a continuous variable based on a question from the *European Values Study* (EVS). The respondents had to place their opinions on a 1 to 10 scale on the following pair of statements: "the state must give more freedom to business/corporations"/"the state must control companies more effectively". High scores in this variable indicate that respondents are strongly egalitarian versus individualist (Carlisle & Smith, 2005).

- *Resistance to innovation*. This variable was built from the factorial analysis of the question Q29: (1) I often take risks to make progress in life, even when unsure of what will happen, (2) I am often open to new ideas and new ways of doing things or thinking, (3) I tend to plan the future in advance, (4) I highly value people who question traditional ways of acting, (5) I try to learn new things all the time, making learning my way of life, (6) I prefer to do important things for myself, without much help from others. The respondents used a scale where 0 means "not at all describing my way of being" and 10 means "yes, it describes me perfectly". This set of questions was extracted from a *Centro de Investigaciones Sociológicas* report (number 3112, December 2015) as a reduced variant of the Schwartz model (Schwartz, 2012) oriented to identify attitudes toward innovation and change.

- *Privacy concerns*. This variable reflects a significant concern about the negative effects of science and technology on the protection of personal data and privacy. It has been built as a dichotomous variable from the results of the question Q.14.9: "If you had to take stock of science and technology considering all the positive and negative aspects on protection of personal data and privacy, which of the following options would best reflect your opinion? (1) "Harms are greater than the benefits"; (0) "benefits outweigh harms" or "benefits and harms are balanced".

- *Distrustful toward the appropriate functioning of science and technology.* This variable was built from question Q18 where the respondents used a scale from 1 to 5, where 1 means that they strongly disagree with the statement and 5 means that they strongly agree with the following statement: "We cannot rely on scientists to tell the truth if they are dependent on private funding".

Finally, the opposition to robotization in the workplace was included as a predictor of the opposition toward artificial intelligence. This variable was built analogous to the dependent variable, as the subtraction between the valuation of the risks less the valuation of the benefits of the robotization in the workplace. The analyzed phrases are the following: *"Using a scale of 1 to 5, where 1 means 'no risk' and 5 means 'many risks', to what extent do you think there are risks in the robotization in the workplace?"; "And now considering the benefits and using a scale of 1 to 5, where 1 means 'no benefit' and 5 means 'many benefits', to what extent do you think the robotization in the workplace has benefits?"*.

Results

Differences among Sociodemographic Groups

In our case of study, one third of the population (33.3%) believe that AI has more risks than benefits, 38.4% believe that it has more benefits than risks and 28.3% believe that risks and benefits are balanced, on a 11 points scale, between −5 and 5 (See Appendices A–C). The descriptive analysis of the dependent variables crossed by the main demographic variables - gender, age, level of education, household income and rural/urban settings- show small differences among groups. Level of education and household income showed significant (but moderate) differences.

As presented in Figure 1, individuals with lower educational levels show a slightly higher opposition to AI. On the other hand, as the level of education increases, the weight of the benefits increases in the perception of this technological sector. In a similar sense, individuals in households with lower income levels are slightly more prone to expressing a critical approach to AI. A theory of competition would expect that lower-skilled workers will perceive a greater competition with technology for jobs, and therefore a greater risk of worsening their working conditions or, even, of losing their jobs since several studies show these workers are (and will be) affected to a greater extent by the disruption these new developments may involve, pointing at a future with fewer lower-skilled jobs available (e.g. Brynjolfsson & McAfee, 2014; Frey & Osborne, 2017; Manyika et al., 2017) and with worse labor conditions (e.g. Fleming, 2017; Spencer, 2018).

Although attitudinal differences by educational level and income are observed these differences are smaller than the competition theory might suggest. We performed a multiple regression analysis to assess to what extent this theory of competition has a high or low explanatory power in explaining the opposition to artificial intelligence.

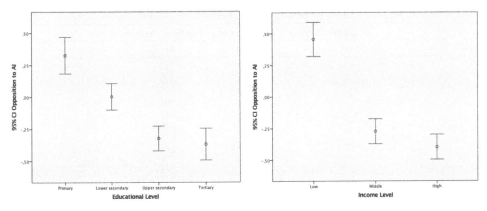

Figure 1. Opposition to Artificial Intelligence, by educational level.
Notes: (1) Values rank between 5 and −5. Positive values mean net opposition. (2) Average net family income in Spain is around 1,100 Euros per month; "high" is considered more than twice that value; "low" is considered less than half that value. (3) ANOVA tests (with Scheffé post hoc test) show that the mean differences between the low-income households and the other two groups are significant at a 0.01 level, as well as the mean differences between the first three groups (primary, lower secondary and upper secondary).

Predicting Opposition to Artificial Intelligence

We fitted a linear regression model to predict opposition to artificial intelligence, introducing the independent variables in blocks (Table 1). In the first block, we introduced the sociodemographic variables as described in the previous section: gender, age, income, work status, and educational level. In the second block, we introduced the "scientific literacy" variable, considering that it has been the main indicator employed in the literature explaining opposition to new technologies by the cognitive deficit model (Bodmer, 1985; Ziman, 1991). In the third block, we introduced the four variables of values and attitudes as described in the previous section: egalitarianism, privacy concerns, resistance to innovation and distrust in the actual application of science and technology. In the fourth block, we introduced the opposition to robotization in the workplace as a predictor of the opposition toward artificial intelligence. As for collinearity, the tolerance values are close to 1, so there are no problems of collinearity (with values of 0.1 or less). The variance inflation factor (VIF) has low values, around 1, so it confirms the previous results.

Model 1 shows that sociodemographic indicators (gender, age, income, and work status) have a moderate effect ($0.021 > R2 > 0.13$), following Cohen's criteria to value the effect size of the adjusted R2 (Cohen, 1988). Nevertheless, college education shows no significant effect ($p > .05$). Therefore, theories of competition and relative vulnerability (H5) cannot be fully supported; only income level ($\beta = -.115$; $p = .000$) and work status ($\beta = .058$; $p = .001$) have a significant effect on the perceptions of AI.

Older people and women are significantly more prone to oppose artificial intelligence. The effect produced by age ($\beta = .083$; $p = 0,000$) is arguably linked to the greater reticence to the use of new technologies – and, therefore, to the technological change in the workplace – among older cohorts. As Westerman and Davies (2000,

Table 1. Linear regression models predicting opposition to artificial intelligence.

Model	Predictors	Beta	p-value	Tolerance	R2
1	(Constant)		.357		
	Gender	0.071	.000	0.993	
	Age	0.083	.000	0.927	
	Income level	−0.115	.000	0.937	
	Economically active	0.058	.001	0.925	
	College education	−0.026	.135	0.930	0.030
2	(Constant)		.035		
	Gender	0.069	.000	0.992	
	Age	0.074	.000	0.915	
	Income level	−0.108	.000	0.929	
	Economically active	0.061	.000	0.923	
	College education	−0.012	.483	0.904	
	Scientific literacy	−0.081	.000	0.932	0.036
3	(Constant)		.074		
	Gender	0.067	.000	0.988	
	Age	0.059	.001	0.907	
	Income level	−0.103	.000	0.925	
	Economically active	0.044	.011	0.899	
	College education	−0.008	.635	0.898	
	Scientific literacy	−0.078	.000	0.929	
	Egalitarianism	0.094	.000	0.949	
	Privacy concerns	0.140	.000	0.983	
	Resistance to innovation	0.060	.000	0.986	
	Distrust in Science	0.051	.002	0.982	0.076
4	(Constant)		.026		
	Gender	0.027	.037	0.984	
	Age	0.047	.001	0.907	
	Income level	−0.044	.001	0.916	
	Economically active	0.041	.003	0.899	
	College education	−0.009	.530	0.898	
	Scientific literacy	−0.024	.072	0.922	
	Egalitarianism	0.018	.175	0.935	
	Privacy concerns	0.057	.000	0.964	
	Resistance to innovation	0.019	.139	0.982	
	Distrust in Science	0.005	.715	0.976	
	Opposition to Robotization	0.619	.000	0.921	0.429

p. 478) showed, "experiential, physiological, and cognitive factors are identified that place older adults at a disadvantage, relative to younger adults, when using new technologies". Moreover, gender differences have been observed repeatedly for other controversial technologies, such as nuclear energy (Davidson & Freudenburg, 1996; Sundström & McCright, 2016). As in that case, this gender gap (β = .071; p = 000) may be explained by the different emphasis that socialization gives to security concerns and the perception of risk to men and women (Bord & O'Connor, 1997; Solomon, Tomaskovic-Devy, & Risman, 1989).

In the second block, we included the scientific literacy indicator, slightly improving the goodness of fit of the model (R2 = .036). Higher levels of scientific knowledge (**H1**) are associated with more positive perceptions of AI (β = −.081; p = .000).

In the third block, indicators of attitudes toward science and values (egalitarianism, privacy concerns, resistance to innovation, distrust in science) increases the goodness of fit of the model (R2 = 0.076), and substantiate some of our hypotheses. In sum, the following hypotheses are supported:

H2: Those with distrustful toward the appropriate functioning of science and technology are more likely to have a more negative perception of AI (β = .051; p = .002);

H3: Those less prone to innovation are more likely to have a more negative perception of AI (β = .060; p = .000);

H4: Egalitarian worldviews are associated with more negative perceptions of AI (β = .094; p = .000);

H6: Those expressing privacy concerns are more likely to have more negative perceptions of AI (β = .140; p = .000).

Finally, in Model 4, we included the balance between risks and benefits of robotization in the workplace to predict opposition to artificial intelligence. This last model reaches a very large effect ($R2$ = 0.429) and substantiate our last hypothesis (**H7**). Perceptions of AI are associated with perceptions of robotization in the workplace (β = .0.619; p = .000). Tolerance values do not indicate any problems of collinearity in this model. The Pearson correlation between our indicators of opposition to artificial intelligence and to robotization in the workplace is 0.652 (p < .001).

Discussion

In the case of the opposition to artificial intelligence, most sociodemographic indicators (gender, age, income, work status) have a significant but moderate effect; less of 3% of the variance in the dependent variable is explained by the independent variables. Furthermore, the effect of having college education is not significant when controlled by these variables. Our results show that traditional explanations of opposition to artificial intelligence, such as competition and relative vulnerability theories, have a very moderate explanatory power of views on AI.

Moreover, age differences may be explained by the "experiential, physiological, and cognitive factors" identified by Westerman and Davies (2000, p. 478) as they place older individuals at a relative disadvantage when using new technologies. Additionally, gender socialization shows a significant but moderate effect on the opposition to artificial intelligence, in the same direction found for other controversial technologies (Sundström & McCright, 2016).

Stronger effects are shown by cultural values and attitudes to science. Those expressing egalitarian (Carlisle & Smith, 2005; Marris et al., 1998) and privacy concerns, as well as those who express less confidence in the actual application of science (Torres-Albero & Lobera, 2017) and those less predisposed to innovation and change, are more prone to oppose both technological applications.

Lastly, we found evidence of a strong correlation between attitudes toward robotization in the workplace and artificial intelligence. This opens the door to new hypotheses that help us explain the formation of attitudes that oppose technological change. The evidence found shows that, beyond the variables associated with established theories, the greatest effect in explaining the opposition to artificial intelligence is in the individual's opposition to robotization at work. We argue that, as in other controversial applications, cognitive shortcuts take place (Brossard et al., 2009; Ho et al., 2008; Scheufele et al., 2009), in this case between both technological applications: the "intelligent machine" as a new threatening or beneficial element.

A significant part of the population perceives AI and robotization in a similar way, subject to the same conditioning factors. Those more favorable to the emergence of the "intelligent machine" are individuals who trust science, do not distrust the influence of the market on science, show attitudes prone to change and innovation, and have individualist values. On the other side, those who oppose the "intelligent machine" perceive these applications as a continuum, subject to the same risks of being misused by companies, and increasing inequality. In this case, there is a cognitive connection between both technological applications that derives in their common social representation: the "intelligent machine" -or the "smart machine" as coined by Zuboff (1988) decades ago- as a new threatening or beneficial element.

Recent studies show that different cultures exhibit more similarities than differences in attitudes toward robots (Gnambs & Appel, 2019; Haring, Mougenot, Ono, & Watanabe, 2014). This suggest that our findings may apply broadly across cultures. Nevertheless, more research is needed to uncover cultural differences in the factors that influence individual attitudes toward AI.

Discussions on AI and the development of robotics have been common in the public sphere since the postwar years. However, some studies have shown that a number of negative concerns have emerged in the last decade (Fast & Horwitz, 2017). This represents a challenge for both the private and public sector. In the case of the former, forecasts about the threatening impact of AI by both media and certain experts might influence the introduction of these new technologies, leading to distrust or even rejection by users. This also implies the necessity of a growing relationship between AI and PR departments in corporations.

Design and PR departments must come up with new ideas to engage users and overcome those fears with new strategies, such as involving the user to help with the acceptance of "intelligent machines" in social life (Reich-Stiebert, Eyssel, & Hohnemann, 2019), or working with the public on other collaborative actions (Brunton & Galloway, 2016). This might not be an easy issue, as PR departments might have underperformed in their communication strategies, acting as "AI cheerleaders" (see Bourne, 2019) and hence obscuring broader perspectives on AI (Galloway & Swiatek, 2018). Regarding the public space, some authors state that it is important to frame a strong public debate about the implications of these emerging technologies to help promote and maintain a public agora (Echevarría & Tabarés, 2018) and to engage and inform the public about the implications of AI.

Conclusions

Despite AI becoming more prevalent in the public debate, little is known about what factors might structure people's attitudes toward this technology. In this study, our aim has been to investigate, for the first time, such factors through the analysis of data from a survey in Spain. We show that common explanations of opposition to artificial intelligence, such as competition and relative vulnerability theories, have a small effect size. Those potentially more affected by the advance of automatization – i.e. lower-skilled workers (Frey & Osborne, 2017; Manyika et al., 2017) – do not oppose artificial intelligence to a significantly greater extent. Similarly, the public understanding of science model shows a moderate explanatory effect, as observed in other cases (Mielby et al., 2013; Torres-Albero & Lobera, 2017).

Cultural values and attitudes to science offer a more effective explanation of this opposition than competition theories: those expressing egalitarian values and privacy concerns are more likely to oppose artificial intelligence, as well as those who express less confidence in the actual application of science and those less predisposed to innovation and change. These results bring to the fore the ongoing issue over who is debating the emergence of AI, and the need for inclusive policies that should be promoted through effective communication from PR departments (Galloway & Swiatek, 2018).

Finally, we found a strong connection between attitudes toward robotization in the workplace and toward artificial intelligence. We argue that a common social representation, the "intelligent machine," emerges as a new threatening or beneficial element. Certainly, some influential literature in which AI and robotics appear deeply intertwined may have helped to blur the differences, and hence, AI are described as smart machines (Zuboff, 1988). However, AI's much broader than just robots, and highlighting the differences remains a pending task for corporations, experts and governments (Galloway & Swiatek, 2018).

The implications of these results are therefore significant for communication in both the artificial intelligence sector of and the robotization sector. These are two distinct sectors; yet, we show that they are strongly connected at the attitudinal level among the public. A first implication is that if there are changes (positive or negative) that impact the public perception of one of the sectors, our prediction is that these changes will be transferred to the perception of the other. The public communication of these sectors must consider that attitudes (favorable or unfavorable) are currently built on an undifferentiated perception: the "intelligent machine" that benefits – or threatens. Furthermore, as mentioned before, this effort should not only involve both sectors, but governments and experts alike.

Notes

1. An example of this gloomy perspective is Elon Musk (the CEO of Tesla) commenting on AI, saying it is like "summoning the demon". Stephen Hawking also expressed similar statements.
2. The questionnaire and the database of this survey are available at https://icono.fecyt.es/informes-y-publicaciones/percepcion-social-de-la-ciencia-y-la-tecnologia-en-espana.

Disclosure statement

No potential conflict of interest was reported by the authors.

ORCID

Josep Lobera http://orcid.org/0000-0002-0620-6312
Carlos J. Fernández Rodríguez http://orcid.org/0000-0002-2959-8195
Cristóbal Torres-Albero http://orcid.org/0000-0001-5630-9101

References

Akhter, S. H. (2014). Privacy concern and online transactions: The impact of internet self-efficacy and internet involvement. *Journal of Consumer Marketing, 31*(2), 118–125. doi:10.1108/JCM-06-2013-0606

Allum, N., Sturgis, P., Tabourazi, D., & Brunton-Smith, I. (2008). Science knowledge and attitudes across cultures: A meta-analysis. *Public Understanding of Science, 17*(1), 35–54. doi:10.1177/0963662506070159

Ball, K. S., Haggerty, K. D., & Lyon, D. (eds.). (2012). *Routledge handbook of surveillance studies.* London, UK: Routledge.

Barak, M. (2018). Are digital natives open to change? Examining flexible thinking and resistance to change. *Computers & Education, 121*, 115–123. doi:10.1016/j.compedu.2018.01.016

Baruh, L., & Popescu, M. (2017). Big data analytics and the limits of privacy self-management. *New Media & Society, 19*(4), 579–596. doi:10.1177/1461444815614001

Beck, U. (1986). *Risikogesellschaft. Auf dem Weg in eine andere Moderne.* Frankfurt, Germany: Suhrkamp.

Bergvall-Kåreborn, B., & Howcroft, D. (2014). Amazon mechanical turk and the commodification of labor. *New Technology, Work and Employment, 29*(3), 213–223. doi:10.1111/ntwe.12038

Bodmer, W. (1985). *The public understanding of science.* London, UK: The Royal Society.

Bord, R. J., & O'Connor, R. E. (1997). The gender gap in environmental attitudes. *Social Science Quarterly, 78*, 830–840. https://www.jstor.org/stable/42863734

Bourne, C. (2019). AI cheerleaders: Public relations, neoliberalism and artificial intelligence. *Public Relations Inquiry, 8*(2), 109–125. doi:10.1177/2046147X19835250

Brossard, D., Scheufele, D. A., Kim, E., & Lewenstein, B. V. (2009). Religiosity as a perceptual filter: Examining processes of opinion formation about nanotechnology. *Public Understanding of Science, 18*(5), 546–558.

Brunton, M. A., & Galloway, C. J. (2016). The role of "organic public relations" in communicating wicked public health issues. *Journal of Communication Management, 20*, 2. doi:10.1108/JCOM-07-2014-0042

Brynjolfsson, E., & McAfee, A. (2014). *The second machine age: Work, progress, and prosperity in a time of brilliant technologies*. New York, NY: Norton.

Carlisle, J., & Smith, E. R. (2005). Postmaterialism vs. egalitarianism as predictors of energy-related attitudes. *Environmental Politics, 14*(4), 527–540. doi:10.1080/09644010500215324

Cecere, G., Le Guel, F., & Soulié, N. (2015). Perceived Internet privacy concerns on social networks in Europe. *Technological Forecasting & Social Change, 96*, 277–287. doi:10.1016/j.techfore.2015.01.021

Cohen, J. (1988). *Statistical power analysis for the behavioral sciences* (2nd ed.). Hillsdale, NJ: Lawrence Erlbaum Associates.

Dake, K. (1991). Orienting dispositions in the perception of risk: An analysis of contemporary worldviews and cultural biases. *Journal of Cross-cultural Psychology, 22*, 61–82. doi:10.1177/0022022191221006

Davidson, D. J., & Freudenburg, W. R. (1996). Gender and environmental risk concerns. *Environment and Behavior, 28*, 302–339. doi:10.1177/0013916596283003

Douglas, M., & Wildavsky, A. (1983). *Risk and culture: An essay on the selection of technical and environmental dangers*. Berkeley: University of California Press.

Echevarría, J., & Tabarés, R. (2018). Artificial intelligence, cybercities and technosocieties. *Minds & Machines, 27*, 473–493. doi:10.1007/s11023-016-9412-3

Edwards, P., & Ramirez, P. (2016). When should workers embrace or resist new technology? *New Technology, Work and Employment, 31*(2), 99–113. doi:10.1111/ntwe.12067

Ellis, R. J., & Thompson, F. (1997). Culture and the environment in the Pacific Northwest. *American Political Science Review, 91*, 885–897. doi:10.2307/2952171

Fast, E., & Horwitz, E. (2017, February 4–9). Long-term trends in the public perception of artificial intelligence. *Thirty-First AAAI Conference on Artificial Intelligence*, San Francisco, CA.

Fiske, S. T., & Linville, P. W. (1980). What does the schema concept buy us? *Personality and Social Psychology Bulletin, 6*, 543–557. doi:10.1177/014616728064006

Fleming, P. (2017). The human capital Hoax: Work, debt and insecurity in the era of uberization. *Organization Studies, 38*(5), 691–709. doi:10.1177/0170840616686129

Foucault, M. (1977). *Discipline and punish: The birth of the prison*. New York, NY: Pantheon Books.

Frey, C. B., & Osborne, M. A. (2017). The future of employment: How susceptible are jobs to computerisation? *Technological Forecasting and Social Change, 114*, 254–280. doi:10.1016/j.techfore.2016.08.019

Galloway, C., & Swiatek, L. (2018). Public relations and artificial intelligence: It's not (just) about robots. *Public Relations Review, 44*, 734–740. doi:10.1016/j.pubrev.2018.10.008

Gnambs, T., & Appel, M. (2019). Are robots becoming unpopular? Changes in attitudes towards autonomous robotic systems in Europe. *Computers in Human Behavior, 93*, 53–61. doi:10.1016/j.chb.2018.11.045

Goldfarb, A., & Tucker, C. (2012). Shifts in privacy concerns. *American Economic Review, 102*(3), 349–353. doi:10.1257/aer.102.3.349

Grace, K., Salvatier, J., Dafoe, A., Zhang, B., & Evans, O. (2018). Viewpoint: When will AI exceed human performance? Evidence from AI experts. *Journal of Artificial Intelligence Research, 62*, 729–754. doi:10.1613/jair.1.11222

Grendstad, G., & Selle, P. (1997). Cultural theory, postmaterialism, and environmental attitudes. In R. J. Ellis & M. Thompson (Eds.), *Culture matters: Essays in honor of Aaron Wildavsky* (pp. 151–168). Boulder, CO: Westview Press.

Haring, K. S., Mougenot, C., Ono, F., & Watanabe, K. (2014). Cultural differences in perception and attitude towards robots. *International Journal of Affective Engineering, 13*(3), 149–157. doi:10.5057/ijae.13.149

Ho, S. S., Brossard, D., & Scheufele, D. A. (2008). Effects of value predispositions, mass media use, and knowledge on public attitudes toward embryonic stem cell research. *International Journal of Public Opinion Research, 20*, 171–192. doi:10.1093/ijpor/edn017

Howcroft, D., & Bergvall-Kåreborn, B. (2019). A typology of crowdwork platforms. *Work, Employment and Society, 33*(1), 21–38. doi:10.1177/0950017018760136

Johnson, B. (1993). Understanding of knowledge's role in lay risk perception". *Risk, 4*, 189–212.

Jones, G. R. (2013). *Organizational theory, design, and change.* Upper Saddle River, NJ: Pearson.

Kumlin, S. (2001). Ideology-driven opinion formation in Europe: The case of attitudes towards the third sector in Sweden. *European Journal of Political Research, 39,* 487–518. doi:10.1111/1475-6765.00585

Leiserowitz, A., Maibach, E., Roser-Renouf, C., Smith, N., & Dawson, E. (2012). Climategate, public opinion, and the loss of trust. *American Behavioral Scientist, 57*(6), 818–837. doi:10.1177/0002764212458272

Lobera, J. (2008). Insostenibilidad: Aproximación al conflicto socioecológico. *Revista Iberoamericana de Ciencia, Tecnología y Sociedad, 4*(11), 53–80.

Lyon, D. (2007). *Surveillance studies: An overview.* Cambridge, UK: Polity.

Lyon, D. (2014). Surveillance, Snowden, and big data: Capacities, consequences, critique. *Big Data & Society, 1*(2), 1–13. doi:10.1177/2053951714541861

Madridakis, S. (2017). The forthcoming Artificial Intelligence (AI) revolution: Its impact on society and firms. *Futures, 90,* 46–60. doi:10.1016/j.futures.2017.03.006

Manyika, J., Lund, S., Chui, M., Bughin, J., Woetzel, J., Batra, P., ... & Sanghvi, S. (2017). *Jobs lost, jobs gained: Workforce transitions in a time of automation.* McKinsey Global Institute, vol. 150.

Marris, C., Langford, I. H., & O'Riordan, T. (1998). A quantitative test of the cultural theory of risk perceptions: Comparison with the psychometric paradigm. *Risk Analysis, 18,* 635–647. doi:10.1111/risk.1998.18.issue-5

Mielby, H., Sandøe, P., & Lassen, J. (2013). The role of scientific knowledge in shaping public attitudes to GM technologies. *Public Understanding of Science, 22*(2), 155–168. doi:10.1177/0963662511430577

Morozov, E. (2011). *The net delusion: The dark side of internet freedom.* New York, NY: PublicAffairs.

Oberson, X. (2017). Taxing robots? From the emergence of an electronic ability to pay to a tax on robots or the use of robots. *World Tax Journal, 9*(2), 247–261.

Priest, S. H. (2001). "Misplaced faith: Communication variables as predictors of encouragement for biotechnology development". *Science Communication, 23,* 97–110. doi: 10.1177/1075547001023002002

Raab, C. (2019). Political science and privacy. In B. van der Sloot & A. de Groot (Eds.), *The handbook of privacy studies: An interdisciplinary introduction* (pp. 257). Amsterdam, Netherlands: Amsterdam University Press.

Reich-Stiebert, N., Eyssel, F., & Hohnemann, C. (2019). Involve the user! Changing attitudes toward robots by user participation in a robot prototyping process. *Computers in Human Behavior, 91,* 290–296. doi:10.1016/j.chb.2018.09.041

Schein, E. H. (1985). *Organizational culture and leadership.* San Francisco, CA: Jossey-Bass.

Scheufele, D. (2014). Science communication as political communication. *Proceedings of the National Academy of Sciences, 111*(4), 13585–13592. doi:10.1073/pnas.1317516111

Scheufele, D. A., Corley, E. A., Shih, T.-J., Dalrymple, K. E., & Ho, S. S. (2009). Religious beliefs and public attitudes toward nanotechnology in Europe and the United States. *Nature Nanotech, 4,* 91–94. doi:10.1038/nnano.2008.361

Schwartz, S. H. (2012). An overview of the Schwartz theory of basic values. *Online Readings in Psychology and Culture, 2*(1), 11. doi:10.9707/2307-0919.1116

Sheth, J. N., & Stellner, W. H. (1979). *Psychology of innovation resistance: The less developed concept (LDC) in diffusion research (No. 622).* Urbana-Champaign: University of Illinois.

Siegrist, M., Cvetkovich, G., & Roth, C. (2000). Salient value similarity, social trust, and risk/benefit perception. *Risk Analysis, 20*(3), 353–362.

Solomon, L. S., Tomaskovic-Devy, D., & Risman, B. J. (1989). The gender gap and nuclear power. *Sex Roles, 21,* 401–414. doi:10.1007/BF00289599

Spencer, D. A. (2018). Fear and hope in an age of mass automation: Debating the future of work. *New Technology, Work and Employment, 33*(1), 1–12. doi:10.1111/ntwe.12105

Standing, G. (2009). *Work after globalisation: Building occupational citizenship.* Cheltenham, UK: Edward Elgar.

Standing, G. (2017). *Basic income: And how we can make it happen.* London, UK: Penguin.

Sturgis, P., & Allum, N. (2004). Science in society: re-evaluating the deficit model of public attitudes. *Public Understanding Of Science, 13*(1), 55–74.

Sturken, M., Thomas, D., & Ball-Rokeach, S. J. (eds). (2004). *Technological visions: The hopes and fears that shape new technologies*. Philadelphia, PA: Temple University Press.

Sundström, A., & McCright, A. M. (2016). Women and nuclear energy: Examining the gender divide in opposition to nuclear power among Swedish citizens and politicians. *Energy Research & Social Science, 11,* 29–39. doi:10.1016/j.erss.2015.08.008

Thomson, R., Yuki, M., & Ito, N. (2015). A socio-ecological approach to national differences in online privacy concern: The role of relational mobility and trust. *Computers in Human Behavior, 51,* 285–292. doi:10.1016/j.chb.2015.04.068

Todt, O. (2011). The limits of policy: Public acceptance and the reform of science and technology governance. *Technological Forecasting and Social Change, 78*(6), 902–909. doi:10.1016/j.techfore.2011.02.007

Torres-Albero, C., & Lobera, J. (2017). The decline of faith in progress. Posmaterialism, ideology and religiosity in the social representations of technoscience. *Revista Internacional de Sociología, 75*(3), e069. doi:10.3989/ris.2017.75.3.16.61

Upchurch, M. (2018). Robots and ai at work: The prospects for singularity. *New Technology, Work and Employment, 33*(3), 205–218. doi:10.1111/ntwe.12124

Ward, K. (2018). Social networks, the 2016 US presidential election, and Kantian ethics: Applying the categorical imperative to Cambridge Analytica's behavioral microtargeting. *Journal of Media Ethics, 33*(3), 133–148. doi:10.1080/23736992.2018.1477047

Westerman, S. J., & Davies, D. R. (2000). Acquisition and application of new technology skills: The influence of age. *Occupational Medicine, 50*(7), 478–482. doi:10.1093/occmed/50.7.478

Ziman, J. (1991). Public understanding of science. *Science, Technology and Human Values, 16,* 99–105. doi:10.1177/016224399101600106

Zuboff, S. (1988). *In the age of the smart machine: The future of work and power* (Vol. 186). New York, NY: Basic books.

Appendices

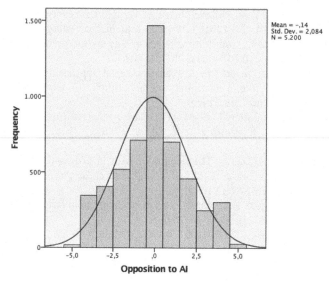

Appendix A. Histogram of the distribution (opposition to artificial intelligence).

Appendix B. Distribution of frequencies and percentages (opposition to artificial intelligence).

	Frequency	Percent	Cumulative Percent
−5: All benefits, no risk	19	.4	.4
−4	345	6.6	7.0
−3	404	7.8	14.8
−2	518	10.0	24.7
−1	711	13.7	38.4
0: Risks and benefits are balanced	1469	28.3	66.7
1	700	13.5	80.1
2	457	8.8	88.9
3	248	4.8	93.7
4	302	5.8	99.5
5: All risks, no benefit	27	.5	100.0
Total	5200	100.0	

Appendix C. Basic statistics of the distribution (opposition to artificial intelligence).

N	5200
Mean	−.14
Std. Error of Mean	.029
Std. Deviation	2.084
Variance	4.343
Skewness	.066
Std. Error of Skewness	.034
Kurtosis	−.314
Std. Error of Kurtosis	.068

Appendix D.

Variable	Categories	Descriptive statistics
Sociodemographic factors		
Gender	0 = Men 1 = Women	51.4% Women
Age	Age (in years)	M = 43.95, SD = 17.951
College education	0 = Without college education 1 = With college education	21% with college education
Work status	0 = Economically inactive 1 = Economically active	% 56.6 Economically active
Household's family income	1 = Much higher (more than 2,200 Euros per month) 2 = Higher 3 = Around 1,100 Euros per month 4 = Lower 5 = Much lower (less than 550 per month)	M = 2.78, SD = 0.910
Scientific knowledge (deficit model)		
Scientific knowledge	Number of correct answers (See Q24 in the questionnaire at https://icono.fecyt.es). Scale from 0 (=none correct) to 6 (=all correct)	M = 4.24, SD = 1.220
Values		
Egalitarism	Scale from 1 (=The state must give more freedom to business/corporations) to 10 (=The state must control companies more effectively)	M = 6.11, SD = 2.933
Privacy concerns	0 = "Benefits outweigh harms" or "benefits and harms are balanced" 1 = "Harms are greater than the benefits"	34.3% states that harms are greater than the benefits
Distrustful toward the appropriate functioning of S&T	Scale from 1 (=Strongly disagree) to 5 (=Strongly agree)	M = 3.25, SD = 1.152
Resistance to innovation	Factor from Q29.1 to Q29.6 (See questionnaire). From −3.805 to 3.0417	M = 0, SD = 1 Cronbach's Alpha = 0,772
Opposition to Robotization	Scale from −5 (=no risk, many benefits) a 5 (=many risks, no benefit)	M = 0.12, SD = 2.166

Making up Audience: Media Bots and the Falsification of the Public Sphere

Rose Marie Santini ⓘ, Debora Salles ⓘ, Giulia Tucci ⓘ, Fernando Ferreira ⓘ, and Felipe Grael ⓘ

ABSTRACT
The purpose of this paper is to discuss if and how Brazilian media outlets make use of automated strategies and artificial intelligence (AI) in order to produce convenient social media metrics about themselves and amplify their relevance on Twitter. We examine how media bots can manipulate online ratings, change social perception of what is relevant and increase engagement with both on- and offline media entities. We extracted three types of data: (i) 530,942 tweets containing at least one URL from Globo Group or Folha Group collected via Twitter API; (ii) URL metadata from 158,690 articles by Globo Group and Folha Group; (iii) Twitter trending topics in Brazil. Profiles that posted links were later sampled and classified using the Botometer. Automated and human accounts were analyzed regarding their posting frequency and speed. In this paper, we assess the hypothesis that the existence of media bots is affecting the Twittersphere in Brazil, where automated accounts, empowered by AI, might be responsible for a substantial share of the links to popular Brazilian media outlets on Twitter. Our research provides quantitative empirical evidence that bots are particularly active in amplifying news media links in the initial moments of spreading. Additionally, automated accounts play an important role in promoting TV broadcast programs in Brazil. Based on these evidences, we discuss the strategies adopted by Brazilian media corporations to sustain their omnipresence online that boosts their online audience.

The phenomenon of media manipulation, which covers an array of practices, including fake news and trolls, has been the subject of much scrutiny and attention in recent years (Marwick & Lewis, 2017). However, little is being said about the possibility of online "manipulation by the media outlets" themselves that take advantage of artificial intelligence (AI) combined with social media vulnerability. A media bot is a specific spammy "bot behavior pattern, represented by a group of online fake accounts programmed to disseminate media links on Twitter" (Santini et al., 2018), forbidden in accordance with the platform rules and policy ("The Twitter Rules," n.d.).

Given the pervasiveness of social media manipulation and automation strategies (Santini et al., 2018; Woolley & Howard, 2019), our aim is to examine how media bots act as artificial audiences and to discuss the role that these profiles play in internet audience measurements. We conducted an empirical research to investigate how these fake accounts use automation to attempt to influence trending topics, manipulate online ratings, change social perception of what is relevant and increase engagement with both on and offline media entities.

The Brazilian media landscape stands out as an emblematic case of ownership and audience concentration. Globo Group is the largest mass media group in Latin America and Folha Group is the third-largest Brazilian media conglomerate (Grupo de Mídia, 2017). We focus on the two media groups, but we suggest further investigations should examine other media outlets in Brazil in order to verify if other online rating manipulation strategies are been used.

Our hypothesis is based on previous research (Santini et al., 2018) that discovered automated profiles that disseminate links to two Brazilian mainstream news media websites (Globo Group and Folha Group) probably in order to amplify their public attention. Given the authors' focus on political discussion, the strategy of this new category of bots was not fully scrutinized. Thus, based on a different dataset, we test the assumption that these accounts are used exclusively to increase audience engagement of certain media outlets. We carry out a case study that confirms the hypothesis that media bots exist in the Twittersphere, apparently as part of a strategy applied to guarantee commercial profit. The concept of media bot opens a theoretical discussion on the activities of these agents and their effects on cultural, social, and political processes. Adopting media bots to disseminate news and attract users to websites is emblematic of a particular case of audience manufacturing and public sphere manipulation, considering the prominent position media corporations hold in the overall news and information environment.

Considering only 41% of the Brazilian population trusts local media companies ("Edelman Trust Barometer," 2018), these manipulation strategies may decrease the confidence in overall news and legacy media outlets. Further diluting media credibility may move more Brazilians away from trusted news sources, making them increasingly vulnerable to polarizing, fake or biased messages from unreliable outlets and strengthen the influence of disinformation and misinformation in the country.

In the first part of the article, we outline the importance of audience manufacturing for news media organizations and lay out the rationale behind the importance of algorithms to online advertising and audience measurements fraud. In the second, we describe the case and context, the data collected, methods applied and research limitations. In the findings section, we first analyze data on the behavior of our collected accounts, considering posting patterns, and then turn to an analysis of the trending topics. In the subsequent section, we position our case study analysis in relation to the use of algorithms and non-human traffic in audience manufacturing and discuss the wider implications of our findings. In the final concluding part, we resume our main findings and identify questions for further research.

The Relationships between Legacy Media and Audiences in the Online Environment

The media environment is undergoing dramatic change since the explosion of the Internet and the rise of social media platforms. New media technologies are providing users with unprecedented control over the media consumption process, from the time-shifting and commercial-skipping capabilities to the personalization of media content (Napoli, 2011). At the same time, changes in the media environment modify how media organizations think about their audiences and deal with market competition.

Given the growing fragmentation of the media environment witnessed in the past decades (Napoli, 2011), scholars have constantly argued that the mass media industry needs to rethink the traditional way of producing and distributing content, and especially update their business models to survive in the contemporary technological environment. With the economic uncertainty surrounding the technological transformations currently taking place, industry stakeholders have initiated a wide range of efforts to preserve the traditional construction of the media audience as self-preservation strategies (Napoli, 2011).

These changes have forced legacy media to provide content online, but the internet is a place where profit is harder to earn, moving these companies toward a more market-driven approach for reporting news (Kalika & Ferrucci, 2019). Against this backdrop, audience feedback and social analytics started figuring as key factors for online content production, distribution, and consumption (Lee & Tandoc, 2017). Notwithstanding, as Carlson (2015) argues, journalistic autonomy and authority depend on a clear separation between editorial and business functions of media companies. Thus, media conglomerates operate online based on a for-profit and advertising funded business model, competing both for attention and credibility.

New digital intermediaries are also modifying the media sector as they start to organize content that, despite not being produced nor commissioned by them, is curated and hosted by these platforms (Gillespie, 2018). According to Bell, Owen, Brown, Hauka, and Rashidian (2017), the public sphere is now mediated by a small number of private companies that operate and organize access and traffic. Legacy media companies need to decide how they want to present their coverage on these platforms, dealing with power relationships in which they do not have the same leverage they once did (Vos & Russell, 2019).

Since platforms such as Google, Facebook, and Twitter have attained an increasingly prominent position in the overall news, entertainment, and information environments (Newman, 2019), it is necessary to revisit difficult questions about how they interact with the old business model of legacy media that still provides the most trustworthy news content according to their users (Newman, Fletcher, Kalogeropoulos, Levy, & Nielsen, 2018).

These platforms are commonly seen as neutral instead of private for-profit corporations (Gillespie, 2014), but their ability to shape the overall media environment has granted these a monopolist power (Kleis Nielsen & Ganter, 2018) and a central role of intermediating ordinary users and a wide variety of other parties (Luo, 2019). As Bell et al. (2017) indicate, about half of the online traffic of news organization websites comes from search and social referrals.

As social media use became pervasive, the ways consumers relate and interact with legacy media have also shifted, presenting both challenges and opportunities for media elites, not yet accustomed to sharing the role of content producer and knowledge broker (Nee & Dozier, 2017). Embodying the connectedness and ubiquity of social media, second screening represents an important aspect of the contemporary hybrid media system (Chadwick, 2013). This phenomenon relates to the use of Twitter to communicate, obtain, and share information and opinions about broadcast programming while watching it, unifying traditional media and online networks. This media use can increase attention and engagement to TV programs as well as promote discussion among users, creating a social media buzz that often generates more viewers, and vice versa (de Zúñiga, Garcia-Perdomo, & McGregor, 2015).

As Giglietto and Selva (2014) indicate the relationship between Twitter and broadcast media is symbiotic, with an increasing number of studies dealing with the practice of using the platform as a real-time backchannel for broadcasting comments while watching a TV program. By commenting, retweeting, liking, and sharing in massive proportions, users enhance the visibility of broadcast messages online, including these topics in the algorithmic selection of most relevant or trending content of each platform (van Dijck, Poell, & de Waal, 2018).

Social media algorithms not only select and personalize what each user will see (Pariser, 2012), but also identify larger trends among its users, creating lists that reflect the high frequency of a particular term and the dramatic increase in its usage (Hargittai & Litt, 2011). van Dijck et al. (2018) argue that these trending lists privilege content that rapidly generates more user engagement, affecting the type of information that becomes prominently visible. As Tufekci (2014) indicates, there is a deliberate gaming of platform algorithms and metrics. Studies have found evidence of artificial trending topics that reflect orchestrated efforts by users to promote content not necessarily new, popular nor newsworthy (Recuero & Araujo, 2012).

Alongside the discussion about audience engagement, the advent of social media raises the need to question the agenda-setting power of legacy media conglomerates (McCombs, 2004). The traditional agenda-setting hypothesis assumes that in choosing and displaying news, media outlets play a crucial role in shaping social reality, by forcing attention to certain issues and building public images (McCombs & Shaw, 1972). Rogstad (2016) argues there are pressing questions about how social media platforms relate to traditional mass media, especially regarding issue salience in each media. As the influence of social media in our understanding of the world continues to grow, scholars are still questioning whether the power of traditional media gatekeepers has been overturned (Groshek & Groshek, 2013) and trying to understand the effects of social media on the agenda-setting process.

Although interpersonal conversations have always been key to the public sphere, only recently scholars began to observe the parallels between online "buzz" and mass media content (Neuman, Guggenheim, Jones - Jang, & Bae, 2014). The intermedia agenda setting extends beyond the original hypothesis of McCombs and Shaw (1972), discussing the ways media content influences and is influenced by other media content. As Harder, Sevenans, and Aelst (2017) argue, although two-way agenda-setting effects have been demonstrated, legacy media organizations remain important players, either in their traditional form or via their online channels.

While some authors indicate that social media, and Twitter more specifically, act as a filter and an amplifier for mainstream media content, rather than an alternative news source (Rogstad, 2016), some investigations suggest reverse agenda effects, that is, salient issues on the Internet could set traditional media agenda (Kim & Lee, 2006). The notion of reverse agenda setting incorporates the influence the public might have on news media (McCombs, 2004), not simply journalists responding to a preceding public agenda

(Neuman et al., 2014). The relationship between social and traditional media is, in general, reciprocal, but social media still have a limited to moderate influence on issue salience in legacy media (Conway, Kenski, & Wang, 2015).

As Casero-Ripollés and Izquierdo-Castillo (2013) indicate we now face a paradox in which online news consumption is continuously increasing, but news businesses are still struggling to monetize from their expanding online audience. While social media creates new opportunities for legacy media companies, from an economical perspective, algorithms redirect advertising revenue from legacy publishers to Silicon Valley platforms (Vos & Russell, 2019).

The traditional business model faces two major challenges: the abundance of free online content and the inability of news companies to monetize from their online activity (Herbert & Thurman, 2007). Against this backdrop, legacy media organizations have adopted different approaches that are similarly reactive and pragmatic (Boczkowski, 2004). A payment-free dichotomy has become the starting point for digital business models, since online advertising revenue remains low (Casero-Ripollés & Izquierdo-Castillo, 2013).

Facing the stagnation of online revenue and ferocious audience competition, media organizations seem to be seeking eyeballs before locating a revenue stream, giving content away for free and granting audience access to aggregators (Ju, Jeong, & Chyi, 2014). Aiming for effective online audience and attention, controversial approaches have been adopted by media players, such as fake news, clickbaits, upworthy headlines, traffic fraud, and social bots. As Fulgoni (2016) argues, fraudsters fabricate invalid traffic as audience to attract advertisers by inflating impressions on websites (Springborn & Barford, 2013). Among the different types of invalid traffic, bots designed to mimic human users are one of the main drivers of artificial advertising impressions (ANA, 2017).

Celebrities, politicians, brands, organizations, and governments are also using social media platforms to reach their audiences and amplify their messages (De Cristofaro, Friedman, Jourjon, Kaafar, & Shafiq, 2014; Ikram et al., 2017; Stringhini et al., 2013). Hence, a supply and demand business opportunity has given rise to a "Twitter follower market" to artificially increase audience metrics on the platform (Stringhini et al., 2013). It represents an underground heated market. For example, Thomas, McCoy, Grier, Kolcz, and Paxson (2013) studied account prices, availability, and fraud on Twitter and found that 10–20% of all accounts tagged as spam by the platform, during their analysis, were generated by "account merchants," yielding them 127,000 USD–459,000 USD. Similarly, on Facebook, a growing industry of "like farms" can be used to artificially inflate the number of likes of a page or profile (Ikram et al., 2017). Selling likes can be quite profitable: for a 1,000 likes package, the cost varies from 59.95 USD to 190 USD for users in the United States and from 14.99 to 70 USD for users worldwide (Ikram et al., 2017).

According to the 2016 Incapsula report (Zeifman, 2017), 51.8% of online traffic is generated by bots, replacing human work power in online traffic sourcing services. In a *pay-per-click* logic environment, a computational routine programmed to click on selected links can execute this action more efficiently than a real person, turning the acquisition of bot traffic more affordable than legitimate human traffic (ANA, 2017). Fake webpage traffic and artificial social media engagement pose a problem for brands by hindering the measurement of marketing efforts. Therewithal, false clicks produce additional costs to advertisers. As Gabryel (2018) argues, the falsification of analytical data, on which advertisers base their marketing decisions, can bias the campaigns' return on investment.

Social bots relate to the exploitation of algorithms and automation, combined with human curation, learning from and imitating real user behavior in order to artificially shape public opinion across a diverse range of platforms and device networks (Ferrara, Varol, Davis, Menczer, & Flammini, 2016). They are cheap tools to make content more popular than they actually are, catalyzing online discussions and stirring outrage and artificial trends (Keller & Klinger, 2019). They are not easily discernible from real profiles, neither by other users nor by platform algorithms (Santini et al., 2018). When acting with the purpose of infiltrating political discussions, they are called political bots that apply a technical and social set of strategies that encompasses misinformation and manipulation efforts (Woolley & Howard, 2019). A growing body of knowledge has developed around the strategies, techniques, and the degree of political manipulation on social media following the results of the Brexit referendum and the 2016 US presidential election (Santini et al., 2018).

Communication scholars have recently begun to recognize and investigate the importance of algorithms to a wide range of processes related to the production and consumption of media content (Napoli, 2014). Research about automated accounts that distribute news links on Twitter have either centered around development opportunities for news organizations and journalists (Lokot & Diakopoulos, 2016), or dealt with the uses of Twitter for news sharing, comparing human and automated account activity patterns (Larsson & Hallvard, 2015). But few efforts thus far discuss online strategies for content distribution, questioning the use of artificial intelligence (AI) combined with social media vulnerability to manipulate ratings and audience measurement.

Methods and Approach

In this study, we analyze Twitter bot accounts that share links to pages of two Brazilian news websites: Globo Group and Folha Group. This section outlines the case and context, methodological approach, as well as research limitations.

The Case and Context

The Brazilian media marketplace is an interesting example of ownership and audience concentration characterized by the low circulation of newspapers, agenda orientation toward the elite, late development of the press, and a huge influence of television as a source of news (Albuquerque, 2012). Diversity of information and perspectives in Brazilian media is also weakened by religious, political and economic interference, and lack of transparency (Reporters Without Borders, & Intervozes, 2019). Family-owned groups, such as Globo and Folha, have adopted a market-driven, catchall attitude as democracy consolidated in Brazil (Albuquerque, 2012), becoming media conglomerates.

Globo is the largest mass media group of Latin America and the world's second-largest TV network, only behind North-American ABC, with its television channels covering 98.37% of Brazilian municipalities. The group figures in the ranking of the 30 major media owners in the world according to the Zenith Top Thirty Global Media

Owners. It controls outlets in all Brazilian media markets, owning nine of the 50 vehicles with the highest audience in the country. Besides operating in the phonographic, movie, and editorial markets, its businesses include free TV network *Rede Globo*; more than 20 pay-TV channels under *Globosat* service; *Globo.com*, the largest Brazilian online news portal, two radio networks, *Globo AM/FM* and *CBN*, among the 10 most important in the country; newspapers of great relevance such as *O Globo, Extra* and *Valor Econômico*; more than 14 magazines; and *Agência O Globo*, one of the main news agencies in the country (Reporters Without Borders, & Intervozes, 2019).

While Globo dominates broadcast channels in a quasi-monopolistic way (de Albuquerque, 2016), Folha Group has held a significant market share of both online and printed news segments (Moreira, 2016) and figures as the third-largest Brazilian media conglomerate (Grupo de Mídia, 2017). Folha controls *Folha de S.Paulo*, the newspaper with the largest circulation and influence; *UOL*, the largest internet content and Internet service company; *Folha.com*, the newspaper site with the most viewers; *Plural*, the largest printing business in Brazil; *Datafolha*, a research institute; *Publifolha*, a book publisher; and *Folhapress*, a news agency ("Know the Folha Group," n.d.).

Thus, cross-ownership is a central dimension of the Brazilian media concentration, with conglomerates migrating toward a multi-platform environment to widen their market share (Reporters Without Borders, & Intervozes, 2019). While the Brazilian media market still features strong broadcasters, the internet has been increasingly used for media consumption and social media platforms have been flourishing. Moreover, the legacy newspaper sector is struggling to find new business models as online news portals, since 61% of Brazilian users share news via social media (Carro, 2018). Despite the prevalence of Facebook and Whatsapp, Brazil has the sixth largest Twitter user-base, as of July 2019, with more than 8 million users (Statisa, 2019).

Additional reasons substantiate our choice for studying Twitter, such as limited privacy restrictions imposed by its users (Zimmer & Proferes, 2014), automated access and extraction of data via the Application Programming Interface (API) (Bruns & Weller, 2014), and a rich dataset that enables different research approaches, ranging from statistical to anthropological (Williams, Terras, & Warwick, 2013). Twitter is also an interesting case of study due to its relationship to mainstream media, either through its agenda-setting power (Skogerbø & Krumsvik, 2015), two-step flow function, especially through news sharing (Kümpel, Karnowski, & Keyling, 2015) or second screening use (Giglietto & Selva, 2014).

Additionally, Twitter plays a key role among social media platforms (Robischon, 2015), especially in the political arena (Isaac & Ember, 2016), making it a pervasive tool in election campaigns (Jungherr, 2016). Twitter has also concentrated a significant body of studies on media manipulation. Most studies thus far have approached the manipulation issue from the perspective of content production such as fake news and disinformation campaigns (i.e. Allcott & Gentzkow, 2017; Benkler, Faris, & Roberts, 2018; Faris et al., 2017; Tandoc, Lim, & Ling, 2017), or focused on automation strategies such as political bots (i.e. Ferrara et al., 2016; Keller & Klinger, 2019). Shao et al. (2018), for example, investigate the role of social bots in spreading articles from low-credibility sources. However, the role of legacy media in this new scenario has not been fully investigated.

Data Collection

To compose our dataset we extracted three types of data: (i) tweets containing links from the Globo and Folha Groups collected via Twitter Application Programming Interface (API); (ii) URL metadata collected from the Globo and Folha Groups' websites; (iii) Twitter trending topics.

(i) Twitter data extraction

We collected tweets continuously using the Twitter Search API from December 1, 2018 to April 12, 2019. Twitter's public streaming API allows access to a random sample of public content published. We extracted links from tweets and retweets using the regular expression module of Python, aggregating a total of 530,942 tweets containing at least one URL from the Globo Group or Folha Group, resulting in a total of 216,507 unique URLs. We listed all Twitter accounts that posted these 530,942 tweets, resulting in 176,438 accounts. During the data collection period, 614 profiles were deleted, leaving 175,824 active Twitter accounts.

(ii) Metadata extraction from links to Globo and Folha Groups

We obtained metadata from the unique URLs extracted from Twitter by accessing the Globo Group and Folha Group websites. The metadata extraction of our initial dataset, comprising of 216,507 unique URLs, was limited due to sources occasionally not providing information regarding time and date of creation for every story published. We used newspaper3k module of Python to index and download metadata from 158,690 articles: 101,203 from Globo and 57,487 from Folha.

(iii) Twitter trending topics analysis.

When some term or hashtag is mentioned repeatedly on social media, its popularity tends to grow. This popularity increase can be manufactured. In view of Twitter rules, which state that any attempt to modify Trending Topic (TT) rankings is considered manipulation ("Automation rules," 2017), we opted to analyze TT data, intending to test the assumption that bot accounts are acting to influence TT ranking algorithms.

We collected Twitter trending topics (TTs) applying the Simple Random Sampling Without Replacement method (Kurant, Markopoulou, & Thiran, 2011). This method allows the extraction of the top 50 TTs for a specific geographic location. The output data are a list containing the name of the TT, the query parameter (hashtag or term), the Twitter Search URL, and the number of tweets for the last 24 h if available. For this experiment, we acquired data every 15 min, referencing Brazilian local time for a four-month period in 2018.

Given the importance of second screening for audience engagement (de Zúñiga et al., 2015) and the cross-ownership of Globo Group (Moreira, 2016), we monitored for evidence of social media metrics fabrication by bot accounts related to trending topics manipulation. In an exploratory manner, we investigated hashtags related to daily live shows that appeared as socially relevant on Twitter in incongruent periods of the day. That is, we were looking for hashtags that became trending in periods different from the broadcast show air timing. Our objective was to observe daily behavior patterns; thus, sports events or sporadic TV attractions were not suitable for this analysis. In order to reduce data storage and processing costs, this assumption was tested based on the hashtag of one daily morning show broadcasted by Globo TV, "Mais Você."

From May 21 to May 26, 2019, we used the Twitter Search API to collect data by filtering for the hashtag #maisvoce (case insensitive). This search was repeated every 5 min. We obtained a total of 1,044 tweets and retweets shared by 576 unique accounts. The accounts were classified with the Botometer.

Data Processing

In order to identify media bot accounts, we employed the following methodological strategies to filter the Twitter profiles on our dataset. We developed a computational routine to automatically classify our population of accounts using the Botometer. During this process, to address time and processing limitations, we defined an account sample able to represent our total account population. We selected a sample size to establish a 99% confidence level (margin of error less than 1%). Hence, we selected a sample of 13,695 Twitter profiles, considering a population of 176,438. We selected the sample accordingly to a uniform probability distribution, meaning that all accounts in our database had the same chance of being chosen, thus avoiding bias.

We used the Botometer to identify the degree of automation of the 13,695 Twitter profiles in our sample. The Botometer is a flexible and accurate tool widely employed to detect bots (Wojcik, Messing, Smith, Rainie, & Hitlin, 2018). It applies state-of-the-art methods to find the extent to which an account has similarities to bot features, collecting, and processing 1,150 pieces of information about a Twitter profile by machine-learning algorithms (Varol, Ferrara, Davis, Menczer, & Flammini, 2017; Yang et al., 2019). Based on Shao et al. (2018), we used a threshold of 2.5 to classify an account as a bot or not. Among the 13,695 accounts in our sample, 2,150 were classified as bots.

Limitations

Quantitative research via Twitter API solutions is limited to a random sample that corresponds to 1% of all public data published on Twitter (Wojcik et al., 2018). The whole stream of tweets (the so-called Firehose) is costly and not publicly available, so the extraction of free data via Twitter Streaming API is the usual choice of researchers and widely used in academic papers.

While the Botometer approach adopted in this research has provided useful insights into the uses of social bots for media engagement manipulation, all automated detection approaches present limitations to what they alone can accomplish (Varol et al., 2017). Botometer produces a 0-to-5 classification scale called bot score in which the higher the score, the greater the likelihood that the account is controlled completely or in part by software (Yang et al., 2019). While we adopt the optimal threshold of 2.5 suggested by Varol et al. (2017), the authors indicate that Botometer produces a false-positive rate of 0.15 and a false-negative measure of 0.11. Other studies found similar limitations with 71% of bot detection accuracy (Bastos & Mercea, 2018). False-positive classification is indeed a limitation of employing Botometer, but false-negative detection may lead to underestimation of the pervasiveness of media bots accounts. Thus, ratings manipulation could be an even greater phenomenon.

Results

Our data analysis is based on a large corpus of accounts that posted links from the Globo and Folha Groups on Twitter, two of the most highly credible news outlet websites in Brazil (Carro,

2018). Regarding the accounts' behavior, our sample of 13,695 Twitter profiles was responsible for 164,839 posts (tweets and retweets). Among these posts, 25% were tweeted by 1% of accounts, and the 16,6% accounts classified as bots were responsible for posting 15% of the tweeted content.

Link Spreading Behavior of the Accounts

We ranked the accounts in our sample by how many tweets they posted with links to the Globo or Folha Group websites and considered the top 1,000 accounts as super-spreaders, based on Shao et al. (2018). Among the super-spreaders, 18.6% of accounts were classified as bots by the Botometer. When compared to the findings of Shao et al. (2018), our "super-spreader" sample has a lower presence of bots, which was expected considering the two different types of source analyzed: low-credibility websites vs. legacy news media.

In addition, we identified that media bots are "early-spreaders": accounts that automatically post links to highly credible media content, tweeting, or retweeting links to articles and increasing the chances that they go "viral." This observation reinforces the results of Shao et al. (2018), showing that bots are more prevalent in the immediate seconds after an article is

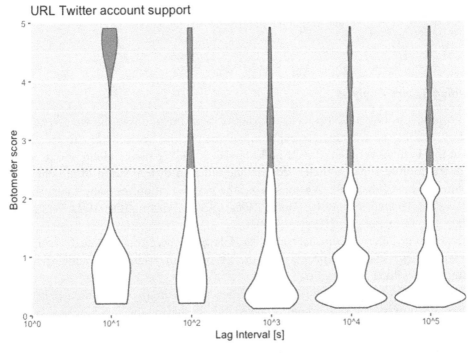

Figure 1. Media bot news-sharing strategy. We use a violin plot to study the temporal evolution of Twitter account support after a link is first shared by the Globo and Folha Groups' websites. We considered 160,650 tweets published by 13,695 accounts in our sample, from which we were able to collect the exact publication time on the source website, and align the times to when each link first appears. We focus on the first 24 h of the spreading phase following each link publication, and divide into logarithmic intervals. The logarithmic lag interval between news links publishing time and Twitter accounts sharing these respective links is plotted in seconds. The plot shows the Botometer score distribution for accounts that tweeted or retweeted during these lag intervals. Data generated by bot activity are represented in a gray color above the horizontal dotted line (Botometer score of 2.5).

first published on Twitter than at later times. To test this, we considered a one-day period after the website published the article. We examined the time lag between the story being published by the Globo and Folha Groups' websites and tweets sharing the story link.

Figure 1 presents the early-spreader behavior and shows bots contribution to links shared on the first day after a story is published on the Folha and Globo websites. We used a violin plot to facilitate the visualization. The violin plot displays a combination of the box plot and of a smoothed histogram and reveals the structure found within the data, adding information to box plots (Hintze & Nelson, 1998). This representation allows one to visualize the distribution of a numeric variable for several groups. For each data group, the width of a violin contour represents the probability of the corresponding value, that is, the part where the violin is thicker implicates that these section values occur more frequently; the violin plot gives more information about the density estimate on the y-axis. This result suggests bot activity on the first moments after a link is shared by a high-credibility media website, which is a strong evidence of the presence of Media bots as "early-spreader" accounts tempering discussion on Twitter.

Regarding the Bot score of a Twitter account, we used Botometer classifier to compute the extent to which an account expresses similarity to the characteristic of a social bot (Varol et al., 2017). Since there are different levels of automation of a Twitter account being employed by bots and humans, Botometer provides a classification score ranging from 0 to 5. When a binary classification is needed, we used a threshold of 2.5 for accuracy maximization (Varol et al., 2017).

Trending Topics Analysis

We propose that bots may play an important role in maintaining the #maisvoce hashtag on Twitter TTs. To test this assumption, we analyze the behavior of the accounts that posted this hashtag between May 21 and May 26, 2019. We used a violin plot to represent the distribution of the Botometer score in the function of the period of the day that the accounts tweeted (Figure 2). We considered the tweet creation time and categorized each post as either shared during the night (00:00– 05:59), morning (06:00– 11:59), afternoon (12:00– 17:59), or evening (18:00– 23:59).

As shown in Figure 2, unusual traffic is displayed by accounts classified as bots during the night hours. This is unexpected since the TV program "Mais Você" audience profile is incompatible with this behavior.

Figure 2 shows evidence of bot activity influencing the metrics of #maisvocê hashtag on Twitter. We observe traffic of accounts tagged as bots sharing the TV show hashtag during the night hours (00:00– 05:59). We classify this as an unusual activity considering the discrepancy with the TV show airing time. "Mais Você" is exhibited in Globo TV from 09:00 to 10:00 (Brazilian time), so this night activity probably does not result of the use of Twitter as the second screen, that is, the use of Twitter as a real-time backchannel for broadcasting comments while watching a TV program (Giglietto & Selva, 2014). Our findings suggest the employment of tools to artificially boost the popularity of hashtags to make them trend. The use of bots to increase #maisvoce hashtag popularity during the night hours could be an attempt to get the audience's attention before the show airing time.

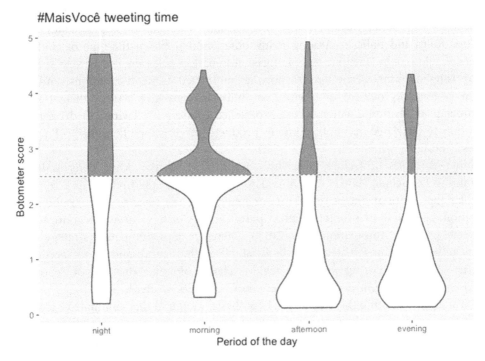

Figure 2. Media bot trending topic strategy. We use a violin plot to visualize the period of the day where tweets and retweets mentioning the hashtag #maisvoce are published. We considered 1,044 posts shared by 576 accounts. Considering the post creation time, we categorized it as shared during the night (00:00–05:59), morning (06:00–11:59), afternoon (12:00–17:59), or evening (18:00–23:59). The plot shows the Botometer score distribution for accounts that tweeted or retweeted during these periods of the day. Data generated by bot activity are represented in a gray color above the horizontal dotted line (Botometer score of 2.5).

Discussion: The Use of Algorithms and Non-human Traffic in Audience Manufacturing

Social media have taken a gatekeeping role between journalism and citizens (Russell, 2019), that is, now social media algorithms and platforms efficiently control the flow of news (Napoli, 2015). In an audience-centric news business, the vulnerability of social media platforms to spammers, content polluters, and malware disseminators (K. Lee, Caverlee, & Webb, 2010) becomes crucial. These threatening agents are being developed into sophisticated algorithms to emulate human behavior and influence the online environment (Ferrara et al., 2016; Varol et al., 2017; Yang et al., 2019). Two-thirds of the links to popular sites posted on Twitter are generated by automated accounts (Wojcik et al., 2018). Social media platforms are beginning to acknowledge these problems and deploy countermeasures, although their effectiveness is hard to evaluate (Lazer et al., 2018).

Policymakers, users, foreign governments, activists, and the press are asking these platforms to both permit contentious speech and curate it, making them take increasing responsibility for policing the activity of their users (Gillespie, 2018). As Gillespie (2018) argues, the governance of platforms is still struggling with the difficult attributes and responsibilities of intermediating online social connections.

The only existing rules are created by the platform itself and automated activity is subject to the Twitter rules. The use of bots, fake accounts, or impersonators violates Twitter Rules and Policies. Among many other limitations on the type of content and behavior allowed by Twitter, the platform automation rules do not permit spamming, comprising duplicate accounts and posting automated content, mentions, and replies. Spam is generally defined on Twitter as "bulk or aggressive activity that attempts to manipulate or disrupt Twitter or the experience of users on Twitter to drive traffic or attention to unrelated accounts, content, products, services, or initiatives" ("The Twitter Rules," n.d.).

Some examples of factors taken into account by Twitter when determining what spamming is, include (but is not limited to): posting multiple updates to a trending or popular topic with an intent to subvert or manipulate the topic to drive traffic or users' attention; and using or promoting third-party services or apps to obtain more followers, retweets, or likes (Automation rules, 2017). Therefore, any automation strategy to reach many users on an unsolicited basis is an abuse of the feature and is not permitted by Twitter. Although Twitter promptly reviews claims of impersonation, or reported bot activity or spamming, it does not actively monitor users' content.

Ultimately, by testing the media bots hypothesis, we found that automated accounts are being used to make articles and other types of news programing more visible to audiences. Although we cannot verify if these news organizations have sanctioned or purchased these accounts for this purpose, our findings show that these bots aim to increase the engagement of Globo and Folha Groups online audiences. This strategy differs from traditional advertising since it is a veiled mechanism that violates the platform's terms of use, hindering proper identification by common users. While Twitter authorizes paid ads, "this means following all applicable laws and regulations, creating honest ads, and advertising safely and respectfully" ("Twitter Ads policies," n.d.).

Communication scholars have recently recognized that social media, due to their convenient and easy-to-use tools for posting content, simplify and facilitate news sharing (Kümpel et al., 2015) and have become a constitutive part of online news distribution and consumption (Mitchell & Page, 2014). Additionally, social platforms have made news-sharing visible and quantifiable (Kalsnes & Larsson, 2018) and online news sites increasingly rely on users' shares and recommendations from social media to improve their website traffic, article views, and ultimately their economic success. Beyond possibly increasing audience engagement, news-sharing practices might have further implications for monetization opportunities for online news media and mechanisms of social influence.

The media bot-spamming behavior pattern found in our research indicates that these automated accounts probably work to boost the Globo and Folha Groups' audiences and amplify their social relevance in Brazil. Our research results converge with the two Pew Research Center reports (Wojcik & Barthel, 2018; Wojcik et al., 2018) which also demonstrate that automated accounts post a substantial share of links to a wide range of US online media outlets on Twitter.

In the online environment, one might expect news sites that were "born on the web" to be more integrated with social media when compared to legacy news sites (outlets that originated in print or broadcast), and thus more frequently trafficked by suspected bot accounts. However, a recent Pew Research Center report (Wojcik & Barthel, 2018), also using the Botometer, found that suspected automated accounts are significantly prolific in sharing links to legacy news organizations. Wojcik and Barthel (2018) showed that "suspected bots shared 60% of tweeted links to legacy sites, about on par with the 59% of tweeted links to digital native sites."

The other Pew analysis (Wojcik et al., 2018) estimates that two-thirds of tweeted links to popular news websites are posted by bots in the United States, and a relatively small number of bots are responsible for a substantial share of the links to popular media outlets. The same asymmetry of news-sharing distribution was found in our dataset considering bot tweets to two Brazilian mainstream news media websites (the Globo and Folha Groups).

Theories of social influence focus on the necessary conditions for individual behavior to be influenced by those around them. Since people tend to follow similar activities as their peers, it is not surprising that the ranking or placing of an article on a given online platform affects its sharing probability (Berger & Milkman, 2012). Li and Sakamoto (2014) found that exposing people to information about the collective sharing behavior positively influences their own sharing practices. Our analysis provides quantitative empirical evidence of the key role played by social bots in the spreading of links to legacy news sites.

Therefore, the use of media bots may have ambiguous social consequences. Primarily, articles afforded more prominence by bots should have a higher chance of being shared, which can generate economic advantages for media companies. However, consumer trust in legacy news sites may decline when it becomes public knowledge that bots are involved in news-sharing practices. Scholars from the Reuters Institute for the Study of Journalism (Newman et al., 2018) showed that the use of social media for reading news has started to fall in a number of key markets (such as the USA and France) after years of continuous growth. Over half of the worldwide news consumers (54%) agree or strongly agree that they are concerned about what is real and fake on the internet (Newman et al., 2018). This is highest in countries like Brazil (85%) and the United States (64%) where recent elections were largely untroubled by concerns over fake content and fake accounts (bots). Newman et al. (2018) show that most respondents believe that publishers (75%) and platforms (71%) have the biggest responsibility to fix problems of fake news and suspicious account activities.

The peer-to-peer circulation of news on social media has been recognized by scholars as a significant new form of agenda setting. In the classic agenda-setting model introduced by McCombs and Shaw (1972), elite news media gatekeepers set the agendas of the citizenry by choosing to cover certain stories over others, increasing the social relevance of the mainstream media. Since then, scholars like Kim and Lee (2006), Sayre, Bode, Shah, Wilcox, and Shah (2010), Papacharissi (2013) and Penney (2017) have identified a "reverse" agenda-setting process on the internet by which social media users, as members of the public sphere, direct attention to an issue in a way that compels the news media to increase coverage. Thus, in the networked digital media era, citizen participation in agenda-setting processes has notably gained weight. As Penney (2017, p. 136) argues, "by lending publicity to favored pieces of journalistic content through various selective forwarding activities (linking, sharing, etc.), citizens contribute to the production and shaping of attention" on particular news stories, reinforcing the common belief in its social relevance.

However, the use of automated accounts for sharing news online may affect the agenda-setting cycle by producing an artificial news echo chamber on Twitter, distorting the real social relevance of each topic. As a selective forwarding and curatorial agency practice (Penney, 2017), the large-scale circulation of news using bots creates a "vicious cycle" of news, characterized by a self-referential media ecosystem which manipulates Twitter algorithms for news recommendations, increasing the power of media outlets for online public influence. As fake accounts are created to be camouflaged, it is necessary to consider how bots, that promote selected media content while appearing to represent common users, are advancing certain political agendas, ideas, and interests.

For Marwick and Lewis (2017), the media's dependence on social media analytics, metrics, and clickbait makes them vulnerable to different kinds of online manipulation. From a political economy viewpoint, scholars have considered that the media industry manufactures and sells audiences as commoditized products to advertisers (Smythe, 1977). This perspective understands that audience measurement is not just a witness of a naturally occurring phenomenon, but rather a rationalization and control strategy amid strong market competition (Lee, Lewis, & Powers, 2014). Rating firms not only check to determine but manufacture audiences through technological procedures for analysis of usage patterns.

The strategies that media organizations and advertisers use to learn about their audiences, to measure their behavior, to predict future trends, and to assign value to different targets change over time and affect the social constructions of media audience (Napoli, 2011). Relying on feedback mechanisms that collect and analyze consumer information, broadcast media had been developed as an advertiser-supported communication industry (Bermejo, 2009) and audience measurement systems became their lifeblood segments (Napoli, 2011). We also draw attention to the fact that this dependence on audience measurements can turn them into online audience rating manipulators. This diagnosis is even more critical if we consider the Brazilian media marketplace, which is highly concentrated among a few influential players, characterizing an oligopoly.

Conclusion

Our research provides quantitative empirical evidence that bots deceptively impersonating humans are significantly prolific in sharing hashtags and news links to legacy media content in Brazil. We analyzed the role played by social bots in boosting the mainstream media audience, uncovering two manipulation strategies. Given our focus on two media groups, namely Globo and Folha, further research should investigate other media vehicles, both in Brazil and internationally, better estimating the pervasiveness of this phenomenon.

Firstly, we found that bots are particularly active in amplifying news media links in the initial moments of spreading (Figure 1). Our hypothesis arose from previous research conducted by Santini et al. (2018) and our methodological approach was based on Shao et al. (2018). While our results are related to the dissemination of content from legitimate, high-quality Brazilian news media sources. Shao et al. (2018) found a similar information dissemination strategy, albeit for the spread of low-credibility content in the United States. Although our purpose did not center on types of content, we demonstrate that the same strategies to increase the visibility of fake news are used to increase the audiences of traditional media.

Secondly, our findings demonstrate that social bots also play an important role in promoting TV broadcast programs in Brazil. Social bots boost hashtags' on Twitter to amplify the reach of the TV audience, disseminating program hashtags in the early hours before the TV show goes on air. This strategy also stimulates the use of Twitter as a second screen platform during TV programs to increase audience participation and interaction. However, bots alone do not entirely explain the success of the Globo Group in Brazil: the use of social bots for news and TV programs probably indicates an aggressive marketing strategy that takes place in the online environment to maintain the leading market share of Brazil's biggest media company.

Whereas there are many studies that focus on the use of social bots to spread false news (Ferrara et al., 2016; Shao et al., 2018; Woolley & Howard, 2019), our findings demonstrate that similar bot strategies are being used to increase mainstream media audience and popularity, promoting selected media content with the appearance of being spontaneous.

A key dimension in discussing media bot action is evaluating the extent to which it compellingly illustrates that the media outlets function as a cultural and political institution, in the sense of the institutional theory framework (Napoli, 2014). This approach involves focusing on what is described as the "institutionalized audience" that considers the audience as socially constructed by media industries, advertisers, and associated audience measurement firms.

While our results suggest that mainstream media groups resort to bots to promote their content online, our study concentrates on two local media companies and considers one single platform. We detected suspected activities on Twitter, but similar phenomena may be taking place on other platforms too. The use of bots to promote legitimate news content and TV programs deserves further investigation considering other Brazilian media players and other countries. Finally, fraud in mainstream media audience measurement and artificial online media popularity using bots may contribute to diminishing trust in the mainstream media, increasing misinformation and disinformation conditions, and other forms of public opinion manipulation.

Future studies can build upon our results by shedding more light on the bot identification challenge with some form of qualitative or mixed-method design in mind, possibly validating our findings by human analysis. Another important agenda is regarding the creation of a local bot repository: Botometer relies on 'common' features supposedly shared by all bots (Besel, Echeverria, & Zhou, 2018). While some similarities can be observed between automated accounts across the world, the framework is limited once Brazilian bots are compared to international ones.

Disclosure Statement

No potential conflict of interest was reported by the authors.

Funding

This work was supported by the Coordenação de Aperfeiçoamento de Pessoal de Nível Superior (CAPES), Brazil.

ORCID

Rose Marie Santini ⓘ http://orcid.org/0000-0003-0657-7217
Debora Salles ⓘ http://orcid.org/0000-0002-3436-6698
Giulia Tucci ⓘ http://orcid.org/0000-0002-1829-2967
Fernando Ferreira ⓘ http://orcid.org/0000-0003-3455-2316
Felipe Grael ⓘ http://orcid.org/0000-0002-9261-379X

References

Albuquerque, A. (2012). On models and margins: Comparative media models viewed from a Brazilian perspective. In D. C. Hallin & P. Mancini (Eds.), *Comparing media systems beyond the western world* (pp. 72–95). doi:10.1017/CBO9781139005098.006

Allcott, H., & Gentzkow, M. (2017). *Social media and fake news in the 2016 election* (Working Paper No. 23089). doi:10.3386/w23089

ANA. (2017). *Bot baseline 2016-2017 | Fraud in digital advertising.* Author. Retrieved from Association of National Advertiser's website https://www.ana.net/content/show/id/botfraud-2017

Automation rules. (2017). Retrieved from Twitter website https://help.twitter.com/en/rules-and-policies/twitter-automation

Bastos, M., & Mercea, D. (2018). The public accountability of social platforms: Lessons from a study on bots and trolls in the Brexit campaign. *Philosophical Transactions of the Royal Society A: Mathematical, Physical and Engineering Sciences*, 376(2128), 20180003. doi:10.1098/rsta.2018.0003

Bell, E. J., Owen, T., Brown, P. D., Hauka, C., & Rashidian, N. (2017). *The Platform Press: How Silicon Valley Reengineered Journalism*. doi:10.7916/D8R216ZZ

Benkler, Y., Faris, R., & Roberts, H. (2018). *Network propaganda: Manipulation, disinformation, and radicalization in American politics*. New York, NY: Oxford University Press.

Berger, J., & Milkman, K. L. (2012). What makes online content viral? *Journal of Marketing Research*, 49(2), 192–205. doi:10.1509/jmr.10.0353

Bermejo, F. (2009). Audience manufacture in historical perspective: From broadcasting to Google. *New Media & Society*, 11(1–2), 133–154. doi:10.1177/1461444808099579

Besel, C., Echeverria, J., & Zhou, S. (2018). *Full cycle analysis of a large-scale botnet attack on Twitter*. 2018 IEEE/ACM International Conference on Advances in Social Networks Analysis and Mining (ASONAM) (pp. 170–177). doi:10.1109/ASONAM.2018.8508708

Boczkowski, P. J. (2004). The processes of adopting multimedia and interactivity in three online newsrooms. *Journal of Communication*, 54(2), 197–213. doi:10.1111/j.1460-2466.2004.tb02624.x

Bruns, A., & Weller, K. (2014). Twitter data analytics – Or: The pleasures and perils of studying Twitter. *Aslib Journal of Information Management*, 66(3). doi:10.1108/AJIM-02-2014-0027

Carlson, M. (2015). When news sites go native: Redefining the advertising–editorial divide in response to native advertising. *Journalism*, 16(7), 849–865. doi:10.1177/1464884914545441

Carro, R. (2018). *Digital news report*. Retrieved from https://web.archive.org/web/20190608205643/http://www.digitalnewsreport.org/survey/2018/brazil-2018/

Casero-Ripollés, A., & Izquierdo-Castillo, J. (2013). Between decline and a new online business model: The case of the Spanish newspaper industry. *Journal of Media Business Studies*, 10, 63–78. doi:10.1080/16522354.2013.11073560

Chadwick, A. (2013). *The hybrid media system: Politics and power*. Retrieved from https://web.archive.org/web/20200213003604/https://www.oxfordscholarship.com/view/10.1093/acprof:oso/9780199759477.001.0001/acprof-9780199759477

Conway, B. A., Kenski, K., & Wang, D. (2015). The rise of twitter in the political campaign: Searching for intermedia agenda-setting effects in the presidential primary. *Journal of Computer-Mediated Communication*, 20, 363–380. doi:10.1111/jcc4.12124

de Albuquerque, A. (2016). BRICS| Voters against public opinion: Press and democracy in Brazil and South Africa. *International Journal of Communication*, 10(20), 3042–3061.

De Cristofaro, E., Friedman, A., Jourjon, G., Kaafar, M. A., & Shafiq, M. Z. (2014). *Paying for likes?: Understanding Facebook like fraud using honeypots*. Proceedings of the 2014 Conference on Internet Measurement Conference - IMC '14 (pp. 129–136). doi:10.1145/2663716.2663729

de Zúñiga, H. G., Garcia-Perdomo, V., & McGregor, S. C. (2015). What is second screening? Exploring motivations of second screen use and its effect on online political participation. *Journal of Communication*, 65(5), 793–815. doi:10.1111/jcom.12174

Edelman Trust Barometer 2018. (2018). Retrieved from https://web.archive.org/web/20191203154903/https://www.edelman.com/research/2018-edelman-trust-barometer

Faris, R., Roberts, H., Etling, B., Bourassa, N., Zuckerman, E., & Benkler, Y. (2017). *Partisanship, propaganda, and disinformation: Online media and the 2016 U.S. presidential election* (SSRN Scholarly Paper No. ID 3019414). Retrieved from https://web.archive.org/web/20200222151719/https://papers.ssrn.com/sol3/papers.cfm?abstract_id=3019414

Ferrara, E., Varol, O., Davis, C., Menczer, F., & Flammini, A. (2016). The rise of social bots. *Communications of the ACM*, 59(7), 96–104. doi:10.1145/2818717

Fulgoni, G. (2016). Fraud in digital advertising: A multibillion-dollar black hole: How marketers can minimize losses caused by bogus web traffic. *Journal of Advertising Research*, 56, 122. doi:10.2501/JAR-2016-024

Gabryel, M. (2018). Data analysis algorithm for click fraud recognition. In R. Damaševičius & G. Vasiljevienė (Eds.), *Information and software technologies* (Vol. 920, pp. 437–446). doi:10.1007/978-3-319-99972-2_36

Giglietto, F., & Selva, D. (2014). Second screen and participation: A content analysis on a full season dataset of Tweets. *Journal of Communication*, 64(2), 260–277. doi:10.1111/jcom.12085

Gillespie, T. (2014). The relevance of algorithms. In T. Gillespie, P. J. Boczkowski, & K. A. Foot (Eds.), *Media technologies: Essays on communication, materiality, and society* (pp. 167–194).

Retrieved from https://web.archive.org/web/20190911024051/https://mitpress.university pressscholarship.com/view/10.7551/mitpress/9780262525374.001.0001/upso-9780262525374-chapter-9

Gillespie, T. (2018). Regulation of and by platforms. In J. Burgess, A. Marwick, & T. Poell (Eds.), *The SAGE handbook of social media* (pp. 254–278). doi:10.4135/9781473984066

Groshek, J., & Groshek, M. (2013). Agenda trending: Reciprocity and the predictive capacity of social networking sites in intermedia agenda setting across topics over time. *Media and Communication, 1*, 15. doi:10.17645/mac.v1i1.71

Grupo de Mídia. (2017). *Mídia Dados*. São Paulo, Brasil: Author.

Harder, R., Sevenans, J., & Aelst, P. (2017). Intermedia agenda setting in the social media age: How traditional players dominate the news agenda in election times. *The International Journal of Press/Politics, 22*, 275–293. doi:10.1177/1940161217704969

Hargittai, E., & Litt, E. (2011). The tweet smell of celebrity success: Explaining variation in Twitter adoption among a diverse group of young adults. *New Media & Society, 13*(5), 824–842. doi:10.1177/1461444811405805

Herbert, J., & Thurman, N. (2007). Paid content strategies for news websites. *Journalism Practice, 1*(2), 208–226. doi:10.1080/17512780701275523

Hintze, J. L., & Nelson, R. D. (1998). Violin plots: A box plot-density trace synergism. *The American Statistician, 52*(2), 181–184. doi:10.1080/00031305.1998.10480559

Ikram, M., Onwuzurike, L., Farooqi, S., Cristofaro, E. D., Friedman, A., Jourjon, G., … Shafiq, M. Z. (2017). Measuring, characterizing, and detecting Facebook like farms. *ACM Transactions on Privacy and Security, 20*(4), 1–28. doi:10.1145/3121134

Isaac, M., & Ember, S. (2016, November 8). For election day influence, Twitter ruled social media. *The New York Times*. Retrieved from https://web.archive.org/web/20200107182903/https://www.nytimes.com/2016/11/09/technology/for-election-day-chatter-twitter-ruled-social-media.html

Ju, A., Jeong, S. H., & Chyi, H. I. (2014). Will social media save newspapers? *Journalism Practice, 8*(1), 1–17. doi:10.1080/17512786.2013.794022

Jungherr, A. (2016). Twitter use in election campaigns: A systematic literature review. *Journal of Information Technology & Politics, 13*(1), 72–91. doi:10.1080/19331681.2015.1132401

Kalika, A., & Ferrucci, P. (2019). Examining TMZ: What traditional digital journalism can learn from celebrity news. *Communication Studies, 70*(2), 172–189. doi:10.1080/10510974.2018.1562949

Kalsnes, B., & Larsson, A. O. (2018). Understanding news sharing across social media. *Journalism Studies, 19*(11), 1669–1688. doi:10.1080/1461670X.2017.1297686

Keller, T. R., & Klinger, U. (2019). Social bots in election campaigns: Theoretical, empirical, and methodological implications. *Political Communication, 36*(1), 171–189. doi:10.1080/10584609.2018.1526238

Kim, S.-T., & Lee, Y. H. (2006). News function of internet mediated agenda-setting: Agenda-rippling ad reserved agenda-setting. *Korean Journal of Journalism & Communication Studies, 3*(50), 175–205.

Kleis Nielsen, R., & Ganter, S. A. (2018). Dealing with digital intermediaries: A case study of the relations between publishers and platforms. *New Media & Society, 20*(4), 1600–1617. doi:10.1177/1461444817701318

Know the Folha Group. (n.d.). Retrieved from https://web.archive.org/web/20200217203423/https://www1.folha.uol.com.br/institucional/

Kümpel, A. S., Karnowski, V., & Keyling, T. (2015). News sharing in social media: A review of current research on news sharing users, content, and networks. *Social Media + Society, 1*(2). doi:10.1177/2056305115610141

Kurant, M., Markopoulou, A., & Thiran, P. (2011). *Towards unbiased BFS sampling*. Retrieved from https://web.archive.org/web/20200222152134/https://arxiv.org/abs/1102.4599v1

Larsson, A. O., & Hallvard, M. (2015). Bots or journalists? News sharing on Twitter. *Communications, 40*(3), 361–370. doi:10.1515/commun-2015-0014

Lazer, D. M. J., Baum, M. A., Benkler, Y., Berinsky, A. J., Greenhill, K. M., Menczer, F., … Zittrain, J. L. (2018). The science of fake news. *Science, 359*(6380), 1094–1096. doi:10.1126/science.aao2998

Lee, A. M., Lewis, S. C., & Powers, M. (2014). Audience clicks and news placement: A study of time-lagged influence in online journalism. *Communication Research*, *41*(4), 505–530. doi:10.1177/0093650212467031

Lee, E.-J., & Tandoc, E. C. (2017). When news meets the audience: How audience feedback online affects news production and consumption. *Human Communication Research*, *43*(4), 436–449. doi:10.1111/hcre.12123

Lee, K., Caverlee, J., & Webb, S. (2010). *Uncovering social spammers: Social honeypots + machine learning*. Proceeding of the 33rd International ACM SIGIR Conference on Research and Development in Information Retrieval - SIGIR '10 (pp. 435). doi:10.1145/1835449.1835522

Li, H., & Sakamoto, Y. (2014). Social impacts in social media: An examination of perceived truthfulness and sharing of information. *Computers in Human Behavior*, *41*, 278–287. doi:10.1016/j.chb.2014.08.009

Lokot, T., & Diakopoulos, N. (2016). News bots: Automating news and information dissemination on Twitter. *Digital Journalism*, *4*, 682–699. doi:10.1080/21670811.2015.1081822

Luo, M. (2019, April 10). *The urgent quest for slower, better news | The New Yorker*. Retrieved from https://web.archive.org/web/20200208152357/https://www.newyorker.com/culture/annals-of-inquiry/the-urgent-quest-for-slower-better-news

Marwick, A., & Lewis, R. (2017). *Media manipulation and disinformation online* (pp. 106). Retrieved from https://web.archive.org/web/20200115043838/https://datasociety.net/output/media-manipulation-and-disinfo-online/

McCombs, M. (2004). *Setting the agenda: The mass media and public opinion*. Cambridge, UK: Polity Press.

McCombs, M. E., & Shaw, D. L. (1972). The agenda-setting function of mass media. *The Public Opinion Quarterly*, *36*(2), 176–187. doi:10.1086/267990

Mitchell, A., & Page, D. (2014). *State of the news media*. Retrieved from https://web.archive.org/web/20180724160540/http://www.journalism.org/files/2014/03/Overview.pdf

Moreira, S. V. (2016). Media ownership and concentration in Brazil. In E. M. Noam (Ed.), *Who owns the world's media?: Media concentration and ownership around the world*. Retrieved from https://web.archive.org/web/20190417234311/http://www.oxfordscholarship.com/mobile/view/10.1093/acprof:oso/9780199987238.001.0001/acprof-9780199987238-chapter-20

Napoli, P. M. (2011). *Audience evolution: New technologies and the transformation of media audiences*. New York, NY: Columbia University Press.

Napoli, P. M. (2014). Automated media: An institutional theory perspective on algorithmic media production and consumption. *Communication Theory*, *24*(3), 340–360. doi:10.1111/comt.12039

Napoli, P. M. (2015). Social media and the public interest: Governance of news platforms in the realm of individual and algorithmic gatekeepers. *Telecommunications Policy*, *39*(9), 751–760. doi:10.1016/j.telpol.2014.12.003

Nee, R. C., & Dozier, D. M. (2017). Second screen effects: Linking multiscreen media use to television engagement and incidental learning. *Convergence*, *23*(2), 214–226. doi:10.1177/1354856515592510

Neuman, W., Guggenheim, L., Jones - Jang, M., & Bae, S. (2014). The dynamics of public attention: Agenda-setting theory meets big data. *Journal of Communication*, *64*. doi:10.1111/jcom.12088

Newman, N. (2019). *Journalism, media and technology trends and predictions 2019*. Retrieved from https://web.archive.org/web/20200104231012/https://reutersinstitute.politics.ox.ac.uk/our-research/journalism-media-and-technology-trends-and-predictions-2019

Newman, N., Fletcher, R., Kalogeropoulos, A., Levy, D. A. L., & Nielsen, R. K. (2018). *Digital news report*. Reuters Institute for the Study of Journalism. Retrieved from the Reuters Institute for the Study of Journalism website http://www.digitalnewsreport.org/survey/2018/overviewkey-findings-2018/

Papacharissi, Z. (2013). *A private sphere: Democracy in a digital age*. Cambridge, UK: Polity Press.

Pariser, E. (2012). *The filter bubble: How the new personalized web is changing what we read and how we think*. New York, NY: Penguin Books.

Penney, J. (2017). *The citizen marketer: Promoting political opinion in the social media age* (1 ed.). New York, NY: Oxford University Press.

Recuero, R., & Araujo, R. (2012). *On the Rise of Artificial Trending Topics in Twitter.* doi:10.1145/2309996.2310046

Reporters Without Borders, & Intervozes. (2019). *Media ownership monitor.* Retrieved from https://web.archive.org/web/20200207194246/https://brazil.mom-rsf.org/en/

Robischon, N.; Noah, & Noah. (2015, March 17). *Twitter's influence problem, visualized.* Retrieved from https://web.archive.org/web/20180518083048/https://www.fastcompany.com/3043788/twitters-influence-problem-visualized

Rogstad, I. (2016). Is Twitter just rehashing? Intermedia agenda setting between Twitter and mainstream media. *Journal of Information Technology & Politics, 13*(2), 142–158. doi:10.1080/19331681.2016.1160263

Russell, F. M. (2019). The new Gatekeepers. *Journalism Studies, 20*(5), 631–648. doi:10.1080/1461670X.2017.1412806

Santini, R. M., Agostini, L., Barros, C. E., Carvalho, D., Centeno de Rezende, R., Salles, D. G., … Tucci, G. (2018). Software power as soft power. A literature review on computational propaganda effects in public opinion and political process. *PARTECIPAZIONE E CONFLITTO, 11*(2), 332–360. doi:10.1285/i20356609v11i2p332

Santini, R. M., Salles, D., Tucci, G., Estrella, C., Orofino, D., Barros, C. E., & Terra, C. (2018). *Online impersonators: Who are they and what do they do? A bot ethnography on Rio de Janeiro's 2016 municipal election.* Presented at the The Internet, Policy & Politics Conference, Oxford, UK.

Sayre, B., Bode, L., Shah, D., Wilcox, D., & Shah, C. (2010). Agenda setting in a digital age: Tracking attention to California proposition 8 in social media, online news and conventional news. *Policy & Internet, 2*(2), 7–32. doi:10.2202/1944-2866.1040

Shao, C., Ciampaglia, G. L., Varol, O., Yang, K.-C., Flammini, A., & Menczer, F. (2018). The spread of low-credibility content by social bots. *Nature Communications, 9*(1). doi:10.1038/s41467-018-06930-7

Skogerbø, E., & Krumsvik, A. H. (2015). Newspapers, Facebook and Twitter. *Journalism Practice, 9*(3), 350–366. doi:10.1080/17512786.2014.950471

Smythe, D. W. (1977). Communications: Blindspot of Western Marxism. *CTheory, 1*(3), 1–27.

Springborn, K., & Barford, P. (2013). *Impression fraud in online advertising via pay-per-view networks.* Proceedings of the 22Nd USENIX Conference on Security (pp. 211–226). Retrieved from https://web.archive.org/web/20200222152552/https://dl.acm.org/doi/10.5555/2534766.2534785

Statisa. (2019). *Countries with most Twitter users.* Retrieved from https://web.archive.org/web/20191217053849/https://www.statista.com/statistics/242606/number-of-active-twitter-users-in-selected-countries/

Stringhini, G., Wang, G., Egele, M., Kruegel, C., Vigna, G., Zheng, H., & Zhao, B. Y. (2013). *Follow the green: Growth and dynamics in twitter follower markets.* Proceedings of the 2013 Conference on Internet Measurement Conference - IMC '13 (pp. 163–176). doi:10.1145/2504730.2504731

Tandoc, E., Lim, Z., & Ling, R. (2017). Defining "Fake News": A typology of scholarly definitions. *Digital Journalism*, 1–17. doi:10.1080/21670811.2017.1360143

Thomas, K., McCoy, D., Grier, C., Kolcz, A., & Paxson, V. (2013). *Trafficking fraudulent accounts: The role of the underground market in Twitter spam and abuse.* Proceedings of the 22nd USENIX Security Symposium, Washington, D.C., USA, (pp. 195–210).

Tufekci, Z. (2014). *Big questions for social media big data: Representativeness, validity and other methodological pitfalls.* Presented at the eighth international AAAI Conference on Weblogs and Social Media. Retrieved from https://web.archive.org/web/20191208144848/http://www.aaai.org/ocs/index.php/ICWSM/ICWSM14/paper/view/8062

Twitter Ads policies. (n.d.). Retrieved from https://web.archive.org/web/20200210233456/https://business.twitter.com/en/help/ads-policies/introduction-to-twitter-ads/twitter-ads-policies.html

The Twitter Rules. (n.d.). Retrieved from https://web.archive.org/web/20200219075941/https://help.twitter.com/en/rules-and-policies/twitter-rules

van Dijck, J., Poell, T., & de Waal, M. (2018). *The platform society.* New York, NY: OUP USA.

Varol, O., Ferrara, E., Davis, C. A., Menczer, F., & Flammini, A. (2017). *Online human-bot interactions: Detection, estimation, and characterization*. Proceedings of the 11th International AAAI Conference on Web and Social Media (ICWSM), Montréal, Québec, Canada.

Vos, T. P., & Russell, F. M. (2019). Theorizing journalism's institutional relationships: An elaboration of gatekeeping theory. *Journalism Studies*, 1–18. doi:10.1080/1461670X.2019.1593882

Williams, S. A., Terras, M. M., & Warwick, C. (2013). What do people study when they study Twitter? Classifying Twitter related academic papers. *Journal of Documentation, 69*, 384–410. doi:10.1108/JD-03-2012-0027

Wojcik, S., & Barthel, M. (2018, June 21). *The news that bots share on Twitter usually isn't political*. Retrieved from https://web.archive.org/web/20190809150142/https://www.pewresearch.org/fact-tank/2018/06/21/the-news-that-bots-share-on-twitter-tends-not-to-focus-on-politics/

Wojcik, S., Messing, S., Smith, A., Rainie, L., & Hitlin, P. (2018). *Bots in the Twittersphere* (Vol. 31). Pew Research Center. Retrieved from Pew Research Center's website https://www.pewresearch.org/internet/2018/04/09/bots-in-thetwittersphere/

Woolley, S., & Howard, P. N. (Eds.). (2019). *Computational propaganda: Political parties, politicians, and political manipulation on social media*. New York, NY: Oxford University Press.

Yang, K.-C., Varol, O., Davis, C. A., Ferrara, E., Flammini, A., & Menczer, F. (2019). Arming the public with artificial intelligence to counter social bots. *Human Behavior and Emerging Technologies, 1*(1), 48–61. doi:10.1002/hbe2.115

Zeifman, I. (2017). *Bot traffic report 2016*. Retrieved from Imperva Incapsula website https://www.incapsula.com/blog/bot-traffic-report-2016.html

Zimmer, M., & Proferes, N. (2014). A topology of Twitter research: Disciplines, methods, and ethics. *Aslib Journal of Information Management, 66*, 250–261. doi:10.1108/AJIM-09-2013-0083

Index

Page numbers in italics and bold denote figures and tables, respectively. Page numbers with "n" denote notes.

account merchants 102
Aelst, P. 101
agenda-setting hypothesis 7–8, 101, 111–112
AI-driven apps 5
AI-related topics 10–11, **11**; Asia and AI 15–17; autonomous driving 17; chatbots and messenger apps 17; computer gaming 18; consciousnesses and a philosophical approach to AI 17; health care 18; mobile devices from China 17; quantum computing 17, 18; robots and football 15; smart assistants 18; tech giants and fake news 17–18; topic modelling 11; Turing-test-related topics 18; warfare 18; writers of philosophical books about AI 18; *see also* newspapers, on AI
Alexa (Amazon) 29
algorithms 5, 7, 103; in audience manufacturing 109–112, 113; computational algorithms 9; deep learning algorithms 5, 15
Alibaba 17
Amazon 5, 7, 29
Apple 7
Application Programming Interfaces (APIs) 5, 104
artificial social media engagement 102
artificial trending topics 101
Ashley Madison 83
audience-centric news business 109
audience manufacturing 109–112, 113
authentic dialogue 25
automated social media accounts 103, 109–110; *see also* media bots
autonomous driving, and AI 7, 13

Badenschier, F. 8
Baron, N. S. 30
Barthel, M. 111
Baruh, L. 84
Baxter, L. A. 29
Beattie, A. J. 42
Bell, E. J. 100
Big Brother scenario 20
big data 5, 83
blissful scenario 20
Bode, L. 111
bonding, in social capital 65, 66
Boston Dynamics 7

Botometer 106, 113
bots 102; political bots 103, 104; social bots 103, 104, 113; *see also* chatbots; media bots
Bourdieu, P. 65
Brazil, Twitter user-base in 104
Brazilian media 3, 99; credibility 99; cross-ownership 104; diversity of information and perspectives in 103; Folha Group 99, 103, 104, 106–107, 110, 112, 113; Globo Group 99, 103–104, 106–107, 110, 112, 113; link spreading behavior of accounts 107, 112; marketplace 103; political bots 103, 104; social bots in 103, 104, 113; trending topics analysis 108–109, *109*
Breazeal, C. 35
Brexit referendum 80, 103
bridging, in social capital 65, 66
Brown, P. D. 100
Bryson, J. J. 27
Buber, M. 25, 31, 36

Cambridge Analytica 83
Carlson, M. 100
Carr, C. T. 32
Casero-Ripollés, A. 102
Cassidy, W. P. 63
chatbots 2, 32; in computer-mediated communication 42–43; contextual-based limitations 52; credibility 46, 49; definition of 41; emoji-use by 45, 46; experimental manipulation 52; future direction 52; humans interpretation of bot behaviors 44; informational and emotional disclosures with 43; information seeking 42; and interpersonal impressions 44–45; operating system variations 52; and social attraction 45, 49
China, social credit system 17
Christian, B. 36
Christian newspapers, and AI news 13
Chung, D. S. 66
citizen journalism, and social capital 65, 66
Clerwall, C. 63
clickbaits 102
cognitive deficit model 81
Coleman, J. 65
Colossus scenario 20
commonsense knowledge 31, 35

INDEX

communication 1, 26–28; AI technologies, human-centric approach to 27; and computer-mediated communication (CMC) 27, 33–34; contexts of 27; technological development and use 26–27; Turing's test 27–28, 36
communicative capital, in AI news credibility 68, 72
competence, and credibility 46, 49
computationalism 9
computer games, and AI 7, 13
computer-mediated communication (CMC) 2, 25, 27, 41; chatbots in 42–43; communication goals and theories 33–34; competence 45, 49, 53; credibility 46, 49; emoji 42; and emoji 43–44; Hyperpersonal Model 31, 33; interpersonal impressions, AI behaviors influence on 53; nonverbal communication 43–44; online message qualities 43; Social Identity/Deindividuation Effect (SIDE) Model 31–32; Social Information Processing Theory (SIPT) 31, 32–33, 35; use of 41–42
Computers are Social Actors (CASA) paradigm 44, 52
Computers as Social Actors (CASA) paradigm 25, 28–29, 34; and Media as Social Actors (MASA) 28; mindless social responses 28; technology triggered social scripts 29
content consumption, in news credibility 62
credibility: computer-mediated communication (CMC) 46, 49; conceptualization of 46; *see also* news credibility
Crevier, D. 20
Crocker, J. 51–52
cultural theory 81–82, 91
cyberpolicing 83

Dake, K. 84
data usage without permission 83
Davies, D. R. 89
Derks, D. 44
digital intermediaries 100
disaggregation, in HMC 35–36
disinformation campaigns 104
distrust toward appropriate functioning of science and technology 81, 86, 89
Dovidio, J. F. 51–52

economic orientation, of newspaper titles 9, 15, 19
Edwards, A. 31, 34, 42
Edwards, C. 31, 42, 46, 64
egalitarian values, influence on opposition to AI 81–82, 85, 89
Eimler, S. C. 45
Ein-Dor, P. 30–31, 34–35
Ellis, R. J. 82
Ellison, N. B. 65
emoji 2, 42, 43–44, 51; human versus chatbots 46; and social attraction 45, 49; *see also* chatbots
emoticons 42, 43
e-WOM channel credibility, in social capital 66

Facebook 14, 20, 65, 83, 100, 102
face-to-face (FtF) communication 33
Fadhil, A. 46
fake news 98, 102, 104
fake social media accounts 98–99
fake webpage traffic 102
falsification of analytical data 103
feedback mechanisms, for audience analysis 112
Feng, B. 52
Folha Group 99, 104; audience engagement strategies 110, 113; businesses 104; link spreading behavior of accounts 107, 112; on Twitter 106–107
Foucault, M. 83
framing, in news agendas 7
Froehlich, K. 8
Fulgoni, G. 102

Gabryel, M. 102
Galtung, J. 8
Gambino, A. 31
Ganster, T. 45, 50
Gates, Bill 18
Gaziano, C. 62
geographical orientation, of newspaper titles 9–10
Giglietto, F. 101
Gilbert, D. T. 28
Gillespie, T. 109
Globo Group 99, 103–104; audience engagement strategies 110, 113; businesses 104; link spreading behavior of accounts 107, 112; on Twitter 106–107
goodwill, and credibility 46, 49
Google 5, 7, 14, 20, 100
Graefe, A. 63
graphical emoticons 43
Grendstad, G. 82
Grice, H. P. 30
Grice's maxims 30–31
Grier, C. 102
Grønning, A. 44
Guenther, L. 8
guiding dispositions 84
Gunkel, D. J. 27
Gvili, Y. 66

Hancock, J. 43
Harder, R. 101
Hauka, C. 100
Hawkins, Stephen 18
health care system, and AI 7
Hentschel, J. 44
Het Financieele Dagblad (newspaper) 9
heuristics 28, 35
Hidden Markov Models 5
high-credibility media website 108
Ho, A. 36, 43, 46
Hovland, C. I. 61
Huawei 17
human-authored news 64

human-human interaction 35; and human-AI interaction, compared 47, 80; and human-chatbot interaction, compared 46–47; and human-machine interaction, compared 46; script framework 32, 44, 53
human-machine communication (HMC) 1–2, 25, 28, 29, 32, 34–35, 53; chatbots 42, 43; understanding of 31
human-machine communication (HMC), application in human-to-human communication 34–36; and disaggregation 35–36; scripts and cues, reliance on 35; stereotypical first impressions 35
human Twitter agents 64
Hyperpersonal Model 31, 33

"I-It" 25, 30, 31, 35, 36
implicatures, notion of 31
information seeking, and chatbots 42
innovation resistance, and opposition to AI 81, 85, 89
institutionalized audience 113
intelligent machine 90
intermedia agenda setting 101
interpersonal attraction 45
interpersonal communication, definition of 35
interpersonal communication (IPC) theories 29–31; Baxter's relational dialectics theory (RDT) 29–30; Ein-Dor's commonsense knowledge 31, 35; Grice's maxims 30–31; O'Keefe's theory of Message Design Logic (MDL) 31; social robot utilizing MDL 31
interpersonal impressions 52
"I-Thou" 25, 30, 32, 33, 35, 36
Izquierdo-Castillo, J. 102

Japan, socially assistive robots in 7
Johnson, T. J. 62–63
journalists, and AI 6, 20–21
Jung, J. 64

Kankaanranta, A. 44
Kaye, B. K. 62–63
Kim, D. 63
Kim, S.-T. 111
Kim, Y. 65
Kismet (social robot) 35
Kolcz, A. 102
Krämer, N. C. 45
Kumar, N. 44

Langford, I. H. 82
language cues 32–33
Lea, M. 31
Lee, K. M. 28–29
Lee, Y. H. 111
legacy media: agenda-setting power of 101, 111–112; and audiences in online environment, relationships between 99–103; consumers' relation and interaction with 100–101; and digital intermediaries 100; market-driven approach 100, 102; reverse agenda setting 101–102; and social media analytics 112; traditional business model 102; and Twitter 100–101
Levy, S. 66
Lewis, R. 112
Lexis Nexis 10
Liu, B. 63, 64
Lombard, M. 28
low-credibility websites 107
Lowrey, W. 65

machine-based news 64; *see also* news credibility
machine learning (ML) 63
Macromill Embrain 68
Major, B. 51–52
manner, Grice's maxim 30
Marris, C. 82
Marwick, A. 112
mass surveillance 83
McCain, T. A. 45, 49, 50–51
McCombs, M. E. 101, 111
McCoy, D. 102
McCroskey, J. C. 45, 46, 49, 50–51
McGrath, K. 62
media bots 3, 98–99; ambiguous social consequences 111; early-spreader behavior 107–108; identification of 106; institutional theory framework 113; link spreading behavior of accounts 107–108, 112; local bot repository 113; and news content 113; news-sharing strategy *107*, 108; spamming behavior pattern 110; trending topics analysis 108–109, *109*; in Twitter 99
media credibility, of news 61
media environment, transformation of 99–100
media manipulation 98, 104
media organizations, types of 8–10
media reliance, in news credibility 62–63, 71
medium credibility, of news 62
message credibility, of news 61–62
Message Design Logics (MDL) 31
Microsoft 5
Miner, A. S. 43
Moon, Y. 28, 35
Mou, Y. 46–47
Musk, Elon 18

Nah, S. 66
Nass, C. 28, 35
Netherlands 6; and AI-related topics and sentiments in press 1, 13, 14–20; and Christian newspapers 9, 11; development of AI in 6, 21; General Intelligence and Security Service (AIVD) 20; national and regional newspapers 9–10, 11; police force 20; societal acceptance of AI, facilitating of 6; *see also* newspapers, on AI
Newman, N. 111

news based on AI: credibility *see* news credibility; public perception of 60–61; *see also* news credibility

news credibility: AI news credibility 2–3, 63–64, 69; content consumption 62; control variables measurement 69–70; measures of 68–70; media credibility 61; media reliance 62–63; and media use 70; medium credibility 62; message credibility 61–62; and newspaper news use 68; and online news site news use 69; and political discussion 67, 68, *71, 72*; predictors 2–3, 68–70, **71**; and public discussion 66–68, 69, *71*; and SNS news use 69; and social capital 65–66; social media credibility 63; and social trust 66–68, 69, *71*; source credibility 61; theorized model 66–67, 72–73; and TV news use 68

newspapers, on AI: and actors and objects 13, *13*; analysis of 1, **12**, 12–14; and building news agendas 7–8; economic orientation 9, 11, 15; and journalists 6, 7–8; national and regional newspapers 9–10, 11, 15; and news media organizations 8–10, 15; and newspaper types 11, 13, *13*; and news selection 8; and news values identification 8; number of articles on 10, 14–15, **15**; popular newspapers 8, 11; publication date 11; related to countries 13, *13*; religious orientation 9, 11, 15; rise of salience for 11, 12, *14,* 14–19, **15, 16**; sensationalism 8; and sentiments in news articles 11, *13,* 14–15, **15**; and singularity 8, 14–15; and societal acceptance 6–7; topics measurement 10–11, **11**

non-human traffic, in audience manufacturing 109–112

nonverbal messages 41, 43–44

NRC Handelsblad (newspaper) 9, 10

NRC.Next 10

O'Keefe, B. J. 31

online manipulation 112

Oppo 17

opposition to artificial intelligence 3, 80; age factor 86, 87–88, 89; and distrustful toward appropriate functioning of science and technology 81, 86, 89; and educational level 86, 87, *87,* 89; and egalitarian values influence 81–82, 85, 89; gender differences 88, 89; and household income 86; negative impacts on employment 83; prediction of 87–89, **88**; privacy concerns 84, 85–86, 89; and resistance to innovation 81, 85, 89; robotization in the workplace 84, 86, 89–90, 91; and scientific knowledge level 81, 85, 88, 89; sociodemographic differences 86–87, *87,* 89

O'Riordan, T. 82

Owen, T. 100

Pan, W. 52

Papacharissi, Z. 111

Paxson, V. 102

pay-per-click 102

peer-to-peer news circulation 111

Penney, J. 111

people's attitude toward AI 80, 90–91; *see also* opposition to artificial intelligence

political bots 103, 104

political discussion, and news credibility 67, 68, *71,* 72

Popescu, M. 84

Postman, N. 34

post-panopticism 83

Prada, M. 44

PR departments, and AI 90, 91

privacy 83, 84, 85–86, 89

professional journalists, in social capital 66

profiling activities 83

Prokopenko, M. 29

public concern on AI 82–84; degradation of labor conditions 82–83; privacy 83, 84, 85–86, 89; quality of jobs 82; usage of data without permission 83; work and employment, effects on 82

public discussion, and news credibility 66–68, 69, *71,* 72

Putnam, R. D. 65

PwC 82

quality, Grice's maxim 30

quantity, Grice's maxim 30

Rashidian, N. 100

relation, Grice's maxim 30, 31

relational dialectics theory (RDT) 29–30

religious orientation, of newspaper titles 9, 15, 19

reverse agenda setting 101–102, 111

robotization in the workplace 84, 86, 89–90, 91

robots: and commonsense knowledge 35; human communication with 28, 29; journalism 20; learning capacity 33; Message Design Logic (MDL) 31; predictability of 29, 33; programming with Grice's maxims 30–31; prototyping 34; selective self-presentation of 33; social cues of 35; socially assistive robots, in health care system 7; trustworthiness 30; uncanny valley effect 8; use of 7

Rogstad, I. 101

Rosen, C. 8

Ruge, M. H. 8

Samsung 7

Santini, R. M. 112

Sayre, B. 111

Schiavo, G. 46

science fiction movies, and AI 6

security breaches 83

selective self-presentation 33

Selle, P. 82

Selva, D. 101

sensationalism, in newspaper titles 8

sentiments, and AI news 8, 11, 13–14, 14–15, **15**

Sevenans, J. 101

Severin, W. J. 62

Shah, C. 111

Shah, D. 111
Shao, C. 104, 106, 107–108, 112
Shaw, D. L. 101, 111
Shelton, A. K. 42
Shevat, A. 46
singularity 8, 14–15
Skovholt, K. 44
smart assistants 7, 13
smart machine 90
Snowden, Edward 83
"social action is social action" *26*, 36
social attraction 45, 49
social bots 102, 103, 104, 113
social capital, and news credibility 68, 72; definition of 65; e-WOM channel credibility 66; formation and maintenance of 65; measurement of 65; role conceptions of professional and citizen journalists in 66; and trust 61, 65–66
Social Identity/Deindividuation Effect (SIDE) Model 31–32
Social Information Processing Theory (SIPT) 31, 32–33, 35
social media: and agenda-setting power of legacy media 101, 111–112; algorithms and platforms 101, 109; and audience engagement in media 100–101; credibility, of news 63; as filter and amplifier for mainstream media content 101–102; for news-sharing 110; peer-to-peer news circulation on 111
social network sites (SNSs) 69, 71
social representations of technoscience 81
social robots: and commonsense knowledge 35; human communication with 28, 29; and individualized communication strategies 33; learning capacity 33; Message Design Logic (MDL) 31; perception of 29, 32, 33; predictability of 29, 33
social trust, and news credibility 66–68, 69, *71*, 72
societal acceptance of AI 6–7
source credibility, of news 61
South Korea, and AI news credibility study 61, 68–73
spamming, in Twitter 110
Spears, R. 31
Spence, P. R. 42, 51, 64
Spitzberg, B. H. 45, 49, 51, 53
stereotypical first impressions 35
support seeker perceptions, in chatbot designing 51–52

Tesla 7
Teven, J. J. 46, 49
Theodorou, A. 27
Thomas, K. 102

Thompson, F. 82
traffic fraud 102
trending topics analysis, media bots 108–109, *109*
trolls 98
trust, in social capital 65–66
trustworthiness, and credibility 46, 49
trustworthy news contents 100
Tufekci, Z. 101
Turing, Alan 27, 31
Turing, A. M. 5
Turing's test 27–28, 36
Twitter 14, 65, 100; agenda-setting power 104, 112; Application Programming Interface (API) 104, 105–106; automated accounts 103; automated activity 109–110; and broadcast media 100–101; data extraction from 105; as filter for mainstream media content 101; media bots in 99; media manipulation 104; in political arena 104; spam, definition of 110; trending topics analysis 108–109, *109*
Twitterbots 42, 46, 64, 108, 113
Twitter follower market 102

Uber 7
upworthy headlines 102
US presidential election (2016) 103

Van Der Heide, B. 51
van Dijck, J. 101
Varol, O. 106

Waddell, T. F. 64
Walther, J. B. 31, 32, 33, 35
Wang, Y. 46
Wei, L. 63, 64
Weiss, W. 61
Weltanschauungen 84
Westerman, D. 35–36, 51
Westerman, S. J. 89
Westley, B. H. 62
Wilcox, D. 111
Windgate, V. 52
Wojcik, S. 111
work and employment, impact of AI on 82
World Economic Forum 82
Wormer, H. 8

Xu, K. 28, 46

Yilma, B. A. 46

Zhou, R. 44
Zuboff, S. 90